ROCK ISLAND: A GANGSTAZ GRAVEYARD

To: Patrick

Thank you for the support

Reality 2019

ROCK ISLAND: A GANGSTAZ GRAVEYARD

BY

N.U.T.T.Y. "C"

www.bookstandpublishing.com

Published by
Bookstand Publishing
Morgan Hill, CA 95037
3144_10

Copyright © 2010, 2017 by N.U.T.T.Y. "C"
All rights reserved. No part of this publication may be reproduced or transmitted in any form or by any means, electronic or mechanical, including photocopy, recording, or any information storage and retrieval system, without permission in writing from the copyright owner.

ISBN 978-1-58909-735-3

Printed in the United States of America

DEDICATION

Shawanda Cross, you were my living proof that Angels exist. I promise to show the world that your efforts will not be in vain, (and that's on everything!)
Jesse B. Lovett: You were more than a Father; you were my best friend, and a bridge to a world I could not see.

HOOD-OG-RA-PHY – A story written about an area or neighborhood, and/or persons that affected such geographical locations.

-PROLOGUE-

"In the name of Allah, most gracious, most merciful, all praise be to Allah, Cherisher and Sustainer of the worlds...."

The short prayer began, as the group of nearly 50 stood in the park of 76th Street, in Chicago. They faced the East towards *Mecca*- the birthplace of Muhammad, and the Holy City of Islam.

"Most Gracious, most merciful; Master of the day of judgment. You do we worship, and your aid do we seek.
Show us the straight way. The way of those on whom you have bestowed your Grace, those whose portion is not wrath and who do not go astray....."

While most of the members of the group weren't practicing Muslims, they were however about to declare *Jihad* (war) against their enemies on 79th.

Their actions would begin to alter the middle-class neighborhood forever.

CHAPTER 1

It was an unseasonably cool May Day, as ten year old Rico walked home from school. Most kids his age were rushing home to catch their favorite cartoon, but he wasn't too eager to get home in a timely manner. Instead he took his time, admiring the graffiti on the wall of the viaducts. The words "Welcome to Rock Island" neatly spray-painted in bold, black letters stood out on the white wall. The stars, moons, pyramids, and canes were all symbols of the gangs that occupied his neighborhood. To most people the graffiti was just eye sores that devalued the middle-class neighborhood but to Rico it was art. Rico loved to draw and had already gotten in trouble for drawing the art that he'd seen on the streets, on his books and on his wall at home.

Instead of going home, he decided to go to his favorite after school hang out, a game room/restaurant called "Lenzy's" that specialized in one dollar pizza puffs with French fries. As he approached, he was happy to see his friends from school, Andre and Willie who were walking hastily towards him.

"Man Joe lets get outta here!" said Andre as they neared Rico, "them Rock Island boys about to move on somebody!"

"Hell yeah, they got bats and belt buckles and stuff" Willie cosigned. Rico's eyes lit up. "Word, man what ya'll spooked of? They ain't gone do nothing to us." Andre and Willie didn't want any part of a gang fight and opted to high tail it back across the tracks where they both resided.

Rico was in dire need of some action, and decided to see what was up with the large group of young men in front of Lenzy's. "We bout to get these bitch ass niggaz," one member of the group said as they descended down the street on both sides. Rico followed, keeping a safe distance, pretending to himself that he was part of the seemingly organized group. Several blocks later, a chase suddenly ensued, and a fight between the Rock Island members and some rivals erupted. It only lasted a few minutes, but time moved slowly for one helpless victim that endured the array of kicks and punches from the Rock Island members. The victim was bleeding and begging for mercy. The fight looked like a scene from a prison riot. Rico's little heart raced as he took cover behind a parked van to get an undetected view of the melee. He wondered *who were these guy's...?. Why were they fighting...? Why did they seem to hate each other so much..?Why did someone just pull out a gun!!!?* ***BLAM! BLAM! BLAM!*** The shots caused the two groups to break back towards their home bases. It was then Rico was able to see one of the young gangstaz lying helplessly in the middle of the street, in a pool of his own blood. He needed to go past the body to make his detour home, but his fear directed him in the opposite direction. He took the long way back to his hood. Rico wanted to hang but knew his mother would kill him if he didn't make it home before her.

As soon as Rico hit the block he noticed his mother's car and thought *"Damn I'm late."*

"Where in the hell have you been Rico?" was the greeting he received from his mother Virginia, as soon as he crossed the threshold of the front door. He thought about lying, but he didn't want to take a chance on getting caught up, especially because his mother was like the C.I.A., she had spy's everywhere. "I went to the game room after school Ma and lost track of time," replied Rico. A little truth was better than none, he rationalized. Virginia was tired and didn't want to argue. "O.K. you go in there and take off your school clothes and get started on your homework."

"I don't have any," Rico said. Thinking that he said something slick, Virginia told him "That's okay… go get your dictionary, I have something for you." She made him look up several words, then use them in sentences. Rico loved his mother but her occupation as a teacher could be vexing at times.

Rico was the youngest of five children and his father and mother were never really together. His other siblings were much older than him, and they had a different father. Virginia never planned on having a fifth child. She was married for twelve years to a decent white insurance agent and it was during her separation she met Rico's father. After Rico was born, Virginia struggled as a single mother while she went back to school to obtain her Master's Degree in Education. Rico found it hard to relate to his biracial siblings as a child. Despite the age disparity, he didn't look like his brothers and sister. His older brother T.J., who at that point in Rico's life, was the coolest dude he knew, was incarcerated; and the twins Cee-Cee and Kaven were the "second parents" while Virginia was absent. After Cee-Cee left and moved in with her boyfriend, Rico discovered that his brother Kaven was gay. His other brother Ray was handicapped with cerebral palsy.

With no one in the house to relate to, Rico often thought of the streets as an escape. And now that he'd seen his first murder, he felt a magnetic attraction to the life-style outside his warm home. That attraction would often lead him back to Lenzy's to do two of his favorite things ear-hustle and play video games.

Rock Island: A Gangstaz Graveyard   N.U.T.T.Y. "C"

****

Lenzy's stayed packed with teenagers after school. All of the neighborhood drug dealers, thugs, hood-rats, and low lives hung out there as well. The small game room only had six games, and Rico's favorite one, Mrs. Pac Man, was being hogged by two teens that were obviously betting on the game. Finally, the boys left to eat their food, and Rico got a chance to insert his quarter in the machine while the two boys were away. After playing for a while, the two boys returned, almost invading Rico's space with their closeness. "Shorty hurry up," one of the guys said with the smell of onions on his breath. "Me and my man on something with this game." Either Rico didn't care or he was simply into the game, because he didn't even reply. This infuriated the two teens. The tallest one, who Rico knew as Mike B, started pushing Rico out of the way while the other one cheered on saying "game over Shorty"!! Rico was heated and in a small fit of rage, he snapped "Fuck you niggas! Ya'll some pussies," then through a half empty can of pop in their direction. He didn't stick around to see what damage he'd done, as he ran fast as he could towards his house, hoping that the two bullies had a short memory.

As he made it back to his block, he noticed all of his friends apparently playing tag. Cordell, Calvin, Lamelle and Red, barely noticed him as they chased each other up and down the block. Red lived across the street from Rico and was the biggest and the baddest of the group. Cordell and Calvin were the same age and Lamelle was about a year younger. Cordell wore thick eye glasses and sported a long jerry-curl. Calvin was a quiet and reserved type and the spoiled brat of the block. "What's up Rico?" Red asked, noticing his friend for the first time. "I just came from Lenzy's" Rico said, trying to catch his breath. "Them fools up there tripping; took my game and everything."
"You know how those Rock Island dudes are," interjected Cordell. "Ain't nothing you can do about it." Rico weighed his options…. none were good. He wished that his big brother T.J. was home, and together they would extract revenge on the bullies. "Yeah, you right." Rico said, "Nothing I could do right now."

Then the group proceeded to play their favorite game. Their version of cow boys and Indians or Cops and Robbers… They split into groups and pretended to be rival gang members. For a whole summer they play-fought and had water wars with each other. They even recruited more members, not realizing the irony of their games. For Rico, it was more than just a game, the idea of being in a gang fascinated him. He did well in school, and was usually smarter than other kids his age. Rico was ashamed of his scholastic abilities. He didn't want to be considered a geek or nerd by his peers. But he took great pride in his knowledge about the signs he spent so much time drawing.

He learned that his neighborhood was called Rock Island and it contained three of Chicago's major street gangs, who were surrounded by opposition gangs, that out numbered them ten to one. Rock Island originally got its name from the rail-road tracks that boarded 75th street. The line was called the Rock Island route. The gang adopted the name and later used it to define the fact that they were surrounded by ops, but they remained hard like a rock.

Rico quickly learned that the gangs in Chicago weren't just some neighborhood kids fighting over colors, although all of the Chicago's gangs had colors. They were able to identify in other ways, such as the way you wore your cap- to the left or the right, hand signals, and of course the beautiful signs and symbols that Rico grew to love. The highly organized gangs even created written laws and policies, in order to maintain order. Some even adopted religious values in their laws. Conversely none of the gangs' original literature promoted violence, drug use or distribution, or criminal activity of any sort; yet obedience to your superiors within the gang structure, loyalty to the members and progressive development.

So in hind sight most gangs in Chicago were walking contradictions, being highly organized like some of the better known crime families and recklessly dangerous like the west coast based gangs that fought over colors.

Rico grew less and less fond of his peers as his awareness of the young men in those street organizations grew. His friends from school both lived on the other side of the tracks, who he knew was Rock Island's rivals' hood. So every time he visited one of them, he paid close attention to his neighborhood rivals comings and goings. He learned their handshakes, slang, clothing that identified them, as well as how they sold drugs and secured their blocks. Willie and Dre were clueless to what Rico was doing, Willie was a short nappy headed cry baby who most people considered kinda on the lame side, but he was seemingly loyal nonetheless. Dre was less introverted than Willie and this made the two more tolerable.

They often spent the weekend at one another's houses staying up all night, doing various activities like making crank calls on the phone. One night while spending the night over Rico's house, they became bored with making crank calls and decided to sneak out while everyone was asleep. They crept out of the back door with their shoes

off their feet like freed slaves. They'd never been out late by themselves. "Man Joe, what we bout to do?' Asked Willie in a meek voice. "Let's go to the park" answered Rico.
"Hell yeah, that'll be cool" Dre agreed.
"What if them rock Island niggaz up there"? Willie curiously warned.
"So what Willie, you scared"? Asked Dre.
"Um Na'll, I aint scared, but…"
"Well we up then" Rico concluded.

CHAPTER 2

At the park located on 76th and Racine, Max and Lil Ed sat in a car across the street, observing the mid-night drug trade in and out of the park, making sure their operation was running smoothly. They were best friends and the two shared leadership responsibilities in the most prominent crew in Rock Island. Their mentor Bam had died in an incident outside of the neighborhood, leaving the two to take the reigns. Bam along with six or seven others were the original founders of Rock Island. Bam controlled the Cons, K. Man the 4Cornerboys, and Black, Tim Conway, and Fin, controlled the Black EEls. But right now Max and Lil Ed were in control of the C's and even though there was a chain of command, no one actually knew who was number one or two. They both complimented each other. Max was considered the muscle and Lil Ed the brain, but on any given day their roles could be reversed without disrupting the order of their organization.

"When we going back out West to cop some more of this shit?" Max said, looking out the window at his workers.
"Probably Tuesday, cuz this shit is moving fast," replied Ed.
"Ed, I'm tired of messing with those West side niggas. Some of them been given me the impression that since the *Brothaz* originated from out there, that we second class niggaz or something, like we ain't real".
"I've been hearing how they been playing some of the Brothas in the County jail. You know Marco called the crib and said when he got on the deck in the county and identified himself as one of the Brothas; the other Brothas looked at him kinda crazy cuz he said that he was from out South. If he didn't know all the laws (literature), those niggas would've moved on him. He represented for Rock Island though." " Na'll man," Ed responded. "It ain't like that as long as he's one of the Brothas and he stands on law, then he all good. You got Brothas from everywhere in there, they just don't know about us yet. We gotta earn that respect out here doing our thang."
Max agreed. "Yeah, that's why security is so vital and we gotta keep buying these heaters and hitting these ops every chance we get just to let them know that we over here."
"Don't you think that'll bring too much heat from the law?" asked Ed.
"Fuck the heat; we're trying to build a dynasty" exclaimed Max. "Let me go see what's up with the Brothas in the park, you gotta stand on those young niggas these days, they'll jag your paper off."
"A'ight Max, I'll rotate with you later then, I'm bout' to go fuck with my lil' bitch Tanesha, so hit me up later."

As Rico and his friends crossed Racine near the entrance of the park, one of the look out men noticed them, and recognized one of them as the slick talking, Mrs. Pac Man playing, pop-can throwing, little nigga from Lenzy's.

"I've been trying to catch this little punk for the longest" he thought to himself.

Now Mike B. had him trapped in the park where the Brothas monitored the entrances and exits like a hawk. Mike B. turned to go over to the park bench where three or four Brothas sat with a short, dark skinned lady, dressed in a pair of spandex shorts and a t-shirt, who appeared to be in her thirties. Her voice was high pitched and whiney. "Ya'll want me to suck all ya'll dicks for just one bag?"

"Pardon me Brothas," Mike B. interrupted. "Um Teeny let me holla at you for a second over here."

The disgust was apparent on Teeny's face as he and Mike B. stepped out of ear shot from the crowd; "Man, wuz up Joe, I'm trying to trick off with this hype…"

"I know T, but I need some aid and assistance" Mike said looking towards Rico as he and his friend played near the other side of the park. "I need you to help me catch one of them lil' niggas."

Teeny immediately became alert, rubbing his hands together. "What's up them some ops?"

"Na'll man, one of them niggas disrespected me a while back in Lenzy's and I've been trying to catch him every since."

"Ok, so he right over there, go over there and handle yo' business."

"N'all man I'm telling you that lil' punk got rabbit in his blood. And you the fastest nigga in the hood, with all of those track medals and shit." Teeny looked back toward the direction of the bench and noticed that all of the bros left with the female hype.

"Man you made me miss my beat, now which one do you want?"

"The dark skinned one with the hat on. Go around the back so they can't escape out of the hole in the fence. I'm gon' walk towards him and hope the little nigga don't recognize me. If he runs, he's gon' run right in your direction."

Meanwhile, as Max collected the money from the previous shift, he noticed that Mike B. wasn't on his post, and called Terry who was the cons Chief-of-Security over to where he was standing.

"Terry why ain't Mike B. posted up at the front of the park?"

"Oh yeah, he about to fuck up some lil' niggaz with Teeny, he'll be just a minute."

"What lil' niggas?" Max snapped. And before Terry could answer, he saw Teeny walking behind the park and three young boys by the swings, and Mike B. walking purposefully towards them with his hands in his pocket. Max couldn't see the boys' faces, but he knew from their size, that they couldn't be no more than twelve or thirteen years old. *"What the hell them lil' niggaz doing out this late?"* He grumbled to himself. "If something bad happens to those boys they could bring the police to the park. Ed would have a fit."

Rico, always conscious of his surroundings, peeped Mike B. looking in his direction on the sly. But he kept the revelation to himself, because he knew that if he told his two buddies, they'd probably panic and do something stupid, so he needed to buy himself some time to think. Then he got an idea. It didn't seem like all of the Brothas were interested in him, just Mike B., and that one high yellow nigga who seemed to have disappeared. So Rico told Dre and Willie what was up and about his three count escape plan. They were to run when Rico counted to three, Willie looked worried. "Rico, you can run faster than us, they gon' catch us."

"Don't worry," assured Rico, "I'm sure he's going to chase me, you just run in the opposite direction as fast as you can."

Mike B. approached the boys with a sinister grin on his face. "Well, well, well, what do we have here?"

Rico quickly took charge standing in front of his friends, "look man, one you don't even know us, two, we minding our own business, and three…" (Rico looked around and Dre and Willie were half way across the park) "And thr--…" Rico pushed Mike B. as hard as he could, causing him to stumble and broke in the opposite direction. He had created a large distance between him and Mike B. "That chump will never catch m…." Then out of no where he was tackled to the ground. "Got yo lil' ass," Teeny said as he secured lil' Rico tighter in his grip. Max along with four other Brothas approached and out of no where a vicious slap was administered across Rico's tender face.

"Hold fast Mike B." Max ordered. "This is a shorty man!"

"Fuck that, he disrespected me Brotha," Mike B. contended.

Over the course of five to ten minutes, both parties explained the events that lead up to that night. Max had heard enough, he was the ranking member and his word was final. "Leave this bullshit alone, and leave shorty alone, and get back to yo post before I have you fucked up out here. Terry I'ma hold you responsible the next time you let niggas play games on security. This shit ain't no joke out here, Brothas gotta be on point."

Max then turned his attention to Rico, "Shorty where you stay?" But Rico wasn't willing to disclose that information in front of his new enemy Mike B.
"Um I live ... I live a couple blocks over, I'm straight, I'll just catch up with my friends."
"Look Shorty, I didn't ask you that, where in the fuck do you live?" Max asked as he grabbed Rico by the arm and began walking him towards his car.
Once away from the crowd, Rico admitted, "I live on Carpenter."
Once inside the car, he thought about the advice about not getting into the car with strangers. But somehow he felt safe with Max whom undoubtedly aided him in escaping the park with only a smack. "Not bad for a full nights worth of action," he thought to himself. "Better than playing tag with Red and nem' on the block."
"What's your name Shorty?"
"Lil Rico."
"Well lil' Rico, yo momma know you out this late?"
"Na'll we snuck out."
"Those other shorties yo' Brothers or something?"
"Oh, you talking about Dre and Will? Na'll those my homies from school, they spending the night over my crib."
Max began laughing, "Well they will remember this night cuz a couple of the Brothas caught they ass in the back of the park and roughed them up a little. I stopped them so they should be straight. You want something to eat before I drop you off?"
"Na'll man, I'll take a rain check on that. You can let me out on the corner."
"How I suppose to know that you gon' keep yo' mouth shut about tonight?'
Rico then decided to share his secret about what he witnessed that eventful day after school." So you don't got to worry bout' me runnin' my mouth about nothing, I know snitches get stitches…"
Max appeared to be impressed with the shorty that seemed to be wise beyond his years, as Rico exited his car and disappeared into the darkness
Meanwhile Dre and Willie sat on Rico's back porch nursing their wounds, while they waited for Rico to return. "Man, I hate them punk ass niggas from Rock Island," Dre said as he rubbed his swollen lip. "I should get my cousins to come over here and shoot they ass." "I wonder if they killed Rico," Willie said with his head down. "I don't care" Dre replied. "I'm never coming back over here anyway."

The two boys were startled as Rico opened the door to the back porch. They noticed instantly that he didn't appear to be injured. "I told you that they were going to catch us," Willie said in his pitiful voice.
"You must've gotten away huh"? Asked Dre.
Rico felt bad for his buddies and didn't want to rub it in, so he simply said "yeah, you know nobody can catch me." (Except that high yella ass nigga Teeny), after getting some ice for his two friends and making sure their actions were undetected, he had to read them their rights.
"Check it out ya'll; what happened tonight stays between us o.k.? Cuz I gotta live over here with these dudes and I don't want any trouble. So if your momma asks what happened to your lip or your eye, just tell her that we were playing football or something."
The boys all agreed and promptly went home the next day.
****

With his friends gone and the idea of going to hang out at Lenzy's discouraging, Rico decided to escape to his second favorite get-away, his grandma's house. Barbra was nothing like Virginia, she wasn't college educated or uptight. She moved to Chicago from the South in the early fifties with Virginia and three dollars to her name. She owned a big home about four miles from Virginia's and flipped big luxury cars every few years. Barbra was by all accounts a straight hustler. She sold candy, chips, and other snacks during the day and forty ounces of malt liquor and loose cigarettes at night. On weekends she cooked large portions of food and sold five dollar plates to the church crowd and anybody else that enjoyed some down home cooked soul food. Barbra, as most Grandmothers are was less strict on her grandchildren, but she had a special affinity forRico, recognizing his displacement at home. They both enjoyed each other's company. They talked like they knew each other for twenty-five years, instead of twelve.

"Rico, what do you want to be when you grow up?"
Rico hated when she ambushed him with pondering questions about life.
"Um, I want to be rich like you Grandma"! Barbra wrinkled her face, "I'm, not rich boy."
"Well how did you get all of this stuff like a new Lincoln and a nice house and you don't even have a job?"
Barbra could only laugh at her grandson's distorted view of life.
"Listen boy, I worked hard for these things, you see all of the stuff I sell, and the work I do? I've been like this since the age of five. I was taught at an early age that beggars get no respect. So I look at every

11

situation as a potential come up. And that's why I don't have a regular job. I've done everything from doing hair to giving out advice for money."
    Just as Barbra was about to conclude her spill to Rico, while sitting on her front porch, two seemingly drunk older gentlemen appeared. Barbra knew one of them as Blue whom she fed from time to time.
"Hey Ms. Barbra, let me take a picture of you and the young man." Rico jumped up, adjusted his clothes, and wrapped his arm around Barbra's shoulders. A picture was taken, and Barbra loved the photo of her and Rico so much that she bought the camera and bought some extra film for him.
"He might become *a professional photographer*," Barbra reasoned. It wasn't the first gift she bought Rico in hopes that he would passionately pursue it. Like the ten piece drum set she bought earlier that year.
"He may become *a professional musician*." Rico didn't know it, but his latest gift would change his life and not in a way in which his Grandmother would've wanted.

CHAPTER 3

Back in Rock Island...

    Lil Ed, Max, Teeny, and Terry sat on Lil Ed's porch in the middle of 76th and May.
Max: "Joe, I'm telling you this weed is bunk as hell. This shit ain't even getting me high no more."
Ed: "Yeah man I feel you, all of the good shit is in Cali."
Terry: "Man, where lil' George at with the food? I'm starving like Marvin. And what did you want to holla at us over here for anyway lil' Ed?"
Ed: I wanted to get all of the Brothas with rank over here because I'm expecting a very important phone call from the joint.
Teeny: Who calling, Marco, or one of the other bros?
Max: Na'll Brotha, *The Old Man!*
Teeny: Talking about the Old man...our Old man?
Ed: Yeah, nigga, *Chief.*

    The Old Man was the Cons highest ranking member, and also the Brothas most respected leader, being that he carried his status long before there were any other branches. Now the Brothas have thirteen branches and each branch has its own Chief. The Old Man governed the Cons on the streets and his rank enabled him to dictate to any branch if they were ever incarcerated. He was serving a one hundred year sentence and managed to convince his followers that the possibility of him getting paroled was inevitable. The Brothas in turn, looked at that scenario like Christians viewed the second coming of Christ.

    "What's he calling us for"? Teeny asked as the rest of the ranking Rock Island members approached the porch. Raulo, Brandon, lil' George and Mike B. all listened as Ed prepared them for the event.
Ed: "Yeah Brothas, in about thirty minutes Chief will be calling to rotate with us. I know that y'all probably heard the stories about The Old man, but now were about to be plugged wit' him directly. Ain't no turning back from this, Rock Island is officially on the map now."
Ed looked at the proud faces of his committee. Lil George second in command sat close to Max, the Co-Chief of Rock Island. Raulo, the short tank like built Con, is the Enforcer, Terry the Chief-of-Security, Teeny First Lieutenant, Mike B. Minister-of-Law and Brandon, the Treasurer.

The phone rang and Ed placed the call on speaker. "Greetings my Brothas, The Old Man said through the speaker.
"I hope that all is well with you and the rest of our beloved Brothas."
"Yes sir, we good over here" Ed exclaimed proudly.
"That's nice to hear and in fact, that's one of the reasons why I'm calling. I've been hearing a lot about the unity that you Brothas have established on the south-side, and I just wanted to rotate with ya'll to let you know that no matter where the Brothas are, we are one. And I'm proud of you Brothas."
Next, each Brotha introduced himself and The Old Man addressed them as a whole and then according to their rank.
"Ed and Max, Brothas, listen to me closely; you are only as good as your followers. You Brothas seem like a close knit family, treat the Brothas with honor and respect and they'll follow you to the end of the Earth. To the rest of you Brothas, Ed, and Max are my ears and we need your loyalty in order to progress. You are the links in the chain of this organization. I will continue to monitor your progress and you will be hearing from someone soon. Until then, your loyalty and unity is greatly appreciated."
"Love," said the Chief, and the group all repeated "love." The proud bunch of young ranking gang members exited Lil Ed's house with a new sense of dedication.

****

Friday afternoon, Lil Rico anxiously waited for the last bell to ring at school, so that he could hurry home, get his new camera, and hit the neighborhood to make some easy money. Friday meant payday for most people and he wanted to take advantage of the temporary surplus that flooded the inner city. Usually he'd hang with Dre and Willie on Fridays, but ever since their encounter with the Rock Island gang, they had been avoiding Rico. The bell rang and Rico raced home. Without changing his school clothes, he hit 76th street and quickly made twenty dollars from the high school kids that were walking home. Rico knew that if he was to make some real money, he'd need to catch the most financially stable group of people in the hood, the hustlers. And from the look of the fancy cars that sat in front of the corner store on 76th and May, hustlers were close by. Rico first decided to wait for the unsuspecting ballers to come outside to their cars then opted to go into the store and catch them, with their money out.

The Arab store smelled like spoiled meat and cigar smoke, but for the poor black families that couldn't afford to drive to the nearest super market, they tolerated the poor conditions and bad services, because they virtually had no choice.

"Get the fuck out of my store, stupid whore," the Arab shouted at the thin dark complexioned lady whom could've passed for Anita Baker back in the days. "You stupid bitch, always causing trouble in my store, you crack head!"

"Hold up man," a deep voice said. "Do you know who you're talking to"? The Arab looked at the light brown skinned, six foot four, two hundred and fifty pound Brotha whose body was attached to the deep voice.

"I don't care, she steal from my store." The seemingly aggravated patron inched closer to the Arab.

"Muthafucka, you better know who the fuck she is, she is my sister!

"Oh, I'm sorry sir, I didn't know that she was family," the Arab pleaded.

"She ain't my blood, but she a black Sista and if your Arab ass disrespect her or anybody else in the hood, the Brothas will be up here to shut this bitch down. We let you muthafuckas work in here, we should have our people in here, providing a better service to this community. Don't get too comfortable."

The Arab didn't even charge the patrons that were waiting in line for their items while keeping an eye on the small army of soldiers that seemed to be growing by the minute in his store.

"O.K. sir, no problem, no problem," the Arab replied.

Rico stood there transfixed on the Brotha with the shiny *Mr. T* jewelry, whom had just given Hakim a verbal beat down.

"Everything all good in here?" one of the Brothas asked their visibly upset Brotha. His demeanor changed as he broke eye contact with his victim, as if he snapped out of a trance.

"Yes sir! Without a doubt or contradiction, I'm straight Brotha!"

Rico identified the group as Rock Islands Black EEl gang and from the look of their attire it was easy to match the cars with their owners. He followed the group outside.

"Excuse me Brothas, would ya'll be interested in taking a few flicks?" The EEl Brotha that had just checked Hakim, asked "how much?" Rico didn't have a set price. He always changed it according to who he was serving. "Um, two dollars since ya'll from Da Island, anybody else, I gotta charge three bones."

With their egos thoroughly massaged, they agreed. Rico snapped four pictures, each one showed the EEl Brothas with their fists over their hearts, which meant they'd die for their Brotha.

Fin introduced himself as one of the Generals for the Black EEls as he gave Rico his biggest payday yet, a fresh fifty dollar bill.
"Where you gonna be later on?" Fin asked as he made his way to his luxury Sedan.
"I'll probably be at the park," Rico replied.
"Oh yeah, that's where we about to head in a minute, so gon' cop some more film and holla back."
After treating himself to one of Lenzy's pizza puffs and some penny candy, Rico bought some more film and headed to the park in hopes that more generous hustlers were feeling photogenic. The park was packed with people, mostly young adults.

At first Rico felt overwhelmed by the amount of people hanging out idly. But then a familiar face put him at ease. Max noticed Rico right away and motioned for him to come to him. That's when Rico saw Fin and the rest of the EEls he had taken pictures of.
"Whatcha doing wit' dat' camera lil' Rico?" Max greeted.
"I'm trying to make some money, that's all."
Fin and Max introduced Rico to a couple more Brothas that paid to have their pictures taken. Ed, the opportunist suggested that they take a lot of pictures to send Brothas in jail.
"Go gather up the rest of the Brothas," Ed ordered.
"All of the Corner Brothas here?" asked K. Man who was in charge of the branch of Brothas called the 4 Corners.
"A few still checking out those new apartments over there on Loomis street," said one Corner member.

That apartment complex would be later known as the complex, as K.Man and Max recruited members to the Rock Island gang out of the apartments. K. Man's presence in the park was a rare sight because he was usually incarcerated or on the run. The EEls and the Brothahood of 4's and C's were allies. The EEls were the only mob that originated from Chicago's south side and although they were a separate entity from the body of Brothas that the Con's and 4 Corners come from, they shared some of the same concepts and identifications. Their alliances gave them a much needed advantage over the oppositions that surrounded them.

As the crowd grew larger in the park, lil' Rico stuck to Max like glue, studying his words, movements and asking every question that came to his young inquisitive mind.
"Why is everybody so deep up here?" Lil Rico asked.
"We about to have a *goal*" Max answered. "It's just a big meeting all the Brothas from the land have every Friday, ya dig? So since you ain't

from the land and you ain't one of the Brothas, you gotta ride up otta here."

The disgust was apparent on lil' Rico's face as Max walked him to the park's entrance. He knew what lil' Rico wanted.

"Right now is not the time shorty. Just wait yo' time, you'll be old enough to kick it in a minute. I can tell from the way that you carry yourself that you got a good head on your shoulders and somebody taught you well. This shit that you see in this park ain't no life for a shorty like you. We out here selling drugs and doing all types of bad shit. For most of us, this is all that we're ever gone do, but you gotta chance shorty and I don't want to see nothing happen to you."

"I ain't trying to hear that shit Max!" a defiant Rico said.

"I see the Brothas act like family and show each other love. I'm gon' be a Brotha from Rock Island, so you might as well get use to seeing me."

"*The nerve of this lil' nigg*a," Max thought to himself. "A'ight Shorty, but you gotta go right now. We gon' rotate." Satisfied with Max's response, Rico decided to go home.

****

The Rock Island high fueled Rico's dreams, hopes, and aspirations. He became more distant from his real family and hung out with Max more and more. A lot of the older Brothas envied Max's new pet. This made Max accept lil' Rico even more. He relished in his power and took advantage of any opportunity to flex his status. Without Max actually sanctioning it, Rico was an unofficial member. His affiliation with the Rock Island Brothas had its advantages, but also had its draw backs. The real gang members that frequented the area of his school didn't take kindly to Rico's endorsement of Rock Island, and harassed him for wearing the Brothas identifying clothing and turning his cap to the left. His friends Dre and Willie were no help because they lived in 7-4 boy territory and most of their families were members.

"You can't be claiming to be a Brotha lil' Rico", Max said to him after hearing about his problems with the oppositions. That's called *false flaggin;* you haven't been blessed to be a Brotha."

"Blessed, what the hell is blessed?" Rico asked.

"It's just a ceremony where you repeat a pledge called the oath," replied Max.

"A'ight then, bless me."

"Na'll Shorty, it ain't that easy. You a little too young for the C's."

"Man I'm twelve years old and I'm damn near grown" Rico joked.

"Listen lil' nigga the C's be on some high tech shit, maybe I'll put in a word wit' K. Man and they'll bless you as a Corner boy."

Rico wasn't impressed; he wanted to be a Con, just like his mentor.
"I could do anything that the old heads can do."
"You don't know shit Shorty," Max argued.
"I know how to get money, help expand the land and I know all about them Ops on 74th street," Rico shot back.
"What you talking about lil' nigga"? Rico went on to tell Max about what he learned from his secret reconnaissance missions during his visits to his soon to be former friends. "And if you give me a gat right now, I bet I can catch those fools slippin and prove to you that I'm a real Con."
"O.K. It's do or die for this lil' nigga," Max thought to himself. Max thought that taking Rico up on his offer would make him realize the severity of the life he was asking to be a part of. After all, the innocent looking, skinny, twelve year old didn't appear to be a killer. Max rationalized that lil' Rico probably never even shot a gun before and once he's in the Ops neighborhood, with a real threat of bodily harm or death in his face, he'd probably chicken out and decided to go back to being the picture boy.

After arming Rico and himself with thirty-eight specials, they headed toward 74th street on foot.
"Aight Shorty c'mon, we bout to creep on these niggas, show me where they at" Max said as they reached the alley before 74th place.
"This is their main block" Rico said observing the landscape like a hungry predator. "They got security at the front of the block, but he usually be snoozing when things are slow, he just be directing traffic to them dudes on the brown porch over there."
"Here, put this mask on" Max said.
"Hell na'll, we can't just walk up this block with a mask on, they'll spot us. We gotta to play it off and get real close."

Max had been on dozens of these kinds of missions and he'd always feel a little nervous beforehand, but after observing Rico and listening to him effortlessly plan a hit without showing the least bit of hesitance made him realize that maybe Rico wasn't wolfing. But he still had to be sure.
"Listen, Rico, these niggas are straight killas, they may have all types of heat up on that porch. You sure you wanna do this? You can still be my lil' homie."
But Rico was determined and without saying a word, he took off walking towards the opposite end of the alley. Max expected him to turn around at any moment to say that he had changed his mind, but knew that it was past the point of no return when Rico turned the corner

and was no longer in sight. Max pulled out his weapon and entered a backyard to go through a gangway that would lead him to the block where his enemies resided.

The young 7-4 boy was totally unaware of his fate as Max casually opened fire on him with the thirty-eight special. The young gang member who was trained to secure his block learned the hard way that his skills were utterly lacking in that department as the hot shells ripped through his small frame. Rico heard the shots, but he was three houses away from his destination and could see the guys on the porch scrambling to make sense of the disturbance. Rico broke out into a slow trout and fired recklessly into the group of guys who were about to come off the porch. "Rock Island Bitch!" Rico shouted as he descended into the cool damp night.

CHAPTER 4

Weeks later: On 76th and May, lil' Ed counted out the money from the previous shift's bundles of crack sells. Business was good in the new spot, an apartment building on the corner, which he rented from a customer.

Lil Ed was only twenty-three years old, but he had lived the life of a fifty year old man. In addition to being responsible for the ever growing Con Nation of Rock Island, he took care of his little sister Corenna, who was eleven years old, as well as his retired grandmother. Lil Ed was extremely detail oriented and had the memory of an elephant. He spent most of his time thinking of ways to take Rock Island to the next level. He wanted Rock Island to be feared, well known, and respected like some of the bigger sets in Chicago.

When Max wasn't around he relied on George, his childhood friend and neighbor well known as cockeyed George, because of an eye deformity. George oversaw the spot most of the time. He wasn't a gangsta type of guy, nor was he an abstract thinker like lil' Ed. With most of his family on drugs, as a child George dreamed of joining the military. Soon Rock Island became his version of the armed forces. He wasn't a natural leader like Ed, Max or even K. Man, yet a seemingly loyal soldier. The only reason he was The Cons second in command was because of Ed's influential presence and his un-canny ability to mimic Ed's persona, during the absence of Rock Island's leaders.

George walked into the room as Ed finished counting the take. He made a mental note that it was fifty dollars light.
"Ay Brotha, why this dust keep coming up short man?"
"Uh I don't know, maybe the workers taking shorts or something" George calmly replied.
"Taking shorts? The nation can't take shorts; get on top of your business Brotha." George listened attentively as lil' Ed vented, relieved that he didn't press further about the missing money and relieved that Ed hadn't suspected him of anything. And once Ed was no longer in his presence, he would extend his relief by indulging in what was becoming a costly habit. He pulled out the small bags of crack and called his guy Teeny. "I got that shit" he said into the phone, come through later tonight."
****

Meantime in the park:
Terry, Brandon, and Max chilled under the warm sun.

"I'm telling you Brotha, we need to put some more pistols out here, cuz them ops been hitting us a lot the last couple of weeks," Terry said as they sat near the sand box.
"Yeah, them phony ass niggas been trying to snap too. I heard one of them got murked a few weeks ago" Brandon agreed.
Max down-played the conversation, because he knew the exact reason why the ops were retaliating and it was about to get their attention.
Pop! Pop! Pop! The three shots startled the members in the park. Everybody was on point as they noticed Rico dashing across Racine Street with a small caliber pistol in his hand. "This Rock Island bitch," Rico yelled to the car that escaped his assault.
"That lil' nigga wild as hell," said Brandon.
"I've been hearing that he been going on missions almost everyday, tell him to put that gun up" said Max, as he entered the park. Rico knew that the group was probably talking about him, as he approached, so as soon as he got in ear shot, he began explaining.
"Man them niggas driving through here with they hats turned to the right, I had to let em' know where they at!"
"You just can't be bustin' out here in broad day light like that shorty," Terry advised.
"Where you get that heater from"? Max asked. Rico hoped that Max wouldn't interrogate him.
"Oh, this ain't nothing, I got it from a hype."
"I guess that picture money treating you good," Brandon added noticing Rico's semi-expensive attire.
"Yeah," Rico lied. "You know how I do, gotta get that dough." But the truth was Rico had a side hustle, one that he could never reveal to his even most trusted Brothas.

Since the mission with Max, Rico felt accepted by the Cons. Max wanted to keep Rico close. Much to the dismay of a lot of the older C's, who felt like Max, was favoring the soon to be youngest member of their gang. Despite the risk, Max and lil' Ed saw a lot of promise in Rico. They would often allow Rico to stay in the spot with George and other workers while they ran errands. The spot was an apartment in a three story building. Hypes (customers) would go to the back of the building and purchase their crack through a slot on the door of the apartment.

George was in charge of supplying the bundles of rocks to the workers on each shift. The workers would be paid for serving the bundles and for being on look-out. But, when Rico started frequenting the spot, the older Brothas took advantage of his low status and commissioned him to do multiple jobs. On any given day Rico could be found in the spot, cleaning up, working the door, bagging the product up and even collecting money. This allowed George and the other workers' to spend their time gambling and entertaining female visitors. Rico would be paid a mere fifty dollars for all of his work, peanuts in comparison to the ten's of thousands that the spot was making every other day.

But Rico supplemented his income well. He would be given a bundle of one hundred bags to sell at a time. With the other Brothas occupied with their extra curriculum activities, Rico would sneak in the bath room and open all one hundred bags and chip a small piece off of each rock. The small pieces would add up to thirty or forty extra bags for Rico who would sell the bundles of rocks and pocket the profit of three to four hundred dollars every time he worked in the spot. He was also good for business because the extra product allowed him to take shorts from customers who didn't have the full ten dollar asking price. He would take the short instead of lil' Ed or Max. To him it was free money with his fifty dollar pay and his supplemental income. Rico was usually making more money than George and the other ranking members from Rock Island. His photography endeavors were now just an elaborate cover up for his more lucrative exploits and he hadn't even been blessed yet. But his time had arrived and Rico was relishing his special day up until the car full of Ops drove by.

"You gon' make it hot up here Rico", Max said as they dipped off from the others.

"We still have to have goal. Have you been studying that literature that I gave you?"

"Yeah, I know it by heart; I'm ready for some more."

"O.K, you better know it because you could get screened at any time. And you know Mike B. is the Minister-of-Literature and he's going to be on you." Rico just gave a faint smirk.

"I ain't worried about it; I'm ready, I'll be screening him in a minute."

The park filled quickly with Brothas as word of a special announcement spread through-out the hood. The goal began as the entire group formed a circle and one member said the opening prayer. After the prayer is said, strict rules were enforced. No talking out of turn, no slouching, and your right hand over the left at all times. Rico witnessed the ranking members at work as they conducted Nation business. After informing the Brothas of the "Old Man's" co-sign, Max took center stage. "Today is a special day, today we will open our doors to a new generation and we will no longer look at a person's age when considering him to be a part of this organization, but we will only judge

their character and heart. This Brotha not only has heart, but he has a good character and he gets on some of our nerves at times. Most of ya'll already know him as Rico the picture boy, but I want to introduce you to lil' Rico "C."
Rico then stepped in the circle and one by one walked around and did the Brothas handshake with each and every Brotha, some even gave him hugs. Afterwards, Max continued to explain the importance of teaching the younger generation, directing most of his conversation to the Brothas with rank.

The 4 Corner Brothas were once again without their Chief K-Man, who got locked up for a parole violation a few days prior. But shortly before he left, a soon to be rising star for the 4's named lil' Mikey was blessed. Lil Mikey was the same age as Rico, but since the 4's had a much more liberal policy on age, he had been a Brotha almost a year longer. Lil Ed explained to the 4's that since K-Man was gone, if they needed any assistance to get with him or any other ranking member of Rock Island. Fin and the other high ranking Black EEls' shared the same sentiments and even added that they began policing their neighborhood for petty crimes, such as crimes against women, and reminded the Brothas of the code of silence. Cooperating with the law was strictly forbidden. Rico was like a little sponge, soaking up all of the dos and don'ts. He quickly learned that the circle of Brothas promoted love amongst each other, that discipline was the foundation of the Brothahood.

"Before we close I want to address one more issue real quick" lil' Ed quickly said as he walked in the circle. He handed Raulo, the enforcer, a piece of paper and with that gesture, everyone held their breath because they knew that it was violation time.

"If I touch you, step into the circle," Raulo said as he stepped outside of the 360'. Brothas dreaded this moment. Ed was a master of this phase. He would often pretend to ignore certain wrong doings of the Brothas during the week, but once Friday rolled around, he almost never forgot. George almost fainted when Raulo touched him lightly on his shoulder, because he knew as a ranking member he'd receive double of that of a non-ranking member (representative).

"George, I know you are wondering why you are standing in the circle right now," Ed said.

"Yeah Joe, what's the deal?" George screamed.

"You've been bought up on charges of stealing from the Nations funds." Brandon the treasurer explained. "Money on your shifts been coming up short and somebody's been tampering with the bags."

George knew that there was no defense for the shorts. He thought that lil' Ed would continue to ignore his transgressions.

"I warned you Brotha and you didn't listen," Ed stated sadly. He did not want to violate his childhood friend, but nobody was bigger than the laws that governed the Brothahood. He suspected that George was using the drugs months ago, now he had to face the truth. Two Brothas beat George from head to toe as Raulo ordered.

Rico was as nervous as a hooker in church, hoping that his exploits weren't detected by his leader.

"Terry will be promoted to the new second in command" and Bo-Bo will be the new Chief-of-Security" Ed said.

The Brothas ended Rico's first goal with a closing prayer. After witnessing George get completely broke up, Rico vowed never to put himself in that position. He also knew that with Terry as the new shift commander for the spot, he'd have to be extra careful, maybe even terminate his side hustle. Terry was a chinky-eyed light skinned, playa type of Brotha that wore his hair in finger waves. Introduced to Rock Island's Cons by his cousins Raulo, Brandon and Calvin, Terry prided himself as a ladies man. Word in the hood was that if the girl was fine, then Terry had her.

"Aey Terry, what ya'll Brothas gon' get into tonight?" Lil Rico asked, knowing that he had to get close to the new shift commander. Terry always favored the young gang-banging prodigy, but he never got a chance to spend any real time with him.

"Man shorty, we suppose to be dippin' wit these hood-rats from 79th street."

"Ain't that Ops hood over there?" Rico asked, bright eyed.

"Yeah so what, I go where the pussy at. I bet yo' ass probably never had no pussy." Terry said laughing as Brandon and Max approached.

"Nigga, I get pussy all of the time," Rico lied.

"Yeah right," Brandon laughed on.

"Put that on something." Rico thought about putting it on the "C", which was popular among gang members to re-enforce the sincerity of their statement. But he knew that lying on the Nation and to a ranking member was a serious offense, and he wasn't trying to see the middle of that circle anytime soon. So he just laughed, as Max pulled Terry to the side for an intense conversation while watching the crowd of Brothas dwindle out of the park.

Rico's attempt to ear-hustle failed, but he could see Terry's facial expression change with each word that came out of Max's mouth. The look of displeasure did not allow Terry to verbalize it to his Chief, instead he just said "a'ight I got you C, I'll be at the spot in an

hour." After Max spent off, lil' Rico decided to probe. "What's up, we on dem' hoez tonight or what?"
"Na'll shorty, I gotta oversee the spot tonight", they have been blowing me up all night" Terry said while looking at his pager in disgust. Brandon was standing by Terry's side saying, "tell dem' broads to come through here, we can kick it wit'em in the spot."
"Hell yeah, tell them to swing through the spot tonight" Rico agreed. Terry seemed to be pondering the idea, as he patted his freshly done finger waves.
"Yeah, that sounds like a good idea."
****

Later that night, Rico snuck out his window and headed towards the spot. "I hope I'm not too late" he thought, noticing another young con named Bo-Bo in front of the building on security. "What's poppin C?" Rico greeted. Bo-Bo was the new Chief of Security and Rico found it odd that he'd be working on a post his first night on the job.
"Yo, it's juking out here tonight, Ed put some big ass bags in the spot, and it's rollin."
"Straight up Joe?" Rico replied. But Rico wasn't interested in the business aspects of the spot right then. He had something else on his mind.
"Who up stairs in the spot right now?"
"Oh yeah, Terry and nem' been waiting on you, they got some lil' bitches from 79th up there, and they descent too." That was music to his young ears.
"I'm in this piece then." Upon entering the spot, Rico was hit with the overwhelming smell of weed smoke and sex. Terry greeted him at the halls entrance. Brandon, Mike B., and lil' Mikey all occupied the couches in the front room with various females.
"Damn, I'm late," Rico thought as he noticed the female to male ratio was about even. The room was dark and that was probably a good thing since the apartment was filthy, and run down. But even so, Rico could see each one of the females shape and sizes and it appeared that everyone had him by at least four years, including the only lone female that sat on the floor near the couch sipping on a cheap wine cooler.
"How ya'll doing?" He greeted blanketly to the female visitors. With no where to sit, Rico flopped right next to the lone light skinned girl on the floor and greeted her again.
"Hey lil' mama, what's your name?" Seemingly uninterested, she answered with a question of her own. "How old are you?"

Rico thought about adding a couple of years to his age to increase his chance, but seeing lil' Mikey nested up on the couch with her friend, gave him a boost of confidence. "Old enough," he shot back in her ear over the rap music.
The Brothas were taking turns using the two bedrooms to have sex with the various girls. After finally getting a spot on one of the couches while Terry and Mike B. entertained the other females in the bedrooms, Rico set his sights on the busty female that he learned was originally there for lil' George.
"They call me Peaches."
Why do they call you that?" Rico said flirtatiously.
"Because I'm sweet and juicy just like a peach."
Even with the lights dimmed, Rico could see that Peaches was very attractive. "You have some soft legs," Rico said as he rubbed the smooth legs of Peaches, hoping she wouldn't stop him from going higher up under her mini-skirt. When she didn't, the wetness inside of her panties caught him by a surprise. When he saw Terry and Mike B return with their girls from the bedroom, he knew that was his cue.

    He led Peaches to the dark room, where she quickly undressed revealing the biggest breast he'd ever seen in real life. Rico was hard and ready; he quickly mounted her and thrust forward sliding inside her juiciness.
"I can't believe that I'm doing this" cooed Peaches as Rico pumped faster in the doggy-style position. He felt like a man having sex that way. She began to moan louder as Rico neared his climax.
"Man, what ya'll on in here?" Mikey said, as he peeked in the dark room with two other Brothas in tow. Rico did not mind because he was finished. But Peaches was just getting started. They all took turns having sex with her for the rest of the night.

    Seeing the various girls stretched out on the dirty mattresses sucking and fucking the The Cons and Conerboyz, Rico couldn't help but think about how many times they must've done this in their own hood, and he instantly regretted not wearing some protection.

    The spot had definitely changed since George's days. Terry allowed Rico, Mikey and the other younger Brothas to come and go as they pleased. Mikey and Rico formed a bond manly because both of them had something in common. They were both doing something that was unheard of from shorties; selling their own work independently, (inside and outside of the spot.)

CHAPTER 5

Over the next several months, Rock Island's membership increased mainly with young Brothas under the age of fifteen. On the east side of the Island, the apartments called the complex spawned a new generation of young Brothas. Wayne, a.k.a Insane Wayne was a transplant from New York, and managed to catch the attention of K-Man just before his arrest. Wayne lived in the Complex and quickly gained a reputation for being one of Rock Island's most dangerous members. Known for his love for double barrel shot guns, Wayne was K-Man's go to guy while K-Man did time down state. As Rock Island's attention focused more on recruitment, Wayne's was on creating chaos. Girls were afraid of Wayne because of his short temper. But Wayne gained more notoriety when he managed to pull one of the hoods most sought after females. Her name was Sheila; she was five foot three, nicely shaped like a gymnast, with light brown flawless skin. She lived in the complex with her mother, little brother and sister. Every dude in the area tried to capture Sheila's attention, but to no avail, including Rock Island's most successful mack, Terry. What Shelia saw in Wayne was a mystery to everyone. She went on to give birth to his first son.

The complex also spawned a lot of other legendary Brothas such as Alvon, a.k.a Pretty Boy. Comparisons of him and Terry soon subsided when Alvon proved that he was much more than just a pretty face. The long jerry curl wearing new Con loved gang-bangin with the Ops' and fought almost daily at school with help from his new neighbors the Hull Brothers which was a new found friendship. The friendship was cemented as the Hull Brothers joined the Cons. The three Brothers looked so much alike, that they became known as the triplets. T-Fly was the oldest by eighteen months and L.T and Antoine were twins. Mike B's family moved to the complex and his sister started dating T-Fly. The Cons benefited greatly from the complex, by increasing their geographical influence as well as their numbers. On the opposite end of Rock Island, 4 Corner boy lil' Mikey decided that the 4's influence needed to increase as well as their numbers.

Whereas the C's and the EEls used intimidation to lure members, lil' Mikey managed to capture the minds of the younger generation, such as the eleven through fifteen year olds. He made the young 4's appear to be a party crew or a fraternity from the hood of some sorts. He and his guys could be seen dressed alike at parties or the skating rinks around the south-side, luring young impressionable minds into the crew. A lot of kids would start off being dancers or fans of the

4's flashy young members while being gradually introduced to the street life that Rock Island had to offer them.

Some of these kids lived outside of Rock Island's small territorial claim, but by the time they found out they were actually from a legit gang, it was either too late or they didn't care. Mikey had that effect on people, you wanted to wear what he wore, eat what he ate, frequent the places that he frequented, and since Mikey was a Brotha, a lot of others wanted to be one too. In just a short period of time lil' Mikey recruited over forty new members, including well known ones such as Travis, Eric, Myron, T.P, Mitch, Marlon, Co-Co, Head, and Kenyatta. It seemed like every week the Corners' numbers were increasing, and the couple of blocks of Rock Island were becoming over crowded.

It seemed like the only ones that were keeping a low profile these days were the Black EEls. Fin, one of the Generals did manage to recruit a few new members, but for the most part, the only members he seemed to be concerned with were the ones that were directly related to his successful drug business. Although as he and Rico became close, he secretly wished the young Brotha that he met over a photo session would have pledged to the Black EEls.

Rico took full advantage of Rock Island's full take over and freely roamed the different blocks to parlay with different Brothas. One day he and Terry would chill on 76th and May, the next you could catch him over the triplets house with Alvon and the rest of the complex Brothas. Another day you'd see him hangin' with the 4's over Mikey's house where Mikey's cousin Bo-Bo also lived. But he valued his time around Fin because unlike Max or Ed, Fin seemed to always have free time, and everything that he did was effortless. Rico also found Fin's conversations enlightening and refreshing, like those that he shared with his grandmother. Fin would always be seen on his block, sitting on his porch. "Why don't I ever see you drinking or smoking weed?" Rico asked, as they lounged on Fin's porch watching the hypes wash Fin's fleet of expensive cars.

"Because that shit ain't for a Brotha like me, ya dig? I have to be on my square at all times."

Fin went on to explain, "You see Rico, I think we're alike. We soldiers and we can't afford to be buzzed and shit; that's how Brothas get caught slipping. When I see you, I notice you be on point wit' yours, noticing everything around you, every sound, every movement, you be on it. Your instincts are very sharp. When you start drinking and smoking all that garbage, it slowly dulls your senses, slows down your reaction time, clouds your judgment."

"Man if I had dough like yours Fin, I'd be chillin' overseas somewhere. Why you still in the hood? You can get a crib anywhere." Fin knew that Rico had a lot to learn about the streets.

"Look Rico, I'm a street nigga, and when you a street nigga, you got five senses, plus one. That extra sense is the sense of danger. You can tell when something is wrong. When you leave the hood, you lose that sense. As long as I got money, there will be danger, being in the hood sharpens my senses, I ain't going no where. That's what the haters want."

It was no secret that Fin was one of the areas biggest drug dealers, but most were unaware that he was feuding with the EEls eternally over a power struggle within their structure. Some say they were trying to extort him, others say he refused to pay taxes to the Nation. Fin chose to distribute his money throughout his community, sponsoring basketball tournaments, and helping poor families.

One family that he assisted was Maggie and her two kids. Maggie struggled when she home from rehab and regained custody of her kids. Her oldest son, Ray, took a liking to Fin, after he bought him a coat a few winters back. Fin also helped Maggie with her bills. Ray and Fin's relationship wasn't like that of Max and Rico's. Fin knew with certainty that Ray wasn't fit for the mob-life. And although he had love for the young unpopular kid, he wasn't prepared to make him a partner in his drug business. Ray was not mentally equipped to deal with the level that Fin was on, and Fin had too much love and respect for Ray and his mother to have him out on a corner selling drugs for him. So Fin spoiled Ray, buying him all of the latest gear and games.

"Look out for my lil' man Ray up at that school" Fin said to Rico during a conversation.
"What he about to be a Brotha or something"? Rico asked in response.
"Na'll, that's like my lil' son, so keep an eye out for him aight?"
"Ain't nobody paying no attention to Ray," Rico responded.
But as they were talking, Ray's little sister could be seen running up the block. "Fin! Fin! Fin! Hurry up, my Mother wants you, she said that it was important." It wasn't the first time that she summoned Fin in an overzealous way. Maggie had become dependant on Fin and he was sort of the man in the house, even though he never even spent more than ten minutes in her home. Fin took a deep breath and looked at Rico, who was obviously annoyed by the young girl's high pitch voice yelling for Fin to come see what her mother wanted.

"Man ride with me over here to see what this Sista want, probably got a rat under the stove or something. She thinks I'm her handyman."
"A'ight Joe, lets ride" Rico replied.

Maggie was sitting on her front porch when Fin pulled up in front of her house. She nervously smoked a cigarette, as she watched Fin stroll as if he didn't have a care in the world up to her gate, with Rico in tow. Maggie's eyes were red, as if she hadn't slept in days.
"Let's go inside" said Maggie, getting up from the porch to greet Fin.
"You got your heat on you Shorty," Fin asked Rico.
"Yep."
"Good, wait for me out here and watch my car." Once they were inside Maggie broke down and started crying uncontrollably,
"It's my baby Fin, my baby!" Fin tried to make sense of her cries.
"What you talking about Magi?"
"They got my baby!"
"Who? What are you talking about?"
"Some niggas got my baby and they said they that wasn't letting him go unless we come with fifty thousand dollars tonight."
Fin weighted Maggie's words. "Did they tell you who they were?"
"No, but they sounded serious Fin, please go get my baby." She handed Fin a piece of paper with a number on it. Fin looked at it with little emotion.
"You going to get Ray back right Fin?" Maggie was becoming more upset by the minute.
"I know you got it Fin, please don't let them kill my baby." But Fin's sixth sense told him that whoever kidnapped Ray was not interested in his money. They wanted to send a message. And more than likely, Maggie was never going to see her baby alive again. He tried to calm Maggie, but that only enraged her even more.
"Fuck you Fin! You gon' let them niggas kill my baby? You ain't shit! I'm calling the police."
Fin knew that was his cue to leave and headed for the front door.

Ray's body was found a day later. He had been dead for two days. Fin was right; Ray was already dead when Maggie sent for him. His kidnappers wanted to get Fin's attention. But Maggie insisted on telling people that Fin was responsible for her son's death, accusing him of being selfish and cheap. News of Ray's death was a popular topic around Rock Island, but not because of Ray, but because of rumors surrounding Fin and him not paying the ransom. Some speculated that Fin was fronting most of the time and that he really didn't have the cash that people thought he had. Ray's mother bashed

Fin's name to anyone that would listen. She even banned him from coming to Ray's wake.

Rico and a handful of the kids from his school attended the funeral. He heard that fin offered to pay for the funeral, but Maggie declined. Rico listened to the pastor say his sermon at the graveyard, as Ray's body was being laid to rest. A fairly large crowd gathered around the small casket. Everyone's attention was abruptly diverted when a parade of cars pulled up. It appeared to be a Presidential motorcade. Then to everyone's surprise, Fin exited the second car dressed in all black. He walked towards an empty plot about fifty feet away from the crowd. Members of Fin's entourage carried large amounts of flowers to the empty plot. One girl placed a large framed picture of Ray beside the plot.

Maggie watched in disgust and tried to encourage people to ignore Fin and his attempt to show respect to Ray.

"Don't let him take my baby's shine, that's just guilt," Maggie said through her tears.

Rico didn't want to be disrespectful, but Fin was his guy, even more so than Ray was, so he excused himself and walked to the area in which Fin was throwing his personal funeral for Ray.

Fin stood by the empty plot stone-faced as one of the EEls approached him with two large grocery bags. Fin then emptied the contents of the bags into the empty grave, and surprisingly it was large bills. After the grave was filled with the money, one of the EEls began pouring lighter fluid all over the money. The crowd held their breath as Fin set the money on fire, the flames were intense, but nobody moved, as Fin said his parting words. "This is for all the people that thought I'd be spineless enough to value money over a human life, a human life that was a friend."

Nobody ever knew how much money Fin burned that day, but it was safe to say that it was substantially more than fifty thousand dollars. That was the last time Rico or anybody else from the hood saw Fin. The rumors flew for months after his disappearance. But Rico just imagined that he was in Jamaica somewhere chillin' under some palm trees. His absence would be a major blow to the EEls and Rock Island. And although Rico learned a valuable lesson to never value money over a friend, he couldn't help but think *"this is what the haters wanted."*

CHAPTER 6

While a lot of kids like Rico joined gangs because of the lack of family structure, Rock Island was unique in a sense because a lot of it's members were actually family and joined the gang as a family. **Calvin, Raulo, Terry** and **Brandon** came in as a family. **Shawn** and **Tommy-Joe** became Cons' together and their little brothers **Myron** and Parish later joined the 4 Corners', as well as their cousins **Eric** and **Marlon**. Other notable Rock Island members that were related were the **Hull Brothers; Alvin, Sony** and **Mike B, lil' Mikey** and **Bo-Bo, Toby, Juan** and **Qualo**.

But no family impacted Rock Island like the **Olley** family. Nobody knew exactly how many of them there were, a new one seemed to appear everyday. They were known for taking over entire apartment buildings, making their home a fortress. Their building on 78th and Morgan became well known as the Olley building, and if you were smart, you'd cross the street before walking past that building at night. But sometimes, even that wasn't enough. Traditionally they were oppositions to Rock Island, and for years struck fear in the gangs. The Olley family was frequently the topic of discussion in the weekly goals, and Brothas dealt with them like they were an entire gang, instead of a group of individuals.

The Olley's stirred up controversy when **Bo Olley** decided to join the Cons from Rock Island. Bo was one of the most feared Olley brothers, because of his size and fearless attitude. People said that he wasn't scared of anything. He wouldn't run or even flinch from the threat of a mob attack. Bo and lil' Ed went to Calumet High School together and remained friends afterwards. Rock Island was the underdog in the new era of gang-bangin', but what seemed to attract Bo Olley and others like him was the fact that despite numbers, they evened the odds by making up the difference in violence and unity.

If you disrespected one Brotha from the Island, no matter the age or branch he was from, the entire mob would retaliate. No other sets had unity like that at the time. Rock Island members were like roaches in the ghetto, if you seen one, you know the others aren't far. So for Brothas like Bo, Rock Island was just like home. Now that he was one of the Brothas Rock Island's life long feud with the Olleys would end.

This was good for young nomads like Rico, who enjoyed patrolling the entire hood on foot, selling rocks, unlike the older Brothas that enjoyed the safe confines of the spot. In fact, a lot of the

35

younger Brothas refuse to work the spot, and began venturing out to sell rocks, taking full advantage of the free enterprise that eluded members on 76th and May.

One of the young Cons named Mario a.k.a Rio became one of the first to see success in the drug game outside of the spot. He opened up shop on 77th and Morgan which was no mans land at the time. That attracted lil' Mikey and his crew of crumb snatchers and before you knew it, Rock Island gained another block. It was an ingenious move by the shorties, being that the Olley building sat on 78th and Morgan and their enemies on 79th. They figured that the Olley building would provide a layer of security for them. Rico would often go on Rio's block just to check on them, because he was one of the few shorties that always carried a gun. Even though he was happy to see the expansion of his gang's territory, he often felt that the shorties were underestimating the enemy.

Nevertheless it seemed like every other week you were seeing Rock Island members on blocks that you never would have thought they'd be frequenting. Like roaches, they came in numbers. For the young Rock Island members it was fairly easy to take over a block. They did it several ways. Sometimes a female on a neutral block would spark the interest of a member, and he'd start visiting her. After a few visits, the roaches were coming. Hustlers like lil' Mikey, took over hype's apartments or houses by feeding the hype crack for weeks on credit, and once they couldn't afford to pay he'd convince them to rent their properties out. These types of spots were like club houses for young Brothas. Unlike the spots of Ed and Max which strict rules were enforced, the hype houses provided a loose atmosphere of drinking, smoking weed and casual sex. These houses started to produce a lot of young delinquents who were often runaways and high school drop outs.

Once the older Brothas got wind of what was going on, they immediately took action.
"All Brothas under the age of sixteen must attend school during school hours, if you are caught on the streets during school hours, you will be dealt with accordingly. Your presence in the hood during that time will only bring unwanted attention to us." Lil Ed sternly said at a goal.
Rico wondered how the Chieves of an organization managed to alter the behavior of a multitude of defiant young rebels, whose own parents even had a difficult time controlling, He'd often visualize how he'd run things if he was a ranking member of the Cons, making a mental note to learn all the inter-workings of the organization. After goals, Brothas would always find something to get into after standing for almost two

hours in a circle. Alvon, Ed, Max, and Rico stayed in the park to discuss nation business. The two leaders wanted their best new shorties to consolidate on a mission.
"We want y'all to go over there and handle that business later on tonight," Ed ordered.
        "We got you Chief," Alvon said in a loyal tone.
"Oppositions have been getting real antsy lately," Max added.
"Don't even trip" lil' Rico added, "we got to give'em what they looking for tonight."
"Alright Brothas, Ed said as he began to exit the park. " Let's go to the spot and get some heat." As the Brothas exited the park, Alvon realized that he forgot his favorite snake skin *Chicago Bull's* hat by the bench. "I'll catch up with y'all in a minute, he said as he ran across Racine Street. But that one minute would become the last minute Alvon would have on this earth. Unbeknownst to the Brothas, the oppositions were one step ahead of them in planning an attack, and in the cover of darkness sent one of their trigger men on a mission. Alvon was an easy target, as he crossed the street. His assailant waited in the alley near the park and walked right up on Alvon, shooting him in the head at point-blank range. The shot instantly got the attention of the Brothas who were only fifty yards away. Rico turned around just in time to see Alvon's life-less body fall to the pavement.
        "Oh shit, it's Von!" Rico said frantically, while taking off running towards the action with his three eighty hand gun out.
Blam! Blam! Blam! Blam! The shots didn't even come close to hitting Alvon's murderer, as he disappeared into the dark alley he initially appeared from. The Brothas gave chase, **"catch that nigga! catch that nigga!** Rico lead the chase undeterred by the shots the dark figure fired upon them as he tried to get away. But he got away once he reached opposition territory. Some of the Brothas were just catching up to Rico as he was returning back to his hood.
        "Did you get that nigga?" A voice yelled from the crowd.
"Na'll, he got away, and I ran outta shells," Rico replied.
The police hadn't arrived yet as they neared Alvon's body again. Alvon was only fourteen and his mother's only son. Sony and Mike B couldn't stand to look at their cousin's body as the police placed the yellow tape around the scene.
"Man, this is some bogus ass shit, Joe," one of the on lookers said.
Rico's heart was pumping, his adrenaline was at its peak and he wanted to cry, but instead he studied the mannerisms of the older Brothas and tried to mimic their energy. But Alvon was Rock Island's first murder victim. This was new to every Brotha, even the older ones.

The ranking Brotha convened on 76th and May to plot their next move.
"Man Joe, we gotta find out who did this shit," Terry said openly,
"I think it was dem' niggas off 79th, they only Ones that'll have the balls to come over here and pull a stunt like this."
"Max, what we gone do?" asked Terry.
"I think we better call Vick and have him bring some of that heavy artillery from the west side," Max responded.
"O.K. who we gone hit Chief?"
"Everybody!" Max answered, with tears in his eyes.
"We go hit everybody in close proximity of us. Kick niggas doors in, shoot up they mama crib and everything. Fuck them niggas up on sight at the school, at parties, wherever!"
  Ed seemed to be the only Brotha who maintained his composure. "Um, I understand how ya'll feel, I wanna get them niggas too, but you talkin' real reckless, innocent people could get hurt, it could get real nasty."
But warfare was Max's expertise and he wasn't trying to hear anything.
"Fuck dat shit, this is for Von, kill em' all and let God sort'em out, I don't give a fuck!"
Chief had spoken and walked away from the crowd of mourning Brothas.

    ****

  Rock Island consisted of three organizations, the Cons, 4 Corners, and Black EEls. The Cons and 4s' were a part of a larger organization called the *Brothahood*. The Brothahood controlled the entire west-side with their thirteen different branches. On the south-side, two organizations were prominent, the largest being the *G boys'*. They originally came from a small area in the Englewood section of the south-side and quickly spread throughout the south side. Like all street organizations in Chicago, they began as community guardians, and in time digressed into criminals who sold drugs and began committing senseless acts of violence.
  The G Boys became so successful so fast the leaders in the gang decided to break up the monopoly and form a sub-division called the D Boys. Together they were known as the "Family". And even though they both came from the same structure, they'd sometimes beef with one another, a lot of times because there wasn't any opposition in their area to beef with. The family's sheer numbers and geographical strong-hold in some areas prevented them from even making contact

with some opposition. But unfortunately that wasn't the case in the area that Rock Islands gangs decided to occupy.

The family surrounded them on all sides. To the north on 74th the *7-4 boys* (G-Boys'), to the south the G-Boys' of 79th, directly west the G-boys formed a notorious set called "killa ward," and to the east near 77th and Halsted the Gs' called their set *"central city."* The D-Boys in the area shared the block of 79th thru 80th and Carpenter. To differentiate themselves from the Brothas organization, the family would represent the complete opposite action of their enemy. If the Bros wore black gold and red, then they wore blue. When the Brothas adopted their signature style of wearing their caps to the left, they wore theirs to the right, anything to distinguish themselves from the *opposition*. The family was cocky and in some areas even bored. But as the Black EELs and the Brothahood grew on the south-side, that would change. They began to tightly secure their hoods which made it extremely difficult to infiltrate one of their blocks. Most of the time, they had armed security posted just for action purposes. They were very good most of the time at detecting non-members or potential threats and was known for giving the flux to those whom they caught trespassing. They took pride in their comfort ability, sometime too much pride.

****

Visibility was low as a thick fog covered most of the city. The G's on 79th took advantage of Mother Nature's little hindrance, hoping that the night shift police would overlook their loitering and drug selling. A group of G's stood quietly in the middle of on of their main blocks.

"Man G, it's slow as hell out here tonight, these hypes ain't coming through," One G-Boy complained to his best friend. "Pass me that weed, I'm about to call it a night, probably gon' fuck wit my baby momma, or something."

"Man, fuck yo' baby momma, she a little runna anyway. You always chasen up behind that bitch," one of the other G's said, in between sips of his forty ounce. The rest of the G's broke out into light laughter. "Dam G, you gone let him get down on you like that?" another G-boy asked from the crowd.

"Man, fuck that nigga, he just mad cuz his lil' broad is a bust down and I heard that she's giving that ass up to Ops and everybody!"

They joked for a few minutes, until one of the lil' G's seen four shadowy figures down the block, the fog concealed their identities. He promptly drew his three–fifty-seven magnum from his waist band. And shouted toward the approaching group, "Who dat?" (No answer.)

The young G looked at his comrades with concern, "Who the fuck--?" Then he heard the familiar voices of the females that his peers were just speaking upon.
"It's yo momma nigga!" One of the girls yelled back.
"Man y'all better stop playing like that, fuck around and get shot one of these days," one G-boy warned.
"Y'all some scary ass niggas," one of the G-girls shot back jokingly. But the G's attention was diverted when a *Chevy Nova* slowed down near them.
"On that car, G!" a voice from the crowd yelled to the three- fifty-seven carrying shorty who was squinting his eyes in attempt to get a good look at the driver.
The car double-parked in front of the building next door to the one that they loitered in front of.

"Excuse me fellas, do you know where this address is?" asked the pizza delivery guy as he exited his vehicle with a large pizza in his hand. "Uh yeah, that's it right their, homie" answered the cautious young G-boy, who quickly tucked the large revolver back in his waist band.
"I told you y'all some scary mothafuckas," the G-girl pressed, opening up a light banter session between the two sexes.

After a number of false alarms and the addition of their female counterparts, the G's let their guards down, just enough for the *Malibu Station Wagon* to go unnoticed as it neared them. By the time lil' G did notice it was too late.
"On that ca...!" Boom! The thunderous sound of a twelve-gage pump sent back shots directly in the crowd of G's striking their bodies with the hot pellets.
Unfazed, lil' G ran towards the escaping vessel and discharged all six rounds in its direction. As he stepped in the street to access the damage, the pizza man came out of the building and opened fire with a *tech nine* semi-automatic into the group of already wounded G's that attempted to hide behind a parked car. Their screams sounded like they were in a horror movie.

The G that emptied his three–fifty-seven on the car full of Ops that sped off into the night, did not notice the movement in the back seat of the Nova doubled parked just a few short feet away from him. By the time he did notice, a familiar face arose from under a dirty blanket on the floor, with a shiny nine millimeter berretta in his hand. The doomed G-boy barely got out two words, "oh Sh--!" before several shots from the berretta struck him down, leaving him in a pool of blood in the middle of the street.

The crowd of G's scattered in every direction as the last barrage of bullets flew from the tech nine, lucky to escape with non fatal wounds. But for those who were trapped in the cross fire of the two assailants, their fate was sealed.

"C'mon get in the car before the police get here," the pizza man yelled to his accomplice. But the young thug's attention had been caught by one of the wounded G-girls crawling towards a building trying to make a safe escape. "Hold up, let me handle this right quick," he responded, remembering what he was ordered to do.

The injured victim had been shot several times and her blood trail could be seen clearly. He stopped her by putting his small shoe on her back, as she attempted to crawl on her stomach, while preventing her from moving, he whispered to the crying young lady, *"this is for my homie Alvon, tell him I said "Rock Island" when you get to where you going."* He pointed the gun to the back of her head, and squeezed the trigger. Click! Click! Click! He was out of ammo.

"Fuck" he shouted, as he tracked back to the car and sped off.

The girl whom everyone knew as Tyra that often used the alias Peaches recognized one of her assailant's voice and just before she passed out she got a glimpse of his face and managed to mutter one word....." Ri--Ri--Rico!"

CHAPTER 7

In the weeks that followed Alvon's death, the violent crime rate in the Rock Island area rose significantly. Shootings were common near playgrounds and commercial areas; assaults were almost a part of the curriculum at most local schools. Rock Island had levied war on every nearby opposition set. It was the only way they would know for certain the right guys responsible for Alvon's death. However, a lot of innocent by-standers became the victims to the random acts of violence. And the spike in violent crimes didn't go unnoticed by the local authorities. The gang tactical unit in the area was starting to work over-time as they attempted to regain control of the streets.

For two officers in the area, it was just another day on the job. Officer Derkensen whom most people on the street called Derk worked in the gang unit for the last decade and was familiar with most active members in his district. He knew most of the first and second generation Rock Island members by name and was shocked at the rapid increase of membership. Derk, a forty year old, Caucasian, college graduate wasn't intimidated by the goons on the street, while working in the all black neighborhoods. Officer Timmons, Derk's partner, a.k.a. Quick, was a twenty-seven year old ex-marine, who joined the force after four years of serving his country. He grew up on the west side of Chicago and was known for his lightening fast speed. He was also known for being personable with the criminal elements that he interacted with. His oldest brother was killed in a drug deal gone badly while he was away on duty in the marines. Quick transferred to the south side to work in the gang unit after three years as a patrol officer. He and Derk had only been partners for two weeks. They both listened to their radio dispatchers as they cruised down 79th street. **Dispatch: ATTENTION ANY AVAILABLE UNITS, WE HAVE A 1032 (mob action) ON THE 7600 BLOCK OF MAY STREET; REPORT OF WEAPONS ON THE SCENE, PROCEED WITH CAUTION.**

"That's those Rock Island punks over there," Derk said to his new partner; whom he treated more like a student. "They've been feuding with the *"family"* in this area. One of their guys got nailed, so they're in retaliation mode. It ain't safe for them because them G-boys don't play. They have resources to give these little fuckers a real hard time."

Quick shook his head and soaked up the intel he was receiving from Derk. "What happened to the multiple shooting cases with that girl in a coma did we get any perps yet?" asked Quick as they neared Rock Island headquarters on 76th street.

"Na'll we still waiting for the female to come out of her coma to give us some details, but I'm sure we'll be able to put some pieces together out here on the bricks."

****

Several Rock Island members leaned on a worn out fence as they heard the call, "Shawntae' Shawntae' coming up the block!" Shawntae' was Rock Island's code word for the police; named after one of the founding members girlfriend who turned him in to the police after being on the run. As the scattered voices yelled out their warnings, one boy carrying a pistol crept into one of the buildings as the group gave him cover in the form of a human shield. "Everybody straight out here; nobody dirty?" One Brotha asked, as the unmarked police cruiser pulled up on the curb, to harass the seemingly laid-back collection of gang members. Derk and Quick jumped out with their guns in hand. "Alright ladies let me see those hands," Derk ordered. "You muthafuckas think ya'll own this block hunh"? This is a residential block; these people don't want ya'll loitering in front of their houses like this."

"C'mon on man give us a break Derk, we wasn't bothering nobody, we just chillin," one of the brave young new recruits said as he was being searched.

"Well you muthafuckas have to go find somewhere else to chill, I told ya'll these are my corners now. Since ya'll want to shoot shit up everyday, I'm going to make sure I come to check on ya'll." Derk looked at the young group of Brothas and realized he didn't know the majority of them and decided to name check. As he retrieved their names, he made mental notes along the way. *"This is Silo, I wonder when he got out, and I just locked him up last month..."* But Quick suddenly noticed a familiar face; he made the hair on the back of his neck stand up. He swiftly pulled his partner to the side and informed him of his revelation. "I know that muthafucka right there," Quick said pointing to one of the oldest members of the group. His name is Victor Smith, also known as Slick Vick; he from the west side and he got some juice for the Corner boy's. His name was implicated in at least half a dozen 9-1's (murders) out west. The Brothas only call him when they want someone killed; rather it's another Brotha or an opposition. I'm telling you, he's bad business."

"Alright," Derk concluded; "let's get this muthafucka off the streets. The two officers let all of the Brothas go except Vick, who was arrested for possession of a controlled substance. They claimed to have found two small bags of rock cocaine in his jacket pocket. Once at the station, Derk and his partner tried to retrieve information from Vick about recent crimes to no avail. Vick was a harden criminal that stuck to the code of the streets-**no snitching.**

But the police weren't the only ones concerned with the recent events of the hood. On 80th and Carpenter (D-boy hood), mid-level D-boys conversed about some of the activities of the family.
"Man fam, shit been crazy round here lately, niggas getting gun't the fuck up Joe!"
"Hell yeah" the second one replied. "But we ain't on shit wit' dem' niggas. The G's and the Ops can kill each other off all I care; I don't give a flying fuck!"
"You right D," another cut in, "ain't any sense in involving our guys in no bullshit war. Let's get this money while those stupid muthafuckas get popped off." The D-boys made it clear that they had no intention on participating in the war between their family's brethren (the G-boys) and the oppositions.

They eventually called for a semi-peace treaty, between Rock Island and some of the D's; which received mixed reviews but nonetheless allowed the D-boys to roam a little more freely in certain areas where known Brothas dwelled, a luxury no G's at the time had. A teenaged D-boy named Beleanie even befriended new Con recruit and hustler Rio, and the two young ambitious drug dealers decided to consolidate their efforts and open up a spot out of Beleanie's basement on 77th and Carpenter.

For all intended purposes 77th and Carpenter was a neutral block that separated the two-feuding groups. Those who weren't fans of the peace treaty considered Rio and Beleanie sell-outs, especially some of the young overzealous die-hard Brothas, who were cautious of going near 78th street. For many it was just too close for comfort, and that was cool with Rio. "Mo money for me" he would say, knowing that some of his peers were reluctant to work that closely with Ops. The Brothas were unaware of the amount of the success 77th and Carpenter was generating. But if the D-boys were good at one thing, it was getting money and taking advantage of a money making situation, as Rio and Beleanie would find out in the near future.
****

Lil Rico had been laying low for a few days after going at it hard in the streets for nearly three months, going on missions and selling drugs. His name was getting hot, so Max and Ed ordered him to just chill for a little while; go to school and stay off the hot blocks.

Rico's mother was very aware of the changes in her son and she and Rico would often have debates and arguments about his behavior. "What are all these signs and stuff written all over your closet Rico? are you in a gang? I don't remember buying all of these shoes and clothes, did you steal this stuff?" Screamed Virginia.

"*Steal,* Rico would think to himself, *I damn near make more money than you."* But Rico didn't have the courage to tell Virginia the truth. He wished so bad that he could, but he rationalized that he'd done too many bad things to tell his mother; her temperament was too unstable to trust. After all, the writing was literally on the wall; either Virginia lacked the capacity to reach her son or like so many parents of troubled youth, she assumed that the old fashion ways of strict discipline would cure all. But like many parents of the time, Virginia was losing her child to the streets, as the new wave of influences captivated their minds. For Rico, this caused him to live a double life; one that balanced the streets with home. He would often wonder how it would be if his father was there with him and often entertained the thought of moving with his dad. But his father had a family, and when ever Rico would visit, they made it clear that he was just a visitor. "Fuck'em" thought Rico, "I got Rock Island for a family. The doorbell interrupted his thoughts. *Ring, Ring, Ring,* "I got it," Virginia yelled as she made her way to the front door. "It better not be for you Rico, I told your friends about coming over all types of night." But Virginia knew that the two men standing on her front porch wasn't friends of her son. The medium built white man next to a tall slim built black guy in the neighborhood could only mean one thing, the police.
"Good evening Ma'am, my name is officer Durkerson, and this is my partner officer Timmons, do you have anyone staying here by the name of Rico Love?"
Virginia wasn't a novice in dealing with the police, thanks to her oldest son, and weighted the situation before answering.
"Um, yeah that's my son," she snapped back. "May I help you with something?"
As good as Virginia was, Derk was even better at doing his job and he wasn't affected by Virginia's indifference.
"Is he here Ma'am?" We just need to speak with him about something that happened a while back."
"Come on in," Virginia welcomed, opening the door. "I've been trying to raise this boy right…"
"Yeah I understand," Quick, responded as they neared Rico's bedroom door; only to reveal that Rico was nowhere in sight. "He was here a

minute ago," Virginia stated as the two men searched Rico's room illegally.

"If you know where he is and you don't tell us..." But Virginia had seen enough.

"I know my rights, and I'm afraid I'm going to have to ask you gentlemen to leave, as you see, my son is not here and you don't have the right to search my home."

"Ma'am, we're just trying to do our job," Derk replied in his faux professional voice. "I know as a parent you don't want to see your son go to jail, but for his own safety, if you see or hear from him, please give us a call." Quick handed her a business card.

"Yeah, sure" she replied sarcastically, as the two officers walked towards the front door. Moments later Virginia returned to her son's room and said a silent prayer. She wondered where her son could be.

Rock Island: A Gangstaz Graveyard   N.U.T.T.Y. "C"

CHAPTER 8

A slight drizzle started to dampen Rico's hooded sweatshirt, as he walked down Aberdeen Street aimlessly. He had been long gone from his home; escaping out of his bedroom window when he heard Derk's voice. He was glad that he grabbed all of the money out of his stash, and the *380* hand gun he carried on a regular basis. He knew he was in trouble, although he wasn't exactly sure what for. He had done enough crimes in the last year to get him several life sentences, so it was no telling. He didn't want to go to the spot or anywhere in the hood, and going to a family member's house wasn't an option. So he decided to go to the only place he knew no one knew about, his girlfriend Yoshawn's house. They met over the phone during one of Rico's cranks, and started seeing each other shortly after.

By definition, Yoshawn was a good girl, whose parents was well off and could afford to send her to private school. But her parents allowed her grandmother to raise her. Her grandmother stayed in G-boy hood, which enabled Rico from seeing her as often as he would've liked. They were both the same age 14 years old; she had medium length hair and full juicy lips. Besides having a few puberty based pimples, she was very pretty and didn't wear makeup on her honey colored skin. She was highly sought after, but she prided herself in being a virgin and Rico respected that.

The rain picked up as he reached the payphone located a block from Yoshawn's grandmother's house. He paid close attention, making sure the Ops didn't become interested in his presence, as he spoke into the receiver. "Hey baby," recognizing Yoshawn's whiney voice. "I need to see you, it's important." Yoshawn was already in bed, prepared for school the next day. "Boy you know it's too late for me to have company," she sighed into her phone.

"I know that's why I need you to open your window so I can creep in tonight." He could hear Yoshawn exhaling sharply and smacking those full lips. "Rico, I told you that I want our first time to be special, and I'm not ready."

"Oh, I'm not on that baby, I'm in trouble with the law, and I need a place to lamp right now. I'm out here bad, and it ain't looking good, so I just wanted to spend some time with the girl I love before shit gets real hectic." Yoshawn agreed.

Rico snuck into her bedroom, a place in which he never spent more than five minutes. Her small twin sized bed allowed a closeness that they rarely shared before, as they laid in the semi-darkness talking

49

about their future together. Rico went on to explain to Yoshawn about his life style and some of the events that lead up to him being on the run. "Damn baby you a bad boy," Yoshawn whispered softly into Rico's ear. "But I see a lot of good in you, that's why I love you, and I'll be here waiting for you when you return."
But Rico was thinking more practically. "But what if I'm gone a long time?"
     "I don't care how long it takes for you to return, as long as you promise to come back to me. I'm a hold you down. Some people wait their entire lives and never find their soul mate. My aunt has been married four times, she is in her forties, and she is still looking for the right man. Why should I waist my time going from man to man when I know where my soul mate is? All I have to do is wait for God to send you back to me." Yoshawn had always had a way with words, and that always impressed Rico, but he still held a pessimistic outlook. "I promise you that I'm going to do everything in my power to get back home to you but…it may take a while. And I don't want to put you in a position to betray me…" Yoshawn cut Rico off in mid-sentence with a passionate kiss on the lips. "I'll never betray you Rico." They made love for the very first time in the small bed and fell asleep in each other's arms.
     The next day, Rico turned himself in to the police. He knew exactly what to expect from listening to the older Brothas and watching cop movies. After being in a holding cell for ten hours, he was placed in a lineup. By the time the detectives finally came to speak with him, he was hungry and restless. He became alert as they explained that he was chosen out of a lineup as one of the shooters in a homicide. They placed him in a small room with a two-way mirror and a small table. The detective that entered the room first appeared to be a Latin American, in his early fifties. His partner was a bald *Montell Williams* looking Brotha, with the earring to match.
Dectective #1: O.k., Mr. Love or do you mind if we call you Rico?
Detective #2: I think he likes Rico.
Rico: It's your world, it doesn't matter.
Detective #1: All right, I'ma get straight to the point, you're in big trouble. My partner and I want to help you, but you must first help yourself.
Detective #2: Yeah, you have your whole life ahead of you and I hate to see you throw it away over some bullshit.
Detective #1: Witnesses put you at the scene of the crime.

The second detective pulled out a large envelope that contained several pictures of the slain G-boy's body, and began placing them on the small table in direct view of Rico.

Detective #2: We know others were involved and we can make it seem like they influenced you. Tell us about the pizza guy and the guys that did the drive by!

Detective #1: We know that you did not plan this hit, so help us out so we can help you.

Rico just sat quietly analyzing both detectives verbiage as they threatened him repeatedly. "I think y'all have the wrong man," Rico said quietly.

The two stunned police looked at Rico as if he had insulted their mothers.

Detective #1: So it's like that hunh? You wanna play hard ball? You're just making this hard on yourself.

"I have nothing else to say," Rico boldly interjected. "Not without my lawyer that is."

Detective #2: Well, I hope you got a good one because you're going to need it. Get this piece of gang-bangin shit out of my face, he's done. He's had his chance.

The police had enough evidence against Rico to book him for a multiple shooting, but they knew he'd be charged as a juvenile. They wanted the bigger fish. But Rico wouldn't take the bait. He was processed and transferred to Chicago's detention center, also known as the Audi home for youth offenders.

****

After a quick strip search, he was escorted to his small cell, where he finally laid down and gathered his thoughts; something he hadn't done in two days. He didn't want to stress out thinking about his case; instead he allowed his mind to wonder back to Yoshawn's room and his last night with her. *"I can't believe she let a nigga like me hit that,"* he thought to himself. He had sex with other virgins before, but Yoshawn seemed special. *"I wonder what she doing right now."* He pictured her in her little Catholic school mini-skirt, smiling, as he dosed off to sleep.

The next few days was spent on adjusting to his new surroundings. He remembered his Brotha telling him that only two kinds of people gets no respect in jail; snitches and child molesters. Rico was neither so he breathed easy; he also learned that respect wasn't being handed out freely in the dayroom/TV area. He had to earn it. He did so by fighting several of his peers. Some fights were won, some were lost, but respect was given nonetheless.

Rico learned a lot about himself in jail. He discovered his passion for writing poetry; his two biggest inspirations were Yoshawn and the streets. When he wasn't thinking about his girl, his mind was on the streets and his freedom. Since he could have neither, he wrote passionately about it on paper in the form of songs or poems. By him being one of the few guys on the unit fighting a serious felony, he seen guys come and go, giving him veteran status on the deck. This allowed Rico to meet tons of young men from all over the Chicago area; from all walks of life. He was surprised to meet many more Brothahood members, including ones from other south side locations. He also learned about networking and utilizing the super information highway. Guys in general usually point the finger at females for being gossip hounds, but incarcerated men talk or gossip far more than any female could ever imagine. For instance if a guy wanted to know if his girl was being faithful or simply wanted some information about someone, it would be as simple as finding someone from her area and strike up a factitious conversation. There was always someone from every area that knew something. "She doesn't mess with nobody from our hood," one G-boy told Rico about Yoshawn. "She barely comes outside." That was music to Rico's young ears.

   No information was better than what was going on in your own hood, and nobody could relay it better than one of your own guys. Rico took pride in seeing any Brotha come on his deck. So when he seen Con member Rodney, come in for a weekend stay; Rico knew that he'd put him in tune with everything. Rodney was one of Rock Island's seediest members and he and Rico never really hung out on the streets but they were both happy to see each other. Rico's nightly cleaning duties allowed him to rotate with Rodney and other guys all night. "Man, all type of shit has been going down since you've been gone. Patrick locked up for a murder. Bo-Bo and Mitch caught attempts," Rodney explained from behind his cell door. "Brothas catching cases like crazy; it's still on with the Ops, but its calming down a little bit. A lot of fresh meat in the complex now, so you know we be over there stalking. All the Brothas spread out now. Silo over on 77th and Sangamon, Ed and Max still on 76th Street. Steve still be getting drunk, shooting dice and shit..." After Rodney was finished, Rico felt like he'd never left.

"I can't wait to get back out there Joe."
Rodney informed Rico that the entire hood had anticipated that he'd be gone for a while. "You go be alright lil Rico, just keep your head up in here. I heard old girl came out of her coma saying your name, and she

and one of them niggas picked you out of a line up." Rico was surprised how much the hood knew about his case and flushed with pride as Rodney talked.

"Just keep to the code Brotha and Rock Island go be here for you." Rico needed that shot in the arm from one of his peers, but his biggest morale boosts came in the form of his family visits.

Virginia came every Sunday and would sometime bring his sister or some other family member. She hated seeing her baby in jail, and couldn't psychologically deal with leaving without him every week. "Ma, did you talk to the lawyer and see what's up?" Rico asked in the small visiting area. "Yeah boy, he's working hard, but I want you to know that regardless of what happens, you need to think about changing your life. I think that God is trying to tell you something." Rico tolerated the preaching of Virginia, so it would not spoil his mood. "I know ma, I'm going to go pray as soon as I get back to my cell." But after his visits, praying was the furthest thing from his agenda.

Yoshawn's letters had slowed down dramatically and after several unanswered letters, he searched his mind for reasons why he hadn't heard from her in nearly a month. He read her last letter over and over for clues:

Dear Rico,
Hey baby, I'm just sitting here thinking about you. I miss you so much. I can't believe you've been gone for a year already. Some people out here don't believe you are ever coming home. It makes me sad to think about it. I wanted to go on my prom with you, but it doesn't look like that's going to happen. I really wish you were here, there's nothing out here for me. I appreciate your poems, in fact, I've turned some into raps, and I won second place in a talent show. I miss you so much, please come home soon.
I Love You
*   -Shawn*

Rico felt bad for Yoshawn, because he knew that, it would probably be a long time before he'd see her again. While staring at his favorite picture of her and stroking his manhood through his shorts, he thought to himself; *"damn, shorty getting thick as hell."* He hated that she had told him that she'd wait for him, now he had to hold her accountable. "Just hold on baby, just hold on," Rico whispered softly to the picture before he fell asleep.

****

One month later: Rico sat at the long table with his lawyer; nervously biting his nails as the large courtroom filled in with witnesses and spectators. He had been coming to the courtroom for over a year now, and today he'd finally have his trial. He made eye contact with Virginia and the rest of his family who smiled at him every time he looked in their direction. The judge seemed to be more interested in the small piece of paper in front of him, as he scribbled and doodled while the mundane proceedings took place. The prosecutor was in his glory as he painted an elaborate picture of Rico's alleged crime. But the whole entire court room gasped when the state's star witness was called. Rico tried not to stare too hard, as Peaches limped to the stand and got sworn in. *"How could I be so stupid?"* Rico thought to himself as he prepared to listen to the damaging testimony.

Peaches: *Excuse me your honor, I have something to say.*

Judge: *Is it pertaining to this case?*

Peaches: *Yes sir, I made a mistake when I said that it was Rico that I had seen.* The courtroom went into frenzy with the gallery of spectators and prosecutors all talking at once. The judge banged his gavel, in an attempt to regain order in the court, as Peaches went on to say that she had deliberately gave a false statement about the incident that left her in a coma for over a month. The state's second witness mirrored her testimony, and added that Rico was a well-known opposition and that he lied in his statements to the police, as an act of malice.

In his last effort to save his case, the state's prosecutor tried to convince the court that his witnesses were under some form of duress. "Your honor, it is obvious that my witnesses have been intimidated by some of Mr. Love's associates; I would like to move forward and convince the court..." But Rico's lawyer was on top of his game and quickly objected. "We move for a direct verdict your honor, due to lack of evidence."

The judge shook his head in disgust, as if he was disappointed that he had to uphold the law, as he granted the motion to dismiss all charges on Rico Love. Rico's family cheered when the judge slammed his gavel for the last time. Rico still couldn't believe what had just happened. But his shock quickly subsided as joy overcame him. *"I'm outta this bitch,"* Rico said to himself as he walked out of the courtroom to be processed for release.

Four hours later Virginia and Barbra waited for Rico to come down to the reception area. "The Lord works in mysterious ways" Virginia said to her mother. "Amen" replied Barbra. "I knew that boy was innocent." As Rico sat comfortably in the family car, he reflected

on how much he learned about himself during his incarceration. He was already evaluating his attributes and how he'd apply them to his life. Rico was diagnosed with the "Amygdale" syndrome as a child, it caused him to be analytical; it effects the part of the brain that processes the expressive qualities of speech, such as rhythm and intonation. In a normal mind this would've caused a person to go crazy, but Rico somehow parlayed his condition by developing skills that many people lack. Because he could not be swayed by verbal theatrics on tone of voice, he could very easily spot liars. In a game in which trust was extremely detrimental, he planned to use his abilities fully. And his first test was just around the corner. He could hardly contain his excitement, as his mother pulled in front of Yoshawn's house. "You sure you don't want to come home first," Virginia said to Rico who was about to exit the car.
"I'll be home in a little while ma, I gotta take care of some business first" Rico replied.

****

It had been fourteen months since he last seen Yoshawn, and he felt his hands shaking as he rang the doorbell.
"Oh my God!" The familiar voice yelled from behind the door. Yoshawn jumped into the arms of her man. "I missed you baby, I'm so glad you're home."
They sat in her living room as Rico explained the events that lead to his early release, but the more they talked the more his eyes became fixated on Yoshawn's mature body. She was dressed in tight gym shorts that revealed her toned thighs and a t-shirt that clearly showed no signs of a bra covering her C-cup breast. "Where's your grandma?" Rico asked, cutting Yoshawn off in mid conversation.

"She's out of town for the weekend; why?" Yoshawn asked with a devilish smirk on her face. "I was just asking" Rico replied, trying not to sound too thirsty.
"So um, what's up shorty? You were writing me all the time talking about you gon' wait on me and shit, and then all of a sudden I stop hearing from you. You found someone else or something?" Yoshawn's facial expression turned animated.
"Na'll baby it's just I was stressed out with school and life in general, but I thought about you each and everyday."
"Thinking about me didn't get my named called during mail-call," Rico thought to himself, as they made their way to her bedroom. It was just like Rico remembered it. Words were cut off with passionate kisses as they backed awkwardly into the soft mattress, and slowly undressed. She moaned; "Mmm baby" as Rico tongue circled her brown nipples.

"Her body had definitely changed" Rico thought as he slid into her, and slowly moved back and forth. "This is yo' pussy" Yoshawn whispered into his ears between moans. Rico came fast, but quickly regained vigor, as Yoshawn surprised him with a wet oral experienced. *"Damn, where did she learn how to do this?"* He thought to himself as he watched her please him. Not wanting to spoil the moment, he enjoyed the physical gratification, instead of bombarding her with a fury of questions. But as they both laid there spent, an obvious uneasy feeling came over the both of them. "I love you. Yoshawn said dryly, as Rico kissed her on the forehead, exiting the bed. "Oh yeah I got something for you" Yoshawn said matter of factly; jumping out of bed running to the closet. She went in the closet and found the small crown royal bag. "You left this over here the night you went to jail."

Rico looked in the bag that contained his .380 handgun and nearly two thousand dollars. "Thank you shorty." He said as he kissed her good-bye.

"Be careful out there boo and come back over here soon."

"Yeah I'll be back, you're going to see me again real soon, I promise." Rico exited her home, armed with his .380 he decided to walk.

CHAPTER 9

Meanwhile in G-boy hood:
Two high ranking G's rotated about nation business. "Everything went according to plan fam" one of the G's said.
"Straight up?" responded his Conrad.
"Hell yeah G", we told old girl to go in there and say that she lied." That's good fam, cuz muthafuckers gots to pay for that bullshit, and I don't want that little pussy to be in the joint getting in shape and living good while my man and nem in the grave."
"Yeah, now that he free, we can murk his little ass. Let the whole family know I got five for shorty's head. And if I can catch him alone, that's even better cuz I wanna know who the rest of them dudes were, especially that fake ass pizza man."
"A'ight G", I'ma make sure the word gets out quickly cuz if the stories about him are true; we need to get him out the way quick.
****

In Rock Island:
Rico's release was also the topic of discussion of ranking members. Lil Ed, Max, Terry, Raulo, Teeny, Brandon, and Mike B., all convened to discuss Nation business. Ed spoke first. "As some of you may already heard, our little Brotha Rico C', just beat his case. I don't know how he did it, but he did. Rico could've taken alot of Brothas down with him, but he followed the code like a real Brotha suppose to do. So I feel like he should be acknowledged and rewarded. We're throwing him a welcome home party Friday and he will be promoted to Minister-of-Justice for the hood. I think everyone would agree that he is capable of that spot and he deserves it."
Max: We're going to give all of next weeks dues to him, as well as take him shopping.
Terry: We have to let that Brotha know now that he about to have a position; he cannot be on all that wild shit.
Raulo: How come he gotta get a high position like that anyway? He just a shorty. I thought I was up for that spot.
Max: Man Joe, its like this, Rico is the new M.O.J. and whoever don't like it, so fuckin what! Raulo you the Enforcer, we need you at that spot. Did you just catch a murder for the hood? I don't think so. So pipe down with that shit, Rico got the spot and it is what it is. Now if nobody got nothing else to add, we can end this.
The meeting ended on that note. But some of the Brothas remained in the apartment and smoked joints provided by Teeny. Toby, noticed

something different with the weed, but he didn't say a word. By the time Max, Ed, Calvin, and others found out what they were really smoking, it would be too late.
****

Back at home, Rico enjoyed his newfound freedom; his mother's house seemed smaller, even his bedroom felt weird. All the things he once took for granted such as going to the kitchen and making a sandwich, or going to use the bathroom facilities in private was a welcome treat now that he was home. Soaking in a tub of warm soapy water, it didn't take long for his mind to drift back to the streets. "I gotta get this money," Rico thought to himself; rationalizing a street business plan. Apparently, word of his release traveled fast, because his front porch was filled with Brothas. T.P., Head, Toby, and Milton all greeted Rico with handshakes and hugs, as he opened his front door. "Man, how you niggas find out I was home?" Rico asked cheerfully.

"Man Joe, everybody know you out, Max and nem' want you to come up to the park." Toby responded.
Rico quickly got dressed and made his way to the park. The warm seasonable weather had many of the Brothas in the park playing basketball or hanging out shooting dice. Lil Mikey, Travis, Kenyatta, Eric and some other Corner boys stopped their basketball game to greet Rico. Max, Vick, Ed, and Terry sat near the back under a tree, trying their best to look serious as Rico approached. "Ya'll niggas look like you ain't happy to see me or something!" Rico said opting to hug his mentor Max first. "Vick you don't ever smile anyway…"

"Ain't shit funny shorty, life too real…" Rico ignored his speech as he admired the gold jewelry Max, Ed, and Terry adored themselves in.
"Man ya'll ballin' like that huh?" Rico said smilingly,
"Hell yeah!" Ed took the chain off and handed it to Rico, and told him to try it on. "That's you lil homie." Rico was flushed with pride as they informed him of his promotion and the new responsibilities that were inherited with it. Max took him shopping and updated his wardrobe, and reiterated the importance of his new position, as well informing him of the fact that not all Brothas like the idea.
"Don't trip." Rico assured, "niggas ain't gotta like me, but at the end of the day as long as they respect me it's cool."

Later that night at his party: Rico entered, with Toby and Milton. The large gold link chain around Rico's neck shined in the dim light of the party. It was filled with everybody from Rock Island and a few neighboring allies. People who Rico hadn't seen in over a year, like Big Bo who was there with his younger brother Duke who was a new Con. Steve sat in the back with a bottle of something wrapped in a paper bag. He was one of the Brothas that always drank too much and had to be carried home by the end of the night. Lil Mikey, Kenyatta, and the Hull brothers were all talking to various females. Myron, Eric, and Travis were sharing a joint. "Rico C" it's your night" Brandon yelled over the music. "Let's get on some of deyz broads in here!" Referring to the abundance of scantly clad young women that were scattered around the party. Many of the females were locals that he was already familiar with or already had sexual encounters with; like Olesha, the red-bone that stayed on 78th street, who Rico, Lil Mikey, and others ran a train on one winter night in the spot, or Porche, the chick from the complex who was known for her oral abilities. One non-familiar face did catch his attention, as she danced to the house music glaring from the big speakers. She was dark like milk chocolate, with long wavy hair, dressed in an all red body suit that left very little to the imagination. Her slim frame had curves all in the right places. She made light flirtatious eye contact with Rico, even though she was dancing with another partygoer. Rio noticed Rico starring at the young lady in Red and put him in tune. "That's Quetta, she a Black EEl Sista from a set called NATION."

"Yeah, I see her staring over here like she wanna get down or something. What's up is she a hood rat or what?" Rico asked

"Man I don't really know." Rio responded. "You know how it is with these chicks, they could be rats in they own hood, but they new booty when they come on yo' joint."

"Hell yeah!" Rico agreed. "But I'ma see what's up cuz shorty moving like she can work a dick." Rio laughed and faded away into the crowd. While Rico approached Quetta and introduced himself, the introduction was swift, but their energy was intense. They made small talk about exchanged numbers. Rico did a little homework and found out she was a Princess for EEL Sistas and that she had a lot of influence in her hood. She was a gangsta chick that didn't take no shit from dudes or females. Her sexual history wasn't too bad for a chick of her caliber. She called Rico the next day, and they talked for hours.

Quetta: So where's your woman?

Rico: Damn, you in a Brotha business kinda early ain't you? I didn't ask you where was your man did I?

Quetta: I don't really care if you got one or not, I just wanna know if I gotta fuck somebody up or not. Rico laughed as his mind quickly flashed thoughts of Yoshawn.

Rico: I got a situation that might not be a situation in a minute, so we shouldn't have too many problems.
Quetta: I ain't trippin' I just wanna find out if the myth is true.
Rico: What the hell you talking bout, what myth?
Quetta: Oh yeah, you ain't heard? They say Rock Island niggas be putting it down in the bed.

Rico knew he had a bonafied freak on his hands and a street savvy down chick. The pros outweighed the cons.

After getting off the phone with Quetta, he immediately dialed Yoshawn's number, informing her that he was on his way over. When he arrived at her home, he noticed her brother and some of his associates chillin' on the porch, and instantly regretted leaving his gun. But he wasn't too concerned with them, his primary concern was with Yoshawn and how she was going to react to the news he had for her. Yoshawn noticed something was wrong as she tried to kiss him. "What's wrong?" she asked, as Rico looked around the house for prying adults. Rico couldn't hold back. His whole demeanor turned violent as he began to drill her with a verbal attack. "You say you was gone wait on me, and wasn't fuckin' with no other dudes, you a lying ass bitch!" Rico's words and tone caught Yoshawn off guard because she had never seen him like this. She began to cry as she attempted to defend herself. "Rico I don't know what you're talking about, I was faithful to you, I'm sorry I stop writing you but I didn't know what to say. So what are you talking about that you have proof?"

"The proof is my dick, you burnt me Yoshawn! And before you deny it, you are the only person I've been with since I came home. I should fuck yo ass up for this shit. I can't believe you gave me a STD." Yoshawn attempted to stand by her word, but quickly faltered after Rico changed his tone a little. He went on to explain to Yoshawn about STD's and how certain ones show no symptoms in females, and that's possibly why she wasn't aware that she was infected. After a while, she wasn't in defense mode anymore and his attitude changed for the better. "I love you baby, and I know you probably made a mistake, it's alright." He gently grabbed her hands, looked into her teary eyes, and asked her "Do you love me?"

"Yes, Rico I love you but…" Rico cut her off and said,

"That's all that matters then. We can get through this together as long as you keep it real with me and promise to never lie to me again. Can you do that?"

Yoshawn's floodgates were weaken by his every word as she began to cry heavily, while Rico embraced her in his arms and stroked her hair. "I'm sorry Rico, I really am."
"I know baby, let's get this behind us. The first thing we gotta do is go to the clinic and get this cleared up. They're going to ask a lot of questions so let's get ourselves prepared for that."
"What kind of questions?" she asked, drying her tears.
"About your sexual history and stuff, it's nothing really. For example, they might ask you how do you think you became infected and who might've infected you. Can you answer that?"
Yoshawn looked down at her hands as she softly spoke. "Well it had to be between two guys- Marcus and Benny." Rico sat quietly as he coaxed all the juicy details out of his first love. Yoshawn felt so relieved now that she had gotten all of that off her chest. "Those dudes didn't mean nothing to me Rico." But Rico's mind was already somewhere else. He had mixed emotions about what was happening. His Oscar winning performance showed him that the one person in the world he trusted could no longer be trusted. And for what he was planning, trust meant everything. For a second he felt bad about tricking her into a confession, he could've easily detected a disingenuous response to any question, but he rationalized that the way he did things was easier than trying to explain to them that their speech patterns and facial expressions gave them away. His condition was both a gift and a curse. He loved Yoshawn and could've easily forgiven her for her betrayal, but he knew if he made a habit of doing that, his chances of survival for the game he was in would be extremely narrowed. Rico left Yoshawn's house promising to return shortly so that they could go to the doctor together. Instead, Rico called Quetta and made arrangements with her, giving her the opportunity to see if the myth was true.

CHAPTER 10
(DA SISTAZ)

Originally, Rock Island started with one female member. Her name was Boonie. She was a tomboy that lived six houses away from Lil Ed. She never really got along with the females her age, and felt more comfortable around guys. Boonie wasn't initially regarded as a "Sista"; she was just a con member. Most of the Brothas forgot that she was a female, because of the way she acted for the most part. By the time she was sixteen, she stood 5 ft. 9 in, and weighed 225 pounds. She grew up in a house full of men that taught her how to fight at an early age. By the time Rock Island took over her block, she was well equipped and adjusted to the street life. Lil Ed did business with guys in her building and he would often let Boonie run errands for him. But Boonie soon became more than a friend to Lil Ed and the rest of the Brothas. She became the big sister and a multipurpose member of a growing organization. She would allow guns and drugs to be held in her house, she helped with bagging up drugs, and sometimes delivering them. She wasn't pretty by most guys standards, and it seemed that she wasn't trying to be. She wore short hair that you could tell was uncombed underneath her ever-present baseball cap. All her clothes were men's attire. But despite her hard exterior, she was a loyal, loving, type, and for a lot of Brothas she was just as much a mother figure as Ed & Max were father figures. She became Rock Island's first Queen.

A lot of people teased that Boonie was gay, but like a lot of the females in gangs, she could be linked to at least one member. And for Boonie that Brotha was Feather, a 4-corner boy, known for his pistol play. The two of them became R.I's version of Bonnie and Clyde. But even though Feather was considered a beast on the streets, he still was just a soldier. Boonie was Royalty, a Queen. As hard as it was for guys to become Cons, its was even more difficult for females.

For years, Boonie was the only female that attended the weekly meetings at the park. Then others gradually became known as Sistaz, usually they were females that were the main girlfriends of ranking members. Since their boyfriends were respected members, they often received the same respect, so it was only a natural progression for Sistaz such as Tanesha (Ed's girlfriend), Lisa (Teeny's girlfriend), and Yolanda (Marco's girlfriend). Unlike Boonie, all of these females were loyal to R.I. primarily for one reason, their men. The girlfriends weren't as aggressive as Boonie, but they did manage to represent, often getting into it with opposition females at school. The same rules applied for the

63

females of Rock Island, if you disrespected one of them, you'd better expect retaliation.

The next Con Sista to be highly regarded came after Ed and Max lifted the age limit. Her name was Lavada. Her skin was the color of a paper bag and she had chinky eyes. She had the body of a grown woman at the age of fourteen, full C-cup breast and a backside that you could easily sit a cup on. Lavada was aware of her beauty yet she didn't carry it around like a badge of honor. She'd purposely down play her looks and even dated unattractive guys just to prove she wasn't shallow. She was raised in a house full of women, who were all hustlers. Most of her aunts were well-known exotic dancers, as well as her oldest sister who mentored her. She gave Lavada the game, teaching her how to manipulate guys to do what she wanted them to do. Boonie befriended Lavada after they got into a fight over what Boonie said was a disrespectful stare. Boonie liked the fact that Lavada didn't back down from her even though she was the bigger threat. She fought with heart. "Like a nigga" Boonie said.

Most people were surprised when they seen that Boonie embraced the pretty girl that every Brotha wanted a piece of. Boonie recommended Lavada to be a Sista, and she would later become the unofficial Princess of R.I's Con Sistas. The Con Sistas were pale in comparison to the 4 corner Sistas, who were seemingly growing in numbers every week, much in part because of Lil Mikey's relentless recruiting spree.

The most notable Sista of the time was Lil Mikey's on again/ off again girlfriend Keshia, who was the oldest of her four sisters. Keshia not only stood out because of her age, but because of her vicious, tenacity and ghetto girl attitude. No dude could control her, and no female would dare cross her. She was cool like a dude, smoked weed, drank, and talked jive with the fellas, yet she was sexy and would often dress up in short skirts and have her hair done. Despite her light skin and medium build, that most guys found attractive, she was a typical hood chick. Keshia, like her male counterpart (Lil Mikey) had an infectious personality, alot of girls wanted to be a cool like her, and since she claimed R.I., most of her peers wanted to follow suit. Even though it was common knowledge that most females gang members initiation included sexual favors with certain male members, the Brothas from Rock Island strayed away from that order of business, opting to just make most Sistas pledge to the gang, even though a lot of the Sistas did have sex with multiple Brothas, including Keshia. But for the most part that was part of the appeal to females that wanted to live the gang life but did not want to be considered promiscuous. Many

Rock Island Sistas prided themselves on the fact that they weren't regarded as hoes or sluts.

Like the Brothas the Sistas were tightly knit or family oriented. Lisa, Tanesha, and Yolanda were best friends. Keshia's sisters and cousins all became members, and had the entire hood buzzing. Her cousin Ko-Ko was well known for starting trouble. And Keshia's sister Nicole was just as bad. Some Sistas often met guys who were oppositions and charm them into coming to pick them up at a destination in which made it easy for the Brothas to ambush them. These "set-up chicks" made their claim to fame by tricking guys. Lavada, Nicole, and Ko-Ko were like magnets for young thugs, who thought with their small head instead if their big one. And they didn't mind being put on display, as they were one hot sunny afternoon, near 75th and Carpenter. The Brothas called it *"trick or treat."*

Ko-Ko: Girl did y'all see them tired ass bitches in Lenzy trying to front today?
Lavada: Hell yeah, I was abut to beat one of dem' hoes down in there talking crazy to my girl Keshia like that.
Keshia: Anyway, fuck that shit. Look at all these niggas out here, trying to trick somebody with their hats turned to the right, throwing up family signs these niggas crazy.
Ko-Ko: Who do y'all think got the biggest dick, the 4's, C's, or EEls?

As they debated about what gang packed the most, Ops started falling for the bait. The Brothas would ambush them by throwing bottles at their cars. For the Brothas it was fun and games. But it wouldn't be for the 2 oppositions in a Sedan. Seeing that the corner was filled with apparent "family" members' on one side and some fine females on the other, the Sedan slowed down. "Pull over fam, let's holla at these hoes" the passenger said to his friend after making eye contact with some of the females.
"Man its ops around here," the driver said.
"No it's not. Dem niggas over there got they hats to the right, this family hood over here. We cool."
"What's up fam?" the driver yelled out the window to the group on the corner.
"What's up fam?" one Brotha shot back.
"G-boy to heart over here." "And you know it."
"I told you, we all good," the passenger said to his partner as they pulled over near the Sistas.
The guys didn't notice that all of the guys on the corner had left, and only got in two minutes of conversation before one Sista approached

the car with a .38 and shot 5 times, striking the driver at point blank range in the head, and hitting the passenger in the arm.

As the car rolled awkwardly down the street with its lifeless driver, the remaining Sistas scattered. The surviving passenger exited the vehicle and fired his gun upon the fleeing group, hitting one Sista in the back. Her name was Sheeky, she was 14 year's old. She had only been a Sista for 2 months. She was later arrested for the crime, but due to her age she was charged as a minor and sent to an out of state placement for teen violent offenders. Sheeky was an exception to the norm.

Most of R. I.'s Sistas weren't going to break a nail for the hood, much less shoot a gun, and commit murder. For the most part, R. I. Sistas eventually could be identified into three different characteristic groups. The first group were *"The Ridaz,"* which consisted of females such as Boonie and Sheeky. They typically weren't fine in terms of looks; they usually were the rough tom-boy types. They'd fight and bang right along aside the Brothas. They sold drugs and spent a lot of time on the block or in the favorite hangout spots of the Brothas.

The next groups of Sistas were called *"Vogues"*, the most stylish and popular Sistas were in this group. A lot of these Sistas were considered fine and desirable. Most were girlfriends if Brothas with status or money. They probably wouldn't strike you as a gang member at first glance; instead, they would wear subtle signs of their affiliation such as an extra earring in their left ear, or gold streaks in their hair, nothing permanent. Because a lot of the Vogues were also set-up chicks, being able to blend in any environment was detrimental. However, these Sistas were the biggest troublemakers, because of their influence and personal relationships within the organization. These Sistas would often start trouble knowing that they could convince the guys to defend them no matter if they were bogus or not. A lot of "Vogues" thought they were better than the other Sistas, which lead to a lot division and internal cat fights, but the "RIDAZ" always kept them in their place.

Lastly, there was a group of curious, ambitious, young women that were more like hood or nation groupies called *"The Cheerleaders"*. They didn't take the gang life seriously. They acted like the gang was their favorite sports team or something, and could be often seen wearing the gang's colors or clothing with Rock Island insignias. They showed their loyalty by going to parties or other affairs representing, but when it came to business, they were highly undependable. In fact, they only usually came around or hung out on weekends or when special events took place. A lot of the cheerleaders were well known for being around one day and gone the next. Some had babies, others were given a dose of reality, and a few just out grew their childish ways.

Very few could play a role in all three groups, but Sistas like **Lavada, Keshia,** and later **Mary-Ann, Ruthie, Java, Bubba,** and **Vicka** did and became female legends of Rock Island.

Rock Island: A Gangstaz Graveyard   N.U.T.T.Y. "C"

CHAPTER 11

Derk and Quick were in route when they got a call of shots fired near 77th and Aberdeen. A large crowd had gathered around by the time they arrived at the scene. "Looks like one of the Rock Island punks got hit this time," Derk said to his partner as they exited their maroon cruiser.
"Yeah maybe those G-boys tired of their shit," responded Quick, paying close attention to the crowd. "Look at this shit, they out here hanging out like they're at a block party or something."
"What we got here?" Derk asked the white uniformed officer. The officer had a small note pad in his hand and referred to it as he spoke to Derk and Quick." Um, the victim, apparently a member of one of the Rock Island gangs was struck by a bullet from one of his own partners. Witnesses say that his friend tried to defend the victim by shooting at some G-boys and the victim, 16-year-old Eric Brown was shot. They say Travis and Eric were close friends, but we can't locate this Travis character as of yet." After being filled in, Derk and Quick decided to canvas the area for Travis.
"It's messed up that he gotta go to jail for killing his friend," Quick said breaking an awkward moment of silence. "Yeah, but you know what I'm starting to hate? Every time I come over here, I'm seeing new faces; all that means is more bodies. And speaking of new faces, you remember that little Con who we booked for that shooting on 74th, with the girl?"
"Who you talking about, Love?"
"Yeah, Rico Love. He's beat the fucking case."
"What? How did he do that with two witnesses that put him on the scene?"
"Fucking witnesses recanted their statements right in court"
"You think he got to em'?"
"He don't have that much juice does he?"
"I'm not sure, but I don't want him on the streets. I heard he's been laying low going to school during the day, and get this, word is that he's selling rocks over there on 77th and Carpenter, with that stupid mo'fucka Mario Lomax"
"Wanna send a couple of undercovers over there to make a couple buys?"
"Na'll, if the fam don't kill him over there, we'll get him. And when we do I want to put him away for a long time."

Later that evening, Travis turned himself in. A lot of people were afraid that Eric's cousins Myron, Parish, Tommy-Joe, and Shawn would hold a grudge against Travis. But surprisingly they all showed up at his court hearings in support of Travis. He eventually pled guilty to second-degree manslaughter and received four and a half years. Eric's death was a somber affair, because there was nobody to retaliate against. "Let's not be sad for our Brotha" Rico said at one of the goals proceeding Eric's death. "Let's celebrate his life, and remember all the things he enjoyed in life. Keep his memory alive and he'll never die." Rico was a prolific speaker, and his presentations at the weekly meetings (goals) not only boasted the morale of young members, but he helped them understand their purpose. He was over exceeding his expectations in his new minister spot, making Max and Ed's job much easier. But his success was slowly creating silent enemies. Enemies that he wasn't use to going to war with. Some accused him of being overzealous with his new status. But Rico knew that he had to rotate twice as hard as the older Brothas because he felt like his spot was still probationary. So he did all the extra things that many others Brothas with spots didn't do. He always took time out to personally see if he could assist any Brotha with a problem or issue. And when he noticed one of his friends Toby not coming around as much, Rico went to him. Toby had been introduced to Rock Island as an Eel from 87th street and later turned Con mentored by Ed and Max. He was once a permanent fixture in the 76th spot on May. But lately he had been seemingly avoiding May Street, opting to stay on his block with another Con Silo. "I ain't really feeling the spot no more," Toby said sitting on the top stair of his front porch. Rico could see the disenchantment in his face. "What's up my nigga, those niggas aint paying you right or something?"
"Na'll man it aint that, it's….man I really don't wanna talk about it. I see you don't be up in there like that anymore either. Man a lot shit changed since you been gone. I've been witnessing some foul shit, and I ain't trying to get caught up."
"Man Toby, you know I've been doing my thang over there on Carpenter and you welcome to come, if you wanna get some money…."
Toby shook his head and lit a Newport. "This ain't got nothing to do wit' no money Brotha, and since you on the committee, I don't know if I could unfold this to you." Rico was starting to become more animated. "What? Nigga, you was my nigga before I even got this spot,

so if there something you need to get off your chest then say it nigga, but don't sit here and front on my name!" But Toby was still hesitant.
"Dem yo guy's Rico, and I ain't tryin to rock the boat."
"Let me tell you something Brotha, we took an oath, we have rules and policies that govern us – nobody and I mean nobody is bigger than these laws. If a Brotha is bogus, he is subjected to the same penalties as the next nigga. I'm cool with a lot of Brothas but I love the Brothahood and what it stands for, so I can't allow my friendships to cloud my judgment. I'm a law man, so if you're aware of something that's not right and you're telling me you don't want to reveal it, then you are part of the problem to. You know I got Ed and Max cuffed, they'll listen to me about any problems."
"Well, what if the problem involves Ed and Max? Who would listen to you then?"
Rico had never thought about that scenario. Even though he'd met higher ranking Brothas from other parts of the city, Ed and Max was all he knew. "I'm telling you Brotha, I could do something" But Toby stuck to his guns and didn't relinquish any more information. It racked Rico's young mind, as he left to check on his comrades on Carpenter Street.*" What could they possibly be doing to cause Toby to feel that way?"* he thought to himself. Once he reached Carpenter, Rio, Kenyatta and Myron were all chillin leaning against Rio's new car. Rico hadn't seen Kenyata in a couple of years, since Kenyatta got locked up for a juvenile armed robbery. "When you get out Brotha?" Rico asked as he greeted Kenyatta with a man hug.
"The other day Joe and it feels good."
"Yeah you know I feel you. But what's good wit' ya'll? Why ya'll hangin out, you know you gotta be low key on this block."
"Well it's like this" Rio said. "I was thinking, since I've been over here getting this money with Belanie and a few of his guy's been coming through on the low serving , I might as well invite a few of my guys too."
"Hell yeah" Myron cut in. "Might as well get that dust. It's a perfect location. We can catch customers going to the ops and Ed & Max spot."
"Yeah, well what if niggas start trippin' about us being over here?" Rico asked.
Rio assured Rico by adding, "We got this Brotha, the D-boys cool, and they ain't like the G's. I holla'd at them already. We got it set up where all of us can get this dust." Me, you, Myron, and now Kenyatta can get this spot juking. The D's that do come down here ain't on shit."

Rico felt like they had already made up their minds, so he reluctantly agreed. "A'ight Joe, let's do this, but I want ya'll to be careful out there. I don't trust no oppositions."

****

Meanwhile, word of K-Man's release from prison was on the tongues of most Brothas. Rock Island's 4-Cornerboy leader had been gone for five and a half years, but his name always stayed in the air. Rumor after rumor flew each year concerning K-Man. Some said that he and Max would beef over control of May Street. Some said that he wasn't too happy about his 2nd in command Wayne's involvement with the Corner Brothas. Others said that he was going to branch off from Rock Island and would attempt to take over the complex creating a separate set. The Black EEls of Rock Island had already did so by transitioning out of the Island to 73rd and May, creating a new set for only EEls called *Brothaville*. But the fact of the matter was nobody knew exactly what was on K-Man's mind or agenda. It was always an event when he came home. Wayne was the first to check in with K-Man to put him in tune with everything. "Man Brotha, everything's been good, we been handling our business out here. I got the complex on lock Joe. The EEls moved to 73rd and May, but they still cool. I think Ed and Max had something to do with that. Them niggas need your help too, cuz lately they ain't been on top of their game. It's a lot of new Brothas...."

K-Man ordered Wayne to tell a 4's to report to the park for a formal meet and greet. An hour later, nearly fifty Brothas and twenty Sistas filled the park, many of whom had never seen their Chief. The crowd watched K-Man exit his jeep, sporting blue jeans and a white wife–beater that illustrated his prison tattoos. He only stood 5'9 but years of prison workouts gave him a muscular physique that made him appear much bigger. He still wore his hair short with waves, and a neatly trimmed beard.

Lil Mikey, Myron, T.P., Kenyatta, and Head all stood near K-Man as he began to speak. "Check it out ya'll, it's good to see ya'll little Brothas, we got a lot to discuss, so if you ain't no real 4, excuse yourself from the park." The crowd of young 4's looked at K-Man with bewilderment, but didn't budge. "All ya'll niggas can't be 4's, who blessed ya'll?"

Most of the crowd shifted their eyes to in the direction of Lil Mikey. Sensing that K-Man was perturbed, Lil Mikey attempted some damage control. "Um, check it out K-Man...." But K-Man cut Lil

Mikey off in mid sentence. "Na'll fuck dat, who gave you the authority to bless all these Brothas?"
Mikey's charisma was no match for K-Man gangster attitude." Brotha you bogus you got all these people claiming to be 4's. That's a breach of security. You walk round here like you Chief or something. You don't have no rank, you ain't shit." K-Man then focused his attention on the crowd of young 4's. "I better not catch none of you mutha' fuckas' claiming to be a 4. All ya'll on ice until I decide what I wanna do wit' ya'll." He then turned and snatched a gold chain with a large 4 medallion off one of the Brothas neck. Although the crowd was filled with young gangstas, no one would alone attempt to stand up to someone of K-Man's caliber. It would be a potential death wish. The young 4's reality check was disturbing, and K-Man didn't know it at the time but his actions would have a profound affect on Rock Island.

The young disenchanted 4's started rebelling. A group of them on 77th and Throop flipped to D-boys. Their block would later become a D-boy set. Lil Mikey expressed his disenchantment to Ed and Max. "This is some bullshit," he exclaimed. "We been holding it down while this mutha' fucka' been in the joint. How he go tell Brothas they ain't from Rock Island?"

In a surprising move, lil Ed blessed Mikey and his entire crew to the Cons organization. T.P., Head, Myron, Kenyatta, and even Keshia followed suit. K-Man seemed to be unaffected by the fact that he had just lost over half of his membership. Surprisingly Lil Mikey and the other new Brothas transition didn't disrupt the harmony of Rock Island's unity. In fact, it seemed to ignite the youthful spirits of old Cons. For Rico, his responsibilities seemed to increase, as Ed and Max became less hands on, leaving critical decisions to Terry and Rico. Something was going on and Rico resolved to get to the bottom of it. His big break came from an unlikely source- K-Man.

In an obvious attempt to deject Lil Mikey and others, he could often be heard speaking against his peers Ed and Max. Rico confronted K-Man, about speaking ill of his leaders.
"Oh you ain't heard? Don't pretend like you don't know what be going on in that spot. All them Cons be smoking laced joints, they might as well start smoking the pipe. I'm telling ya'll now it's only going to get worse." K-Man seemed to be on a mission like a politician on a campaign trail, trying to gather votes. "That's why all ya'll need to turn to Corner boys and be on a winning team."
Rico felt like K-Man's words were inappropriate. "But we all Brothas" Rico pleaded, "So if one suffers, we all suffer."

K-Man wasn't use to being confronted and his tone became indignant as he directed his words towards Rico. "Do you think dem' niggas give a fuck about ya'll? All they care about is getting high. Ed, Max, George, Teeny, all of them niggas, they fucking with that shit. I'll take care of ya'll Brothas, we'll do this the right way, and the way real Brothas suppose to do it."

Rico couldn't believe his ears. He instantly hated himself for not seeing it for himself. He prided himself in being observant and now some of his most admired and respected peers were abusing drugs right under his nose and he didn't catch it. Still loyal to his members he gave K-Man an ear full before parting ways. "Nigga, if you a real Brotha, you'd be trying to help those Brothas instead of talking behind their backs, trying to get niggas to follow you. You knew these Brothas before we did and now you trying to outcast them. Them my niggas and I'm gon' see what's up."

K-Man responded with a brief laugh, "Yeah good luck nigga, cuz the problems those Brothas got bigger than all of us."

K-Man's campaign had a minimum affect. Con members Nelson from the complex pledged to the 4 Corner Chief, followed by two young hustlers Wacky and Menace. Rico didn't like what was happening, *"Brothas couldn't be just flipping back and forth changing branches."* He vowed to get to the bottom of the situation before other Brothas were affected. He wanted to re-route on Toby and start his investigation from there. When he arrived at Toby house, he met Silo on Toby's front porch. Silo was a high-ranking Con who introduced Toby to the gang. But shortly after Toby was blessed, Silo went to the joint for a couple of years, leaving Toby's to be mentored by Ed and Max. Silo was a top-heavy bulky Brotha who also benefitted from all the weights he lifted in the joint. Since his release from the joint, he had been lamping, trying to stay out of the spotlight, which was kind of odd to Rico because with his former status, Silo could be just as powerful as Ed or Max. Rico figured if Silo wasn't messing with Ed, something had to be up. Toby, Silo and Rico all sat on the porch and discussed the problems of R.I's beloved leaders.

SILO: You know Ed my nigga, we grew up together came into the Nation together, so when I first found out I didn't want to believe it. Then when Toby told me what happen, I just told him to stay out the spot.

RICO: Man Toby, what the fuck happen Joe?

TOBY: I was in the spot with Ed and nem' one night, and everybody was drinking, having a good time. Then muthafuckas starting rolling up

some bud.....I hit the weed and I knew something was wrong but I didn't say shit. I think them niggas was trying to turn me out.
SILO: They gave this Brotha a laced joint, had em' down there smoking cocaine. Dem Brothas bogus, we don't get down like that ya' dig. I wasn't raised like that, ya' feel me.
RICO: I feel you, but what we gon' do? We can't just go and violate dem Brothas and kick em' to the curb, everything gotta be done by law.
SILO: We gotta go over their head. Go to the Brotha they have to answer to.
TOBY: How in the hell we go get up with the Old Man?
SILO: Na'll, the Old Man is at the top of the chain of command, but there's a Brotha in place that governs the entire south side. You see, Ed and Max are smart. They don't want Brothas to know that they have to answer to someone beside the Old Man. They want all you young Brothas to follow them and them only. They try to preach *"No big I's and little U's"*, but in reality they make the rules and the rules are put in place to control the membership, not the leadership. But I know how this shit goes, and if we gon' deal with Ed and Max, we gotta be prepared to go against the grain, and we go need the assistance of somebody with more juice than them. That's the only way we can overthrow Brothas like them.
RICO: But before we bring in any outsiders, we gotta try to deal with this internally. I think I'll go holla at Max and Silo you drive on Ed and maybe we can try to convince them to stop what they doing and get some help, if not we'll move to plan B.

****

   Silo, Toby and Rico wasn't the only ones with intervention on their minds. On 60th and Winchester, the Cons that controlled that area were on high alert as Big Bo, Lil Mikey, and Steve sat in a parked car waiting. "Man you think this a good idea?" Steve asked, as they waited. "Ed and Max gon' have us killed if they find out we over here to holla at Chief behind their backs."
"What the fuck we suppose to do?" Bo shot back.
"Yeah Joe, this is the only way to fix shit" Lil Mikey added.
"Chief ready to see ya'll now." One of the shorty Cons said in the passenger side window.
Big June the Cons south-side Chief, was a twenty-nine year old drug dealer, who made a name for himself after moving from the west side. Now he controlled the entire south side that contained over 40 different Con sets. He was a liberal leader, with a selfless attitude. He didn't dress overly flashy, and still sported his jerry curl, a hair style that had been out of style for years. A lot of people said he looked like the

rapper *Ice Cube*, back in his N.W.A. days. He greeted the Rock Island Brothas as they passed his two armed security guards. "What can I do for you Brothas?"

CHAPTER 12

"*These dudes must be crazy*" Rico thought to himself as he pulled in front of 76th and May, where Max, Terry, and a new Con named T.Y. stood talking. "How in the hell could they possibly think they can beat crack. Most of these zombie ass crack head mutha' fuckas' started off the same way."

As he parked, he practiced what he would say to Max over and over in his head. "*I don't want to sound too preachy, but I gotta let this Brotha know that with him on that shit he's a liability, and Rock Island can't afford to have a crack-head leader.*"

"What's crackin' Brothas?" Rico greeted, as he approached the group of Cons.

"Nothing much" Terry said. "Just waiting on Ed to come drop this work off."

"Max what you bout to do?" Rico asked.

"I'm just chillin, why what's up?"

"Come ride with me to get something to eat, I gotta holla at you about some business." Max agreed. "Alright Joe, C'mon Terry let's roll."

They got in Rico's black Chevy Caprice, and cruised down May. Rico didn't want to come out and be direct with his leader about the probing issue, so he made small talk as they listened to Rap music. "I feel like getting some *Hurold's Chicken* that shit the bomb Joe."

"Hell yeah," agreed Max as he looked at his pager. "Damn this Big June paging me, he said out loud." Max meant for his comment to be directed to Terry, but Rico made it his business to steal the show.

"Big June?" Rico said, playing naïve. "Ain't that one of the Brothas with some juice? What dat' nigga on?"

Max thought to just brush Rico off and was glad Terry answered for him. "Big June cool, he got the south-side, but ya' know we been doing our own thang, ya' dig? It's crazy cuz when we was only one block niggas not making no noise, mo'fuckas wasn't trying to fuck with us, but I just play my role, leave all that shit to ya' boy right here. Ain't dat right Max?'"

"Man fuck you" Max said jokingly. "The whole south-side just getting on the map, not just us. So you know the Old Man had to appoint somebody to organize all the sets. Big June have to rotate with all the sets out south just to make sure we cool. That's his job as overseer, you know this thang is bigger than Rock Island, we a whole *Nation* of Brothas…" Rico felt that Max's little speech was a perfect segway to the topic he wanted to address. So he cut in. "Yeah you right

77

Brotha, this is bigger than just Rock Island and that's what I've been wanting to holla at cha' about." Rico turned the music down to have Max's full attention. Rico continued to explain what the streets were saying about R.I.'s top dogs. "You know that drug use is forbidden amongst the guy's; the only exception is weed."
Max immediately became defensive, and tried some reverse psychology as damage control. And he began bombarding Rico with an array of irrelevant questions. "Who told you that shit, who been talking behind my back?"
But that didn't detour Rico. "It don't matter who told me," Rico sighed. Wuz up wit' you and dem' Brothaz messing with that shit?" Max conceded that he wasn't going to win a war of words with his Minister-of-Justice. "I know you just trying to do the right thang Joe, but it ain't like that, it ain't that serious. Mo'fuckas probably just hit a mac joint every now and then, but that shit don't do nothing."

"What you mean it don't do nothing? You smoking crack Brotha, that ain't cool. What kind of example you setting for the younger Brothas?" Max knew he was in the wrong, but he got tired of Rico's interrogation. "I'm straight lil' nigga, don't worry bout me, I got a strong mind and I don't care what mo'fuckas out there saying, we straight." Terry sat in the back seat, concealing his disdain for his leader and friend, pretending not to hear the conversation that was taking place; as he did not want to ruffle the feathers of the man that was feeding him. In reality, he knew exactly of Max's and other Brothas transgressions with cocaine, and he secretly shared Rico's sentiments about drug use among the Brothahood. But he kept his mouth shut. Now he wondered about Rico's fate, now that he just boldly confronted his own Chief.

As the group arrived at Harold's Chicken, the realization that they were smack dead in the heart of G-boy territory overwhelmed them. They instinctively paid close attention to their surroundings, looking for any indication of potential trouble. This was common for the Brothaz. On the south side, it was required for you to develop certain skills essential to your survival, such as visiting ops neighborhood undetected, securing one another outside the hood, and being able to spot an ambush. For members of Rock Island something as simple as going to their favorite restaurant to retrieve a meal could be compared to a navy seal operation. "You got yo' heat Rico?" Terry asked with concerned.
"Yeah Joe I stay strapped"

Max got out the car first. "Got to be careful over here," he said. "These niggas will pull it."

"I know man" Rico said. "Let's just get our food and get the hell up outta here." He then removed his black and gold Pittsburgh Pirates cap that would easily identify him as a Con. Looking around the restaurant, they scoped for any hostiles. It was fairly empty, only one guy and two females occupied the establishment. Max entered first, and approached the counter that was surrounded by bulletproof glass. Terry and Rico casually roamed the front entrance, pretending to be interested at the menu on the wall, while keeping a close eye on the street leading up to the restaurant. "What ya'll want?" Max asked his two subordinates.

"Get me a 3 piece and an order of gizzards with mild sauce, and a grape pop," Rico said.

"I'll take 5 wings and some fried mushrooms and a large coke," Terry responded, noticing one of the females admiring his lady killer looks and slick swagger. He was use to women admiring him, which usually played well to his narcissistic personality. But he wasn't trying to further his playa status, he just wanted to get his food and get back to his hood.

Rico was being checked out as well, and it wasn't because he was being admired either. In fact, the lone male patron was unsuspectingly eyeing Rico with contempt. For months, his guys had been trying to get at the elusive Op who was rumored to have shot several "FAMILY" members. The G-boy desperately wished he had a gun. After getting his order, he made his way to a pay phone and quickly dialed one of his guy's number. He informed his Comrades, who were only two blocks away of the Rico sighting. "Yeah G, that pussy ass nigga up here right now, ya'll better hurry up for he get ghost."

The G's acted instantaneously calling two of their new recruits to the task. For these two new members, making a hit like this would solidify their membership in their gang. The two best friends had gone on missions before, but nothing like what was about to happen. "Ya'll two niggas run up in there and murk that nigga, we got yo' back" said one of the ranking G-boys. They were given a description of what Rico was wearing, as they marched out the G-boy clubhouse armed with .40 caliber semi-automatic handguns.

Despite their keen awareness and precautions, the three Cons were oblivious of their seemingly critical fate. "Man what's taking these mutha' fuckas so long," complained Max. "I hate that Lenzy's be closed at 10, gotta be over here risking my life for some gizzards and shit." As if on cue, their orders were called, and the group exited the restaurant... just in time for the two young G's who had orders to kill to spot them as they turned the corner on foot. "There dem' niggas go right there" one of the G-boys said under his breath as they walked purposefully towards the group.

"Just play it off "G" so we can walk right up on these niggas and give it to em' point blank range. Remember we gotta get the one with the black t-shirt on."

As they made their way out of the Harold's Chicken joint, and moved towards Rico's car, Rico could see the shadowy figures walking towards them. They were at least 25 feet away, when conventional wisdom told him that getting in the car was a bad idea. If the dudes were intent on doing them harm, they'd have a better chance defensively outside of the car. Getting in a car would only make them sitting ducks.

"Hold up ya'll" Rico said. "Let these two dudes past before we get in the car. I'll first act if I'm looking for my keys.

The G-boys were only 15 feet away, when Rico put his hand on his 17 shot .9MM berretta, and slowly began easing it out from the small of his back. The G-boy also grabbed their weapons from their waist bands as they made eye contact with Rico. "Oh shit that's Rico!" one G-boy said placing his gun back in his waist ban. The two G-boys walked right past the group of Cons without even firing a shot. Rico, who was ready to shoot first, and ask questions later was also struck by surprise, as his brain was slow registering what had happened. "What tha...?" But his thoughts were short-lived as the G-boys back up arrived and began shooting. Plow! Plow! Plow! Even though they froze up, the other hungry G-boys weren't about to be so passive. Pop! Pop! Pop! Pop! Rico shot in the direction of the G's. "Start the car!" he yelled throwing Terry the keys. As they got in the car the G's continued their onslaught, hitting Max in the arm, and shattering the back windshield. The group laughed nervously as they made their get away, not because they were happy about being abused, but because they were happy about escaping the ordeal with their lives. However, Rico didn't take the assault so lightly; he knew he was supposed to be dead. He couldn't believe what had just happened, or what he had just seen. Now this was personal to him. He looked his would be killers directly in the eyes with a shocking familiarity.

"Aw shit, my fucking arm" Max complained, as the shock wore off on his way to the hospital. "Rico make sure that shit gets handled, I want them niggas dealt with." But Rico was already two steps ahead of him. "Don't worry "C", you just get that arm fixed, I got this." Over the next several days different Cons attempted to retaliate, by shooting up the ops neighborhood. Max fell back and nursed his gun shot wound.

CHAPTER 13

The young G-boy finally got a chance to relax, as he smoked a blunt. It had been a long week for him. After the Harold's Chicken incident and the violation he received behind it, he was a little off put. But the fine piece of ass he was about to get was a good way to relieve his mind (and body). He couldn't believe his luck; coming out of his best friends house, seeing the thick voluptuous, beauty, wandering hopelessly in search of some weed. After showing her where she could get the drugs, she offered to show her appreciation buying him something to drink. After a few drinks, she asked him if he wanted to get a room. He wasn't old enough to get a nice motel, so she suggested the *NEW HALSTED MOTEL* on 83rd and Halsted, one of the seediest motels on the south side that never checked I.D.

He was lounging on the bed enjoying his blunt, as the chinky eyed freak, poured some *E & J* into plastic cups. "This E & J make me a lil crazy," she said in a matter-of-factly tone, with a seductive smile on her face. "I hope you can handle all this," she cooed, lifting her skirt up just enough to reveal her heart shaped ass.

"Don't worry baby, I won't let you get too wild. I want you to be able to enjoy all this," he said laughingly, as he approached the dime piece, kissing her and grabbing a handful of ass. *"I'm gon tear this pussy up"* he said to himself, as they both made their way to the bed and began undressing each other.

"Baby could you get me some ice for my drink?" she asked him in between kisses. But the G-boy was hard enough to cut a diamond and didn't want to discontinue their make-out session that was surely leading up to some mind blowing sex.

"I got you shorty…just let me…"

She stopped him from removing her panties.

"Trust me, daddy, the ice ain't just for my drink, if you knew what I could do with some ice in my mouth, you'd be running to that ice machine."

And that's all that it took, the "G" grabbed his pants and an ice bucket and was out the door.

"Hurry up baby" she groaned to him. Dressed in only his pants and shoes, he swiftly made his way to the ice machine that sat in the corner of the first floor of the motel. *"Wait till I tell fam and nem' bout this shit",* he thought to himself as he scooping the ice out the machine. His bucket was almost filled when he felt the unmistakably cold feeling of a large automatic handgun pressed against the back of his head. The G-boy's entire life flashed before him, as he tried his best to hold his bodily wastes within him. "Drop that ice bucket bitch!" a deep voice growled "And don't make no sudden moves. Now slowly walk yo punk ass back to yo room." The G-boy complied. When they arrived to the motel room, the realization and gravity of what was happening really hit home. There was no sign of the young tender he had spent the last few hours with. Only a chair with a roll of gray duck tape on it remained. That was the last thing he saw before being knocked out and tied up.

****

Meanwhile in G-boy neighborhood, another G-boy was calling it a night. It was still early, but he didn't feel like hanging out. His guys was upset at him and he didn't feel too comfortable about being around them, after what happened at Harold's earlier that week, and the beat down violation he received as a consequence of his actions. The events caused him to think about his decision to join the gang. The street life wasn't his forte', but every since his best friend's uncle got shot a couple years back, he was forced to ride with his partner, who's agenda was to avenge his uncle's death. The two friends were inseparable, so he wondered where his friend could be that evening as he walked in his house. Immediately, he noticed that his mother had company, seeing one of the nice drinking glasses on a table half filled with red Kool-aid. His mother was sitting on the couch mulling over some papers.

"Hey boy, where you been? We've been waiting on you all day."

"*We?*" he thought to himself. But he wouldn't be in suspense for long, hearing the toilet flush in the bathroom down the hall, and seeing his old friend walk towards him, adorning that sly sinister grin he remembered him having as a kid. With a look that implied shock, horror, and fear, he managed to call out his name still not wanting to believe his eyes. "Ri-Rico?"

"Whut up Willie?" he replied, with just a hint of sarcasm in his voice. "Long time no see, huh?" Willie's mouth became dry as sandpaper, and his hand started shaking. "Um yeah-yeah, it's been awhile, Ri-Rico."

"Seems like yesterday," Rico added. "Come give a Brotha a hug!" Rico laid it on thick in front of Willie's mother, making small talk about the old days as if he was 50 years old. "So you see Ms. Jones, it ain't nothing out here in these streets, but death and a trap to fail," Rico went on. "So many of our young Brothas dying out here over nothing. That's why I'm here to try to encourage my friend to do something with his life." Willie's mother seemed to be impressed with Rico's theatrics, nodding her head as he spoke. "You see, Willie, I hope you're listening to Rico" Ms. Jones said. "You ain't doing nothing but hanging out with that no- good nigga Andre everyday, getting in trouble. Tell Rico how you got jumped on by some *GANG-BANGERS* the other day."

Willie was powerless. He had one of the most feared and dangerous young men in the area sitting in his living room with him and his mother drilling him about getting his life together.

"Ms Jones, I hope you and Willie could look over these packages about job corps. They accept guys Willie's age; Job Corps could help with the skill that will make him become a responsible adult. Please promise me you'll look into this because I'm tired of losing my friends."

Willie was thinking Rico could easily give Denzel a run for his money as he watched Rico's performance."

"If I didn't already have a scholarship for college next year, I'd be gone myself Ms. Jones."

"Yes, baby" she replied. "I will look into this, I promise."

As soon as Ms Jones left the room, the real Rico resurfaced. "You bitch ass nigga; you tried to murk me the other night!" Rico sternly said to his old friend and new enemy. "I should change yo pussy ass" he threatened, brandishing the handle of the fire arm in his waist band. Rico was counting on the fact his childhood friend still possessed some of his cowardly ways. But he knew it was a gamble, because he was well aware that a so-called lame could become a gangsta over night; giving the right influence. A lot of his Rock Island friends were examples of that. Fortunately, for him, Willie showed he had not changed that much despite his obvious affiliation with one of Chicago's most notorious street organizations, Willie began trying to reason with his ex-friend. "Rico, I swear to God Joe, we didn't know it was you that the FAMILY was talking about, on my momma, I swear!" Willie cried. "You see we didn't even shoot when we seen it was you. They beat our ass for not completing the hit." Willie went on to tell Rico that he found out about the reason the G's wanted him dead after the failed attempt on his life. He told him about Peaches and the G-boys change of heart testimony. "So why didn't you get up with me and put me up?"

"Man, it.... it was Dre, man. He said fuck you after we got violated. I don't know what's wrong with that nigga. He told the G's that he know how to get you and to give him a couple of weeks. But they still violated us. Please Rico, this my momma house, man, why you had to come here?"

85

"Just in case" Rico said. "Just in case you want to show yo guys where I lay my head, I want you to know that I still remember where you stay too. And my guys know too, so if anything happen to me...well you know how this shit go."
But Willie didn't, he wasn't on the level Rico was on. Rico was a shark and Willie was a gold fish. Nonetheless, he was still a liability.
"I ain't gon' do you like that Rico, I swear, what you want me to do?" Willie pleaded. "I want you to go over that package and pick a job corps facility and get the fuck out of Chicago on the first thing smoking. This life ain't for ya' dawg, it's bout' to get real ugly round here. So I urge you to consider my offer, cuz some of your guys ain't gon' be so lucky."

As if luck would have it; one of those friends was being held in a motel room against his will. His captors were awaiting a phone call. Lavada had seduced and lead the young man into a trap in which there was no escape. Dre wasn't like his buddy Willie, he was considered a *real* gangsta. He hated ops with all his heart, every since the night they beat him silly at the park on 76th. He hated Rico for letting it happen. And after his uncle was killed, his hatred only intensified. He regretted not killing Rico earlier that week, and would've done it if he hadn't frozen up at the sight of Rico. After being violated, he vowed to kill Rico himself. But right now he had bigger problems. After being tortured, his body was set on fire, and left in an alley two blocks from his home.

After hearing the news of Dre's death, Willie's mother sent him to his aunt's house in Michigan, where he joined a co-ed job corps. He dropped all his gang affiliations. But that did not take away from the fact that the **family** still wanted Rico dead, and Rico wasn't bothered by that fact. He endorsed a *"to be aware was to be alive"* attitude. But he also knew that he couldn't take the **family** for granted. He became more mechanical in his maneuvering of the streets, playing close attention to everything and everybody, attributes he already had, but now it was dire that he utilize. Some say it made Rico a little paranoid; others figured it was just a matter of time. *"It ain't nothing you can do when it's your time to go"* Fin use to tell him. *"God already knows when you go punch the clock of life, you can not escape death, so there's no sense in walking around scared."* But Rico didn't necessarily believe Fin's sentiments to be accurate. He believed that God gave every human free will and choice; therefore, if one chooses to put oneself in a dangerous position, the consequences of their actions will determine their fate.

Being aware of the set up game, even the number of females Rico interacted with was limited. The EEl princess, Quetta, provided him with superb sexual gratification, and the freedom to do his own thing on the streets. He knew a female like Quetta could not demand he commit to her. He knew she was more than likely seeing other guys, which was fine by him, as long as it wasn't any of his own guys. He had several encounters with other females, but Quetta was efficient, expendable, and convenient, and she could definitely move in the bedroom like she moved on the dance floor. In addition to her prowess Quetta also proved to be the quintessential ride or die chick. She accompanied Rico when he made drug pick-ups and drug drop offs, and even sold weed for him at her school.

Although she had her share of so-called *"real niggas,"* she was definitely infatuated with Rico. He was everything she wanted in a man smart, handsome, and thuggish. She had never met a young man with his swagger. Her friends teased her saying she was sprung, but Quetta knew it was much more than physical attraction. She finally admitted to herself that she loved him. But loving a guy like Rico was a dilemma to say the least. Quetta knew he cared for her, but she also knew that he couldn't attach himself to anyone, for his love belonged to the streets, and so confessing her love to him would only scare him away. So she loved him from a distance, never showing any real public affection, such as kissing, hugging, or holding hands. But when they were alone in the bedroom, she would go all out, giving him everything she had, pleasing him the only way, she knew how - sexually. She did things with him she never did with anyone else. She had never put so much effort into satisfying a man. *"He has to know its love,"* she thought. *"A girl don't just do these things for any ole nigga. He has to know he's special."*

But Rico had a wealth of other issues on his mind. Ed, Max, and other elder Brothas were now smoking crack, and no longer in the closet. And Rico feared their influence could corrupt the younger Brothas. Rico's mother was threatening to kick him out if he didn't take a college offer that would relocate him down south. But the money he was making on Carpenter with Rio, and had gotten too good. His stress levels were at an all time high.

"What's wrong, baby?" Quetta asked when she came up for air, noticing that Rico was somewhat distant and unresponsive to her supreme phallic skills. "Nothing shorty, just got a lot on my mind." As usual, she had no comforting words or advice, so she only did what she knew best, hoping to ease his mind through her calculated strokes and pelvic thrust while riding his manhood in the cowgirl position. She softly moaned the forbidden words *"I love you"* from between her lips as she climaxed. Rico pretended not to hear her.

CHAPTER 14

If Rock Island was a machine, Max and Ed was the oil that made it run smoothly; and the drugs that they were using was a monkey wrench. What started as a slight social indulgence was now a full-fledged addiction. The money that was usually reserved for buying guns or helping Brothas had mysteriously been misappropriated. The once lucrative spot on 76th and May was now becoming a safe-haven for crack-head members. Some of these members resulted to selling dummy bags to support their habit. Disenchanted customers who knew Ed, Max, and Terry would complain, and usually heads would roll. But even the soft spoken, charismatic Ed, turned into a temperamental rude, sociopath, causing even loyal customers to do business elsewhere. But the customers weren't the only ones dissatisfied with the leadership and rapid personality changes. Lil Mikey and other Brothas were reporting all of Ed and Max's transgressions to Big June. He was the only one that could rectify the ills of the unrighteousness ranking Con members. Bo Olley, Lil Mikey, and Toby reported weekly to Big June, and unbeknownst to Ed and Max, they were secretly being investigated. June was fair with the two leaders, and gave them mild warnings. But the Ed and Max everyone once loved and respected were long gone. The only Brothas who now respected Ed and Max were those who had been seduced by the poisonous whispers of that dragon. Terry, and Brandon were not only dealing with their Elites doing drugs, but their cousins Calvin and Raulo were now addicted

June threatened Armageddon, but Rico didn't like the idea of destroying and rebuilding. So he sought out to help his leaders, before they fell too far from grace. But a major event would stagnate his efforts.

R. I. members, Marlon, Toby, M-Dubb, and others all stood around near the corner of 79th and Sangamon while Officer Timmons grilled them about their life-style. He often sought out the troubled and at risk youth in hopes of curbing violence in the hood. Since his own brother's death, he did this to ease his mind, often to the disliking of his peers. But he figured if he could deter one gang member from doing something stupid he was saving a life. He didn't say enough when he saw his brother going down that path. And vowed not ever be silent again. Unfortunately, for the officer, everyone came to know as Quick, it would be his own life that would be in need of saving as FAMILY members shot into the crowd hoping to score on unsuspecting Brothas, striking the officer in the neck, right above his bulletproof vest. The crowd dispersed into the night, leaving the wounded officer to fend for himself. He never got a chance to draw his weapon; he collapsed, and died in the middle of the street.

As a result of a veteran officer being scourgely gunned down, due to gang violence in an area where gang violence was on the rise, after the media cameras left, the police lead by Officer Derkerson started acting like a gang themselves. They extracted their revenge on all of the areas gangs. They targeted gang members; beating them, planting drugs, guns, and even unjustifiably shot some gang members. Since it was suspected that G-boys were behind Quick's shooting, they received the most attention. Everyday for weeks they harassed, provoked, and arrested FAMILY members. But their big break may have come from the Brothas of Rock Island – Marlon, Toby, and M. Dubb. Their statements lead to the arrest of two FAMILY members.

For Officer Derkenson, that was not enough, the gangs in his district were at his mercy. And Brothas such as Rico, Rio, Ed, Max, Lil Mikey, and Silo were on his shit list. One by one they were taken off the streets. Lil Mikey was the first to go. After being arrested for a bogus murder on an Arab store owner. Rio was arrested on drug charges, Silo for robbery, and Rico for possession of a firearm. For Max and Lil Ed, their fate would be left in the hands of their south-side Chief. On a warm autumn day, several carloads of Cons pulled up in front of the 76th street spot. June entered and placed everyone under arrest, demanding that they produce Ed and Max. Once Ed showed up, he was made aware of his doomed fate. Three burly Brothas beat Ed for several minutes with bats, wooden boards, and golf clubs. They broke both of Ed's arms and one leg, several ribs and fractured his skull. The Brothas of R.I. had never witnessed this type of brutality against one of their own. Blood was all over the apartment. June dragged Ed's limp body out of the building where a small crowd of Brothas had gathered.
"You see this?" June yelled to the large group of spectators. "This is what's going to happen to any Con that gets out there on that shit. This was ya'll Chief, now he's a nobody, because he chose drugs over ya'll, so don't feel sorry for this nigga. He is officially no longer a part of this organization."
Some of the Brothas had tears in their eyes watching Ed lay helplessly on the ground bleeding. Lil George was the only one to speak, not caring about June's entourage who were all armed with automatic weapons and appeared to be ready to shoot anybody that wanted to protest or play hero. But George ran to Ed's side and attempted to pick

him up. "Ya'll bogus Brotha" his eye's teared up. "Let me take him to the hospital, he gon' die out here."
"If you help him, then you're no longer a part of this organization either," June said bleakly. But Lil George helped him anyway, sealing his own fate in Rock Island.

After hearing about the events that took place, Max took refuge with the Black EEls near his home. The EEls had love for Max and as long as he was on their turf, they would never let no harm come to him. June chose not to put a hit on him, declaring that his disgrace was enough. Ed remained in the hospital for nearly a month. Bo was appointed to take his place. He was on house arrest at the time. And his house arrest location would play a pivotal part in the new generation of Rock Island members. Bo's family moved into another large apartment building on 79th and Green. In traditional Oley fashion, they took over the building in no time. Some how, tenants just abandoned their apartments and no new ones moved in. The new Oley building sat on one of Chicago's busiest streets. And what was once forbidden territory for R.I. members, was now infested with the Brothas.

Sitting in his new multi-purpose fortress, Bo began recruiting local young men and women across 79th. His sister, and long time "family" affiliate, flipped and pledged to the Cons, and Bo rewarded her with a "Queen" title. Boonie was cast aside to the side because of her loyalty to Ed, under suspicion that she also indulged in the forbidden drugs. Bo had Boonie violated because of her actions, and Boonie was forced to fall back. The move was unpopular among many of the Sistas and Brothas, but Bo clearly made his intentions be known. "If niggas don't like how I get down, fuck'em."

****

An incarcerated Rico heard it all while sitting in Cook county jail awaiting trial. Lavada and other disenfranchised Sistas would visit him every week, and bring him up to speed. Lavada's boyfriend at the time (Al) was a new corner Boy from the hood, and he'd often accompany her on her visits to the jail. It baffled Rico that a seemingly broke, unpopular dude like Al could even stand a chance with a chick like Lavada. *"But that was just Lavada,"* he rationalized to himself, as he sat on a stool, watching Al and Lavada search for him in the crowded visiting cage. Heads turned as she passed the inmates, sporting skin tight jeans and a baby blue sleeveless blouse. She wore her hair in a style that covered her right eye. "How you holding up in here my nigga?" she asked through the thick bullet-proof.
"I'm cool; this is the county so you got to be on your P's and Q's 24-7." "Well it's been crazy around the crib; Bo got the hood on smash.

Everybody hangs on 79th now and since T.Y, Nelson, Wayne and the triplets caught that murda, nobody hangs on May that much. A few Brothas still hang on 77th, but they ain't on shit."

Rico enjoyed his brief county visits, but the adult jail was a much different environment from the audey home. The gangs controlled the entire complex, which consisted of 12 divisions (all separate buildings). Most of the buildings were designed to house 700-800 inmates per building. But due to overcrowding, they usually held twice as many. Unlike some county jails or prisons around the country, Illinois typically doesn't separate its inmates according to their race and gang affiliation. Instead, they leave it up to the inmates to police themselves. Rico had to learn the rules of the jail right away; the written ones and non-written ones. The first thing the gangs do upon inmates entering a unit in any division is screen inmates. Rico could remember hearing the calls as he approached the door of his unit that contained at least 150 inmates. *"On da new, On da NEWWW."* Alerting other inmates to the new arrivals. As the inmates walked in the door, they are greeted by a welcoming committee of sorts. "What you is, Lil Homie?" One guy yelled out to Rico obviously trying to appear intimidating. "I'm a Con!" Rico replied profoundly. "We got a Brotha over here," the man yelled to no one in particular. And as if on cue. A tall stocky, bald Brotha approached Rico and introduced him as being the Minister-of-Literature for the Brotherhood on the unit. "What up Bro.? They call me Big Ghost; did you have any status in the world?"

"Yeah, I had a Minister spot for my set- Rock Island" Rico replied.

"Ok, that's all good Bro. but we don't recognize that function in here," Big Ghost informed Rico. "We only honor Brothas that were Chieves on the street, as ranking members in here." Ranking Brothas received special treatment such as personal security, bottom bunks, and a piece of any action that the Brothas were involved in., "Do you know your laws and literature?"

"Yeah, I know my shit" Rico replied. He was proud that the Rock Island elites enforced that all members learn their laws and literature and after spitting some lit for Big Ghost, convincing him that he was indeed legit, he was formally introduced to the rest of the Brothas on the unit. He was then given the customary care package containing a variety of hygiene products.

The next day, Rico was given a home made knife for protection. As a rule, most feuds are to be squashed in jail. The leaders do not allow members to carryout personal vendettas on oppositions in the jail system. So Rico was semi-safe from the "FAMILY" hit on his head. Nevertheless, the gangs do fight over trivial matters, and the possibility of being stabbed or seriously injured is present everywhere.

Rico's cellmate was another Brotha from a different branch located on the west-side, his name was Lil Mafia. He was twenty-four years old and had been to the joint twice. He only stood 5'8, but he had broad shoulders that gave him a wide appearance. He wasn't highly regarded in the Brothas organization, but with a seemingly young and impressionable mind such as Rico's, he probably felt he could tell him anything. "Man Joe, I was checking ugly paper out there you know what I'm saying? These bitches put a pack on me, ya feel me? I would've bonded out for 10 stacks, but they got a probation hold on me. I was just bout to cop that new Lexus and come hard for the summer ya feel me?"

Rico loved hearing guys war stories, even though he knew most of them were embellished, or flat out lies. He knew that was how a lot of guys passed their time in jail. But jail was also as a good place to network. Rico met a lot of influential ranking Brothas in jail. And they all took a liking to the young Brotha from R.I. He exchanged information with a lot of them, promising to stay in touch once he gets out. He loved talking about R.I. to any Brotha that would listen, like a promoter promoting a special event. Rico made sure that people knew he was from the south-side set.

However, after he received prison time, and was shipped to the penitentiary, his boastful ways almost caught up with him. Rico learned that after Ed's brutal violation out of Rock Island, he relocated to Minnesota and reestablished himself. Most of Ed's loyalist followed him there, including his long time girlfriend and Con Sista Tanesha. The ones that remained, that stayed in R.I. were considered outcast for the most part. They refused to abandon their affiliation, despite the Brothas disdainful attitude towards them. Before Bo could get off house arrest and deal with them, he was arrested again, and sent to prison. Big June had all but forgotten about the remaining members of Rock Island, due to his own personal conflict within the organization. He was murdered by one of his closest aides. Some believe it was a hit ordered by the Old Man.

This caused Rock Island and other south-side sets to feel disenfranchised. They eventually turned against any authority that came from an outside entity. This did not sit well with the powers that be, including the old man. As a result, orders were given to eliminate, neutralize, and punish any and all members of renegade sets. Since the orders were initiated in the jail and prison system, the sanctions were enforced there first. It didn't take long for the word to reach the joint where Rico was. "Listen Brotha; niggas getting dealt with for going against the grain" one of the Elites explained to Rico. "We are taking dem' niggaz off count." Knowing the Brothas from Rock Island that were incarcerated for an extended period of time would be spared, Rico tried to bargain for mercy for his guys on the streets. "I know how this shit go, treason is only punishable by death, it's the law," he attempted to reason with two Elite Brothas incarcerated with him. "But let me get out there and put those Brothas back on track. I know I can do it, they just need the proper guidance."

"Lil Rico, Rock Island days are numbered, it's over fo' dem' niggas" one Brotha said. "The Old Man already laid it down, we can't go against that."

But Rico wouldn't be detoured; he talked for hours with high-ranking Cons, hoping to persuade them. "I know you can get in touch with the Old Man. Let him know I'll take sole responsibility for Rock Island's actions once I get out, if he spares them. I'll get shit together, I promise, on da 'C' Joe!

After intense thought, the two Elites decided to run Rico's proposition by the Old Man. "Alright Lil Bro. we'll see what he say bout it, but I hope you know what you getting yo'self into."

Two weeks later… Rico received the news. He was to be appointed Rock Island's new Cons Chief; however, he only had 2 months to get the set back together. Rico wasn't too excited about his new status, he was more grateful for Rock Island's much needed reprieve. He still had months to do on his sentence, so he spent a lot of time formulating his strategy to revive his beloved set. He knew as a leader, he had to have a supporting cast. He thought about whom he could trust, and what needed to be done to rid R.I. of its vices. He knew if he failed his mission to save his Brothas it could cost him his life. He heard about the changes and new faces that made R.I. synonymous with other renegade sets, but his primary concern was the remaining original members. His passion to help Brothas affected by drugs was pushed aside, due to a sense of urgency; a sense of urgency that would not tolerate any resistance from anyone. He developed a *"Ride with me, or collide with me"* mentality.

Rico began lobbying support from his close friends and trusted members from R.I., such as Head, who was a former Lil Mikey protégé. Head and Rico built a repoire, just before Rico was arrested, and Head kept Rico in tune with everything that was going on in the hood. "Man Joe, niggas ain't on shit out here "C", mutha fuckas is lawless", Head said over the phone. "Brothas ain't honoring shit no more, niggas out here bad man. That nigga Bo had us on some "fuck da world shit", and I felt him, cuz mutha fuckas don't care bout us, it's Rock Island or nothing". The Brothas killed Chief (June) for nothing, so fuck da' Brothas."

Rico was surprised to hear his usually mild mannered friend speak so colorfully about the streets, but he also knew Head and the rest of the members of his set was a little naïve about the bureaucracies of the Brotharhood.

"Check it out "C", Rico responded. "All that shit sound good, but rather you like it or not, you are a Brotha as well as the rest of them niggas out there. I can't get into the details over the phone, but believe me when I tell you; ya'll niggas ain't ready to go against the mob."

"So what you saying, Rico? You went to da' joint and let them Brothas fill yo' head with some bullshit?"

"Man, stop it my nigga, if you only knew the sacrifices I've made to ensure we straight... It boils down to this; I'm bout to come home and get shit back to where it needs to be. I got the blessings from the Old Man to come home and do whatever needs to be done. I got a plan and vision and I'm gon need good Brothas like yo'self on the team. So are you going to ride wit' me or not?"

"Fo'sho Brotha, you know I got yo back. I'm with you Joe, and umma let niggas know you on the way to the crib, and to pipe down till you touch the bricks. But you know you still got them outcast niggas thinking they on something, and a few other hatin' ass niggas...."

"Don't even trip on that Head, all that gon be handled; that's something small to a giant my nigga. Just get the word out and gauge niggas reactions. If I need to rotate with you about anything else, I'll just send word through Quetta."

"Man, Rico, you still mess wit' that chick?"

"Yeah, you know how it is, she ain't going no where."

"You want me to drop off some ends or something?"

"Naw man, she's a hustle bunny, she carries her own weight, but you can drop off a couple of magazines, nothing hardcore, something light. She comes up here every week."

"A'ight, Brotha, you'll have yo' magazines this week. I'm glad you got a female in yo' corner dawg, especially while you're in there"

Quetta was indeed there for Rico during his incarceration, she came to see him every week. And every week she bought him drugs, mostly marijuana or as Rico called it "magazines" for him to sell.

****

Quetta was already seated in the visiting area when Rico arrived, trying to appear frustrated. She wore her hair in a long ponytail, which she knew Rico hated. She wore jeans, which kept him from enjoying his under the table finger-action, a sign she was obviously trying to tell him something. But Rico had become a master in handling her temperamental episodes. As he approached, she tried to avoid eye contact in attempt to maintain her mean mug. But it was extremely challenging for her, because Rico's mere presence made her glow and his touch often over stimulated her. She hated the way he had her, she felt powerless.

"What's wrong with you?" Rico asked as he embraced Quetta for a hug. "Nothing," she lied, hoping he would push her for more information. So Rico played along with her for a while. "What's wrong, shorty?" he asked in a gentler tone, looking into her eyes, and holding her hand. "Tell Daddy what's wrong" He touched the side of her face, and gently kissed her on the forehead. She felt like a baby around him. She couldn't keep her act up. She felt her nipples grow hard and wetness in between her legs. But she still had a point to prove. "Stop Rico, I'm mad at you" she said unconvincingly as she put more distance between them and broke eye contact.

"What I do?" Rico asked, preparing himself for whatever.

"Head, got up wit me, and gave me those extra magazines. My pussy sore as hell, for packing all that shit. I put everything in the regular spot, but I'm tired of this shit, is that all you want me for?

"Naw baby, it was a last minute thang, and this is the last time, I just wanted to stack a little more paper before I come home." Quetta smacked her lips, and crossed her arms. "You ain't gon do nothing but come home and try to fuck everything in a skirt. You probably ain't gon have no time for me." This was not the Quetta Rico liked when he first met her; she was confident, cool, and independent. Now she was weak, insecure, and apparently sprung. "Look, Quetta, we been through dis shit a million times. Ain't shit changed with us, you act like you didn't know who I was when you got with me. I respect you shorty, cuz you've been down with me, so don't get on no soft shit with me, ok?"

Those weren't the reassuring words that Quetta hoped for, but she accepted them, she had no choice. "Ok, baby, but I'm just saying…." Rico interrupted her with a passionate kiss on the lips. She closed her eyes and relished the brief joy that she only received once a week. "You know I'm gon' tear dat' pussy up when I touch down right?" He whispered in her ear, as they hugged for the last time during their visit.

"I can't wait baby" she replied, as she reluctantly separated herself from his embrace, and made her move towards the exit.

Rico was happy about coming home this time and not being obligated to any one female. But he knew Quetta cared for him, and he couldn't just dismiss her. After all, she was in his corner throughout his incarceration, and unlike his ex, Yoshawn, she was a street person just like him. She banged, sold drugs, and hung in his hood. He could now focus all if his attention on Rock Island. By the time his release came, he was well informed and prepared for his Rock Island takeover.

CHAPTER 15

Rico was released on a Thursday, and 24 hours later he called a meeting with the entire Rock Island gang. Brothas were anxious to hear what the newly appointed leader had to say. "I called this goal to let you Brothas know that we're about to get our stuff back together," Rico said confidently as he stood in the middle of the large circle of members.

"All that renegade nonsense is over. And you Brothas that are doing drugs, I'm giving ya'll a choice right now. You can either choose the drugs or choose the hood; you can't have both if you're even suspected of doing drugs, it's on, no probation or nothing."

The entire circle started buzzing, which annoyed Rico. "T.P, you are the new Chief enforcer, walk around this circle one time, and if anybody interrupts me again while I'm talking, hit they ass in the mouth!" His tone let them know he was dead serious. "I'm giving you Brothas the opportunity to walk out of this park without any questions right now if you feel like you ain't with the program." The circle of Brothas and Sistas stood in complete silence, as they watched George, Calvin, and at least 20 other Brothas fall out of formation and exit the park.

With Ed and the rest of the defunct original members of R.I. long gone, Rico was left with a group of young men and women none over the age of 21. To him, it seemed like only yesterday that he was the baby of Rock Island's Cons, and now he was one of the elders at the tender age of 19. The next few days Rico worked on forming his new committee. Toby, Milton, T.P., Head and Myron were all ranking Brothas now. He used his connections from the prison system to acquire guns and large amounts of drugs. He required that all R.I. members buy their drugs from him, "keeping the money in the family," he called it. Since most of the Brothas had abandoned 76th and May as a means of a money making opportunity, he gave young Brothas who typically couldn't afford the weight he was selling, packs, and encouraged them to sell them on 76th and May. Each pack was worth a grand. They would sell the rocks and give Rico $650 back. A win-win situation for everyone involved, but he didn't limit his economical strategy just to 76 Street; he'd pass out packs to anyone who wanted them, to sell wherever they wanted.

His most lucrative endeavor was the spot on 77th and Carpenter. Myron, Rio, and Kenyatta all worked the block, but some of the D-boys also benefited much to the dismay of Rico. And it didn't take long for him to initiate a full take over plan, despite Rio advising him against such. But Rio's long time friend, Beleanie, started using; giving Rico the leverage he needed to over-rule any suggestions contrary to his plans.

Beleanie's house was becoming very popular with crack customers, who took refuge in the large multi-story home after they purchased their drugs. The D-boys would often send a brave member to sit in the home and sell large amounts if crack to the hypes who wanted a second, third, or fourth high. Most initial purchases were made outside of the home from the Brothas that stood on the block. "The hypes can stay but the ops gotta go" Rico told Myron, Rio, and Kenyatta, standing in front of Beleanie's house. "Fuck a peace treaty; if they come back down here trying to work, do what you gotta do. What dem' niggas gon do? They can't fuck wit us"

But unbeknownst to the semi-naïve new Chief, a power shift was in progress on 79th street. A lot of the hardcore G-boys that once gave R.I. the flux, had consolidated with **KillaWard**, or either **Boystown**; the larger G-boy sets to the east and west of R.I. and most of the G's that remained converted to D-boys bringing their hatred for the Brothas with them.

But the D's leadership still remained extremely diplomatic, and after hearing about R.I.'s hostile attitude, they reached out to Rico attempting to curb potential violence. "It's too much money out here, man" one D-boy leader said to Rico over the phone. We all grew up together; ain't no sense in us killing each other over some bullshit. If dem' shorties wanna get into it, just let'em fight, ain't no sense in shooting up the blocks, attracting the police and shit. Maybe we can arrange a little fight between the shorties and let them get that animosity off they chest."
The D-boys had no idea why R.I. had suddenly turned hostile towards them, but they knew that a war would cost them money. "Yeah, I'll look into that" Rico responded, "but for now it's best that niggas keep they distance, you know the code, if somebody get caught out of bounds it's fair game. You don't have to worry about nobody coming down there on 79th and Carpenter shooting shit up," Rico lied.

Despite Rico reading the D-boys leader his rights, the stage was set. The D's had to act. "We ain't no hoez, Joe" one D-boy said at a meeting shortly after hearing about the comments Rico made. "Who the fuck dem' bitch ass niggas think they is? Dem' niggas is some pussies fam, I'm telling you if we let dem' niggas get away wit trying to lay they lick down, they gon' think we soft."

"Yeah!" answered a D-boy who had recently flipped from a G-boy. "We should kick it off wit dem' niggas just to let'em know they don't run shit." The leaders agreed, "We gon' do something, they forced our hand."

****

Meanwhile, Derk and his new rookie partner cruised the streets. Since the death of his old partner, he was determined to make the lives of gang members a real nightmare. But most of the gangs adjusted to his tactics. Feeling that the gangs were always a step ahead of him, Derk took alternative methods of doing police work. Some say that it was Derk that influenced the G-boys to abandon 79th and Carpenter, leaving it solely to the D-boys. But now it was 76th street who he had his eye on. The R.I. members spotted Derks maroon Chevy Caprice two blocks before he hit their block. Derk wasn't trying to be inconspicuous, he was looking for someone. And he found the light skinned, hazel-eyed Con, walking down 76th street. Derk hit the brakes and pulled up right beside him upon seeing his new friend. "Aww shit!" the young Con exasperated as Derk and his partner exited their vessal with their hands on their guns. "Get yo' hands out yo' fucking pockets asshole" Derk said as he grabbed the Con by the collar.
"Come on man, I ain't doing shit, I ain't got nothing on me Derk" he cried.
"Yes you do muthafucka!" Derk responded. "You got some information for me."
"Come on Derk, don't front me off like this, somebody might see us out here. I told you I'll call you. I'd page you if something comes up."
"Well something came up" Derk snapped. "And you wasn't worried about being fronted off when I got yo' ass out of that drug case last week." Derk cuffed him up and transported him back to the station, where the ranking Con member filled Derk in on everything that was going on in R.I.
"So you mean to tell me that Rico is calling the shots over there now? Derk ask rhetorically. "Son of a bitch! Tell me everything… Where is he getting his dope from? What about the guns? …Who shot that dude on 79th last month…" The questions continued for over an hour before the snitch was released. Armed with an informant, Derk seemed confident that he could destroy the R.I. crew as he did with the G-boys on 79th. "These snitches practically do our job for us. There's no real honor among these muthafuckas, when it comes down to it, I can get the information I need. Nobody wants to go to jail."

Later that night, police raided the 77th street spot; arresting six R.I. members, charging them with an array of gun and drug charges.

After hearing about the raid Rico was extremely critical of his operation. "How in the fuck the police catch us slipping like this?" he asked a group of Brothas that avoided arrest. "We was just about to change shifts" Kenyatta replied. "They just got lucky."
But Rico didn't believe in luck that much, he was much more practical. "We're going to have to switch shit up again! Find a new place to hide the guns, and put security on the corner." Despite the minor set back, Rico, Rio, Myron, and Kenyatta wasn't about to shut down the spot, it was too lucrative. On a good day the spot could generate up to $20,000 dollars. The Brothas fancy cars could be seen lined up and down Carpenter Street like a ghetto car show, attracting large amounts of opportunistic females, who sought to capitalize off the success of the new neighborhood ballers. No one benefited from this more than Myron, who wasn't the most attractive choice for females, but certainly now one of the most popular. Some of his peers called him a "trick", but his liberal ways with money won the hearts of many fine young ladies.

CHAPTER 16

Under Rico, R.I. made great progress, despite the absence of experienced Brothas. But Rico still felt a void in the hood. After unsuccessfully trying to convince his former mentor Max to come back to the hood, he reached out to the Brotha who use to run the spot for Ed and Max – Terry. He had already convinced Brandon to come back, despite knowing that both of his cousins Calvin and Raulo were outcast. He hoped that Brandon would influence Terry to come back as well. He didn't do drugs and his experience could be used on the committee.

Terry moved to the north-side where he owned a condo. Rico wasn't sure what kind of hustle Terry had going on but from the looks of his crib, it seemed to be very profitable. He hadn't seen Terry in years, and didn't know what to expect, as he, Brandon, and Head entered Terry's apartment. The apartment had a strong incense smell, and was adored with African tribal Art, leather furniture, and large plasma televisions. A large fish tank filled with colorful fish sat in the middle of the living room.

"This how you doin it huh?" Rico greeted, as he and Terry embraced one another. "Aw man, dis' ain't nothing" Terry modestly replied. "Just trying to live my nigga. But it's good to see you Lil Rico. I guess you ain't so little no more. I heard you over there in da land making major moves."

"Yeah Brotha", Rico replied. "That's kinda what I wanted to holla at cha' about. I know you salty about what happen to Ed and nem', but we gotta move forward. The hood need Brothas like you Terry."

Terry sat on his couch rolling a blunt, seemingly weighing the gravity of Rico's words. "You wanna hit this Bro.?"

"Nawl man, you know I don't fuck wit dat' shit," Rico said hostily.

"Oh yeah I forgot, my fault." Terry lit the blunt and passed it to Brandon and Head. "So was up Joe, you gon' get back in rotation or what?"

Terry leaned back on the couch and exhaled. "Rico, Rico, Rico, you see, that's always been your problem dawg, you too uptight, you take life too serious. You don't smoke, drink, or nothing." The group all laughed at Terry's pun. A person could listen to Terry talk for hours. But Rico only wanted to hear one thing come out of Terry's mouth. "You know I ain't goin' no where homie" Terry said. I'm going to start rotating again, just for *you* man. But right now my presence is needed up here. My Jamaican buddies trying to put me in tune with some important people. So if everything go right it could be real beneficial." They all agreed that a month was sufficient.

"I'll holla at you then," Rico said as he left Terry's apartment. It felt good to have one of the originals back on the team. However the next elder Brotha Rico encountered wasn't greeted with such fan fare and admiration.

****

"Hold that nigga down" Rico yelled to two large Brothas holding Mike B's arms, while others took turns punching him in the face and head. "I neva did like yo' bitch ass anyway, Rico said with hate in his eyes. " If we catch yo' ass over here again, its curtains for you," Another Brotha said, in the complex parking lot, where Mike B's blood was splattered all over cars. They continued to beat Mike B for at least five more minutes, until his sister Neecy ran out her house and pleading with his assailants not to kill him. "STOP!" She cried, "Please stop! What he do? What he do?" The crowd dispersed swiftly into the complex, and Rico jumped in his car. "Ask yo' baby daddy" Rico said out the window and drove off.

Neecy's baby's father, T-fly, was currently incarcerated for a beat down murder, along with his two brothers, Wayne, Nelson, and Ty. Mike B. allegedly cooperated with authorities by implicating the Brothas in the crime. While out on bond one of the Hull brothers confronted Mike B. and attempted to reason with him, in light of their relationship. But Mike B. took this as a sign of aggression, and went to the police. The Hull brother's bond was revoked for *INTIMIDATION OF A WITNESS*. When Rico learned of Mike B.'s actions, he jumped at the opportunity to eradicate his long time silent foe.

At a goal, Rico stressed the importance of an important law. THE CODE OF SILENCE. "You Brothas better know to keep yo' mouth shut around the police, we don't cooperate with the police." But despite the enforcement of laws, Rico's, words fell on deaf ears of a few Brothas.

Even though Rock Island was on the verge of achieving it's former glory, a vicious cycle was brewing; one that threatened the stability of Rock Island, one that could ultimately cost Rico his freedom and possibly his life.

"We can't force nobody to be a Brotha" Head said, as he and Rico cruised down Carpenter. "If niggas ain't down, fuck'em, we don't need'em!"

"You right Joe," replied Rico. "It used to be a privilege to be a Brotha. Imma' let niggas do them." So Rico discontinued his search for the original Brothas, and his efforts to reinstate them.

He did make a couple of exceptions, one being Con member, Steve, who didn't frequent the hood much since he landed a job on the riverboat, and when he did come around, he was usually drunk. As Rico approached 77th street, he noticed Steve, and a small crowd of young Bros lingering in front of the dope spot. Some of the Brothas were bent on one knee picking up fists full of money, indicating that a dice game was in progress. "Look at these niggas Joe!" Rico said to Head as they got out of the car. "What ya'll Brothas doing?" he asked, trying to appear concerned.

"Breaking these fools" Chad responded.

"Hell yeah, you want to get down 'C'?" asked Darnell. Chad and Darnell were the younger brothers of Mitch, one of Rico's closet friends who was incarcerated at the time. Both had been exposed to the gang life since they were 9 or 10.

"Break this shit up before ya'll have Chantae out here."

Rico's rant caught the attention of Kenyatta who was in the back seat of a car with a young female. He tried to discontinue his activities before Rico saw him, but he was unsuccessful. "Ain't dis a bitch!" Rico exclaimed. "I remember when most of you muthafuckaz was spooked to even walk past this block, now ya'll so relaxed that ya'll shooting dice, fuckin wit bust-downs in cars, straight snoozing!"

"It's cool Rico, we decent over here, niggas know better than to come over here," Chad said, brandishing his new 9 MM pistol. Chad didn't appear to be the type to carry a gun. The 5'6, ego inflated young Con, was considered a pretty boy. Products of biracial parents, Chad and his brothers were all light skinned with "good hair." Chad kept his short and wavy. He played close attention to what he wore, and would never leave the house if he didn't match, or had one wrinkle in his clothes. If he scuffed his shoes, he discarded them. Yet he was becoming one of R.I.'s most feared triggerman.

Darnell was more low- key; and mainly concerned himself with taking advantage of the free enterprise of R.I.'s drug business. He would send his brother Mitch, large portions of his profit every week. Rico found that to be noble because he also supported a brother in prison, as well as other members from R.I. Rico made sure that even the Brothas families and girlfriends were taken care of. After leaving Carpenter, he needed to stop at Kiesha's house to take care of some business, so he decided to walk across from the alley, and cut through a gang way that led him to his destination. Keshia was sitting on her porch with Lavada and some of the other Sistas chit-chattering when he walked up. The ladies were always happy to see Rico. But this visit wasn't going to be a friendly one for Kiesha. She vowed to take care of Lil Mikey's affairs, and act as a wifey. But it had been over a year since Mikey's arrest, and she was already starting to show signs of disloyalty. She had not visited Mikey in months, she hadn't responded to none of his recent letters; and she didn't even send pictures of his sons 2nd birthday.

Rico didn't have any children but, he imagined how he'd feel if he was incarcerated and not able to see his seeds. But more importantly he knew the importance of having that outside support.
"Hey Rico!" the young Sistas all said singingly.
"Whad up, Whad up" he responded in his cool tone. "What ya'll getting into tonight?"
"Finna go to that concert at the Regal" Lavada said, "We waiting on our ride."
"Oh yeah, well take some flicks for me up there.
Keshia was uncharacteristically subdued, probably because she knew what was next.
"A Ke-Ke, let me holla at cha" Rico said, as Keshia got up and entered her house, holding the front door for Rico to enter, and quickly darted to her room. Her room was filled with pictures of Mikey, and Mikey Jr. As well as cards that Mikey had sent her over the last year. She let out a deep breath as if she was annoyed by his presence before she began to speak. "I already know what you bout to say Rico, so don't go there. I know I'm bogus for not going to see him but...." Rico cut her off. "But nothing! Get on top of yo' business Ke-Ke, Mikey need you. Here's a few dollars for lil' man, make sure you take him up there to see his father. You don't have to stop living yo' life to be loyal to him. You know if that nigga was out he'd be holding you down, so don't leave him in there like that. Being locked up is hard enough, and having to worry bout you and the shorty complicates things. Don't make me have to come back over here for this ok?" Keshia seemed to absorb what Rico was saying, and promised to start doing a better job as a baby's momma. As they both stepped back outside, Rico instinctively clutched his .40 caliber underneath his shirt as a truck full of males slowed down in front of Keshia's house. "Who da fuck is that?" he asked loud enough for the guys in the Chevy Suburban to hear. "That's our ride Keshia said, as she tried to signal them to park. Rico never took his eyes off the vehicle, letting its occupants know that they shouldn't get too comfortable. "Ya'll better not be having no ops coming thru here",

Rico said to no one in particular, as the Sistas made their way to the truck.

"Boy shut up", Lavada laughingly said as she passed Rico. "These are some EEl Brothas from the east side." "What up Brotha?" one of the EEl's yelled out the car, feeling safe that he was amongst an ally. "Ain't shit up, my nigga. Thought I was gon' have to swiss cheese some vics coming thru here. It's all good though, ya'll Brothas be careful and take care of my Sistas, ya dig." The EEls all put their fist to their chest, and drove off, just as Rico's pager went off. It was Quetta's number with 911 behind it. *"Damn!"* he thought to himself. *"I wonder what dis bitch want. She constantly blowing me up all day. Fuck dat I ain't callin' her back,* he finally concluded.

Walking back to his car, Rico was spotted by Al (Lavada boyfriend) "A Joe, um you seen Lavada?" Al yelled from his hooptie. Flashbacks of Lavada jumping in the truck with a bunch of dudes minutes earlier flooded his mind. But Rico knew a jealous dude when he seen one. Lavada was his homie, so he opted to spin Al, who would be lucky just to have sex with a vixen like Lavada, much less a relationship. "Uh, na'll I ain't seen her, dawg," Rico lied. "I was looking for her myself. If you see her, tell her to call me, I need to see if she gon' help cook for the NATION PICNIC."

Rock Island: A Gangstaz Graveyard   N.U.T.T.Y. "C"

CHAPTER 17

Gangs in Chicago routinely meet in their hoods, and even the leaders sometimes convened at undisclosed locations. But when the entire organization wanted to rotate, they did so at highly organized picnics, usually held in the local forest preserves. They called these picnics **"Nationwides"** For the Brothahood; each branch sponsored a picnic every other year. The Cons picnic was one of the most anticipated events of the summer for most young members. Due to restructuring it had been 4 years since their last nationwide.

The C's spared no expense in planning and organizing the event. Hundreds of pounds of meat and chicken were ordered, along with other picnic favorites. Local rappers and R&B singers were commissioned to perform. Brothas from everywhere were invited. It was mandatory for Brothas with rank to attend. Someone from each set had to represent their prospective hoods. Thousands of Brothas and Sistas attended.

Most of the Brothas from Rock Island had never attended a Nationwide; so this year was special to them. Even though a lot of "Nation Business" was conducted at the picnic, the event was quite festive, and could be enjoyed by anyone, from any walk of life. So Rico invited several corner Brothas and some eye candy. Other Bros had even invited their idols, older and ranking members took the opportunity to network and issue directives. Leaders from different locations shared their recipes for success.

Rico knew that he would be one of the main topics of discussions amongst the heads. But he didn't burden his R.I. peers with the potential threat. Instead he watched as they mingled with Brothas and Sistas from sets such as the "THE HOLY CITY", "THE LECLAIR COURTS PROJECTS", '"THE WILD 100's", "HOWARD STREET", and even "GARY INDIANA". He also noticed a group of Sistas that seemed to be isolated from everyone else. Big Saw was the "Queen of Queens" for the Cons Sistas. She was a dark skin, large woman, unattractive by most men's standards, but she was extremely wealthy, and had an impeccable taste in clothing, cars, and jewelry. At 36, she had 25 years experience within the organization. Her reputation for taking virtually unknown up & coming C'z and using them as her personal boy toyz, and putting them on in the drug game far exceeded her. She was one of the Old Man's most trusted liaisons. Many believed it was, Big Saw that kept the organization up and running, and not the cycle of Brothas that held high positions. But the catch-22 was if you became involved with Big Saw, you would gain wealth and power, but if she became disenchanted with you, you could come up missing.

"Who is dem' chicks over there wit' Big Saw?" Rico asked Pons from 89th and Cottage. "Dem' some of the Sistas from out west" Pons replied. "You don't want to fuck wit' none of dem', they bad for business." One of them is the Old Man's daughter too, so they outta yo' league my nigga, you be better off tryin' to holla at one of these other young Sistas." Thinking to himself; *"Ain't nobody outta my league."* "I ain't on shit; I'm just tryin' to network" he said, as he made his way over to the group of older Con Sistas that occupied two picnic benches and looking unimpressed with the large group of Brothas that surrounded them.

While a lot of the other females were busy being in awe of some of the flashy drug dealers and street legends that were abundantly present at the picnic, Big Saw's girls sat quietly, talking amongst themselves only speaking to Brothas when they were being spoken to. "How ya'll lovely Sistas doing today?" Rico asked as he approached the forbidden group.

"Fine," one Sista replied.

"Do ya'll mind if I take a couple of flicks wit y'all?" Rico asked. "Cuz ya'll are the perfect examples of what Sistas should be." The newly flattered Sistas took a liking to the courageous young con.

"Where you from" Val (Saw's right hand) asked. "Rock Island" Rico replied.

"They from the south side" Big Saw interjected.

Rico met Big Saw on a couple occasions with Max and Ed. "Look at you boy, all grown up and shit. What have you been on lately? I heard you The Man in Da Island now. The conversation seemed to spark the interest of the other Sistas. After Rico flirted for a while, he introduced them to a few Bros form R.I.

The usual hard faced, unimpressed ranking Sistas were under Rico's spell, laughing, joking, and horse playing with the guys from R.I. Rico favored Val, a 32 year old, short, medium built mother of two. She wore her hair in a short bob style, dyed blond. Her Gucci sandals revealed her freshly French manicured toes. She wore diamonds on every finger, and her necklace shined brighter than the hot July sun. But it was Big Saw, who seemed more interested in Rico. She kept asking him questions about his drug spots, commenting on how much money he could be making. But Rico was satisfied with the money he was making. Rico could only listen as she promised him fortune and fame, if he invested in heroine, and drop his crack trade. "You need to upgrade, Brotha, and let me give you 200 grams of this China White, I promise you; your life will never be the same." Given her reputation Rico didn't want to deal with Saw on that level, but given the same reason he knew that he probably didn't have much choice. He took her number and promised to call.

The Brothas that held positions for the Brothahood also took notice and congratulated Rico for turning his hood around. "We gon' inform the Old Man of your progress" the overseer of the City told Rico. "Keep up the good work," the newly elected south-side Chief Chinaman added. "I'll be rotating with you regularly to make sure everything good."
Chinaman was Big June's right hand man, and some believed for a long time that he was somehow involved in Big June's death. So when he was appointed to his new position, he wasn't met with much fan fare. The majority of the south side Brothas respected his position more than they respected his persona. Rico felt relieved now that his set was off the hook with the Brothahood. But he knew his job as R. I.'s leader was far from over.

After the picnic, it was business as usual for Rico and the Brothas. 77th and Carpenter was becoming a gold mine. Rico accepted Saw's offer to purchase heroine. She fronted the drugs to Rico as "NATION WORK," drugs given out in large quantities, by a trusted leader to be distributed. The profit was so great. The leader would demand a percentage be donated back to the Nation. If anyone on any level messed up with the Nation Work, a severe punishment would be handed down. Rico passed out his Nation packs periodically. The packages were usually sold for free by rookie members or by Brothas performing "NATION COMMUNITY SERVICE", a form of punishment for Brothas that have committed minor rule infractions, that didn't require a beat down or a monetary fine.

Head had positioned himself as Rico's right hand man. Their friendship transcended the organization. He selflessly supported and assisted Rico in all endeavors. He never asked Rico for one cent; despite Rico's fortunes. Rico was honored to have a friend like Head.
"Nigga when you gon' get some of this paper with a nigga" Rico asked Head as they counted over 50 thousand in small bills, while sitting in front of the 77th street drug spot.
"Man, you know I'm not a hustler like that" Head responded. "I'm here for you if you need me to do something. I didn't get in this shit for the money, as long as you cool, I'm cool."

Kenyatta approached the car, and tapped on the passenger side window, indicating for Rico to get out and holla at him. "We finished shaking that work up, when you wanna open shop back up?" Rico looked at his watch, and it read 4:30p.m. He closed down the spot during school hours when school traffic was heavy. He didn't like the fact that kids had to walk past lines of sick heroine addicts on their way from school. Even the kids next door to his spot had to be exposed to the business. He would always try to shield them from the madness that surrounded the business, by advising them to go in the house if he felt they were in harms way. And he even rewarded them by buying ice cream when the ice cream truck came on the block and even gave them money. Alot of the parents didn't mind, some of them were his best customers. But for one mother her attitude wasn't so relaxed. She felt that Rico had crossed the line. Roselyn was the mother of an 11 year old girl name Waheeda and an 8 year old boy name Abu, two of his favorite shorties. Rico had never seen their mother, who was walking swiftly towards him with each child in tow. From the look on their faces, Rico could tell they had done something wrong. As Rico, Rio, Kenyatta, and Chad all loitered in front of Roselyn's house; they could hear the woman's scowling voice.

"Which one is it?" she asked the children. They pointed to Rico. Roselyn looked at Rico from head to toe and stepped to him. "Excuse me, sir! Did you give my kids some money the other day?"

He observed the older woman, who appeared to be in her mid to late thirties. Her long black curly hair blew in her face as she stood directly in front of him. She wore a long sun dress that fought hard to reveal what was undoubtedly a curvy figure

"Um who are you?" Rico said trying to figure her out angle.

"Dis my momma Rico," Waheeda cut in.

"Shut up girl" Roselyn shot back, as she focused her attention back to Rico.

"Aaw yeah, I remember now," I gave'em a couple dollars to get some ice cream, it's cool I didn't mind." Roselyn stood there with her hands on her hips, visibly unimpressed and annoyed with the sound of Rico's voice. "Well I don't need you or no other man to be giving my kids no money!" She exclaimed, as she reached in her purse for a ten dollar bill. "I told these kids bout' talkin to strangers... They know better..." She held the money out to Rico. "Here's your money back sir, now please stay away from my children." Roselyn, despite her overzealousness, was quite amusing to Rico. Waheeda even tried to reason with her mother. "Ma, he ain't no stranger, he—" Roselyn cut her off. "Didn't I tell you to shut up? Now go in the house and wait for me."

Rico, noticing Roselyn was becoming upset, pulled her aside near the front entrance of her home and away from the growing crowd of spectators. "Look miss, I apologize if you feel disrespected by my actions. I see kids out here everyday playing and having fun, and a lot of parents can't afford to get them ice cream or any extra treats. The day I gave your kids some money, they would've been the only ones out here with nothing. you were a kid before, and you know how kids can be. I didn't want to subject them to that."

Roselyn found herself briefly transfixed on the young hustler. She had seen Rico before and knew that he had to be a drug dealer, but she also noticed that he stood out amongst his peers. She never saw him with the customary 40 oz. or blunt in his hand, and he always seemed poised and meticulous. And she concluded from his brief conversation that he was some what intelligent. Not what she was use to seeing from the typical drug dealers and gang bangers in her 13 and half years on the Chicago police force.

"Um, I was just saying... You could be crazy or something. And I just don't want my kids to be indebted to anybody out here in the streets. So are you going to except this money so we can be even or what?"

Rico just smiled and grabbed one of the large rolls of money out of his pocket. "Na'll I don't need that, but thank you anyway."

Roselyn couldn't believe the audacity of the charismatic gangbanger. "Well since you won't accept my money, how bout some food, it looks like your skinny butt could use a home cooked meal."

"Oh you got jokes huh?" Rico chuckled, relieved that he elicited a smile from the cold-blooded vet.

"So you think you can get down in the kitchen huh?"

"I do a little something" she said coyishly. Their conversation lasted nearly 30 minutes. She promised to let Rico sample some of her fine culinary inventions. She also expressed her disdain about the Brothas loitering in front of her house, leaving trash and broken bottles.

"I'll see what I can do," he said as he was cut short by the presence of an apparently annoyed Quetta. She noticed Rico talking to Roselyn and just stood about 15 feet away, as if she had been waiting for hours, rolling her eyes and smacking her lips, like she was auditioning for the roll of hood rat of the year.

Kenyatta and Head tried to run interference by making small talk with her, in an attempt to buy Rico some time, but Rico knew Quetta was a drama queen, and their efforts wouldn't sustain. So Rico ended his conversation with Roselyn. "Who da fuck is that?" Quetta

spat, pointing towards the area she last seen Rico and Roz standing. Rico didn't answer her question. She wasn't really expecting one anyway. "What da fuck you want Quetta? I told you bout coming over here like this," he shot back trying to seem unconvinced. "Why haven't you answered any of my calls?" she cried. "You make me sick Rico, Eww-- I swear to God you be pissin' me off. You can't pick up the phone and call me back now? After all we've been thru?" This was the second female to confront Rico today, and the Brothas just stood around and shook their heads. Some were use to Quetta's tantrums and break downs. "I swear Rico, on everything I love, if I catch another bitch all in yo' face again..."
"Quetta don't come over here trying to start a fight wit' me today, cuz I'm not in the mood" Rico calmly said. "I've been busy, and that's all you need to know. I don't have to answer to you. You better quit coming at me like this..."
She didn't need to hear no more, she was satisfied that she got his attention. "I'm sorry Rico" she replied in a babyish voice. "I just be worried about you sometime." She wanted to kiss him, but knew better. "I wanna kick it with you today," she whispered in his ear. "And then I can make you happy later on tonight."
Rico looked at his watch, it now read 5:30 p.m. "Let's just skip the kickin' it part, and I'll just get up with you later tonight. I still gotta' lot of shit to do today."
Head came to Rico's rescue. "Um, ay we gotta' go 'C'".
"Here I come." Quetta knew the deal. "Umma get up wit' you later shorty, I gotta get little." Rico headed toward his car with a slight variation of contempt for Quetta. *"This bitch crazy,"* he thought to himself. The motorcade of Brothas drove south on Carpenter, towards 79th street.

CHAPTER 18

As the motorcade approached 79th, they noticed several D-boys scurrying in response to their presence. "These niggas don't want it with us" Rico yelled to the car behind them. "Fuck deyz niggas!" Rico tried to convince his group to keep going, but it was too late. A few Brothas had already exited their vehicles and began fighting with the D-boys. "Rock Island killa!" one young D-boy yelled, as he challenged the rest of the Brothas to exit their cars and fight. Rico thought about his previous conversation with the D-boy leader. "C-mon, let's get deyz niggas!" Rico hadn't had a good ole gang fight in along time, so he put his pistol under his front-seat, and jumped in the crowd of guys, throwing punches at each other. He was punched instantly on the side of his face. He fought timelessly as if his life depended on it.

The scene became chaotic as the two groups filled 79th. Word of the fight spread like a wild fire, as more and more cons, 4's, and D'z ran to 79th to assist their brethren. For the D's this was a golden opportunity. Two D'boy leaders drove up to the scene and noticed Rico. "Aye fam, change that bitch ass nigga, Rico" one of the leaders said to 2 of his young subordinates, passing them two small semi-automatic hand guns out the window.

The fight was subsiding and the Brothas were making their way back to their cars. Rico, Kenyatta, Myron, and T.P. all jumped in Rico's car. "Come on, ya'll get in before Shawntae' come."

Rico let Myron drive, because his hand had been hurt in the brawl. He noticed the 2 figures running towards them with their weapons out in his peripheral vision. "Oh shit! Dem niggas' got heat! They bout' to bust, drive off, drive! Get the fuck outta…" BLAM! BLAM!,BLAM! BLAM! Bullets hit the side of the car, as Myron tried to back into traffic. The glass from the windows shattered as bullets whizzed by their heads. One of the triggermen made it to the intersection as the car gained momentum and squeezed off the last few rounds in his clip. Pop! Pop! Pop!

Rico could feel the blood running from the top of his brow. "I think dem' bitches shot me in the head" he said shockingly. But most of the blood in the car wasn't his. "Ahh, I'm hit too" Kenyatta said weakly. His moans and groans filled the car's cabin. He was shot in the upper torso and in the shoulder. Rico's wound was just a graze, and he managed to control the bleeding. However, Kenyatta was bleeding out, and started to lose consciousness.

"Drive to the hospital!" Rico yelled in the front seat to Myron. "You gon' make it Brotha, just hang in there. You gon' be alright Yatta, just hold on my nigga." Kenyatta's cries sent chills up Rico's spine. He continued to talk, despite his injuries.
"Make sure you... get, get dem' niggas fo' dis shit Rico." Rico felt so helpless. "We gon' get dem' niggas together Yatta, just hold on." Those were the last words Kenyatta heard, as his lifeless body grew colder in Rico's lap, as they neared the hospital. "Niggas gon' pay for this shit" Rico said to the rest of the occupants of the car. Kenyatta was pronounced dead on arrival. He was 17 years old.

After Rico was treated for his injuries, he was immediately taken into police custody after being questioned by homicide officers for hours. He relinquished no valuable information. But this was Derk's first time seeing Rico since his last arrest years earlier. "Do you know how serious this is muthafucka? We could charge you with obstruction of justice if you don't tell us what you know."
"I told you, I didn't see the shooter," Rico shot back. "I'm tired, I just want to go home."
"You mean to tell me that a guy or some guys can shoot over 20 rounds into your car from a distance no farther than 5 feet and you didn't get a glimpse?... That's bullshit and you know it Rico. I'm tired of your cocky bullshit!" But Derk knew he'd get no where being temperamental with Rico. "Ok Rico, have it your way. I know how you guys operate, and I know that you're one of the shot callers. I'ma find out who did this, cuz that's my job, with or without your help. I know you're not a snitch, so I'm not going to sit here and play cat and mouse with you. So here's the deal. I know you guys are upset about what happen, but I can't allow you young punks to hold court in the streets. So since you wanna be Chief, I'ma hold you responsible for every muthafuckas actions in your hood. If one of the D-boys gets shot tonight or any other night in the near future I'm coming to get you. As a matter fact, a D-boy better not even cut himself shaving or I'm gon' be all over your ass. So you better go out there and put those little radical sons-of-bitches on ice. And if you think I'm joking; try me."
Derk had placed Rico in an awkward position. For the first time since he took his top position, he was torn about what to do.

He was released after being held for 10 hours. The blood on his clothes had dried, and he was tired and in dire need of rest. He expected to see his mother in the down stairs lobby of the police head quarters. But to Rico's surprise, waiting for him was Roselyn. He had to adjust his eyes when he noticed her standing in the waiting area. "What you doing here?" Rico asked curiously.

"I heard what happen, I'm sorry about your friend. I was calling you all last night." (She explained to Rico that she was a police officer on the west side.) "When I got to work I did what I had to do and I found you. I knew that your car was impounded and figured you'd be released soon, so I thought you'd probably need a ride."

"And why would you go through all this trouble just for little old me?" He asked in his signature sarcastic tone.

"I don't know, I guess I'm just crazy" Roz replied, "Besides, I owe you and this was the only way I knew I could repay you."

He and Roz made their way to her grey Honda Accord. Once inside the car, his mind was still racing, and Roselyn took careful notice. "Um, Rico I'm not going to get in your business or nothing, so I'm not going to ask you what happen. I just want to know are you alright? The soft R&B music put his weary mind at ease. "Yeah, I'll be alright" he responded in a hoarse voice.

Her soft voice and the slow melodic music provided the perfect back drop, as he closed his eyes for the first time in almost two days and 45 minutes later... "Rico, Rico, Rico... wake up!" Roz urged. Suddenly Rico stirred and yawned himself back into consciousness. "I didn't know where you lived, and you fell asleep so fast I... I...just... well I just bought you here. I hope you're not upset, I can take you where you wanna go."

Rico looked around and realized that he was back on 77th street, in front of Roselyn's house. It was nearly dawn, and not too many people stirred about. She informed him that the police had been sweating his guys real hard, and they left. "They'll probably be back" she added noticing he was in observation mode. If you want, you can get cleaned up and get some rest here and we can take it from there."

Rico accepted her offer. He needed time to regroup, and get his mind right.

After a hot shower, Roz made him a breakfast fit for a king. Rico feasted on blueberry pancakes, cheese eggs, hash browns, turkey bacon and grits. He called Head and informed him of his whereabouts, and requested some clean clothes, just before he nodded out again on Roselyn's soft leather couch.

Roselyn couldn't sleep, instead she crept about in her house, struggling with the decision she'd made to let Rico in her house.

"You got dat' nigga just layin' up in yo' crib?" Carmen, one of Roselyn's best friends yelled into the phone after receiving the latest 411.

"Bitch are you crazy!? Ain't that one of them niggas that sell drugs on yo' block? You don't know that nigga like that; he could be a killer or rapist. And you just…?"
Roz knew Carmen was right but every since Rico said two words to her she was intrigued by the sharp tongue soldier. "Listen Carmen, I'ma big girl, I can handle myself. I'm not worried about that Lil boy. He just went through some hell, and I feel like he needs a friend."
"How he look girl, is he cute?" Carmen asked devishly. Her question made Roselyn giggle. "There you go, Ms. Thang. That boy in there is young enough to be my son. I haven't looked at him like that"
"Bitch stop lying!" Carmen laughed. "Is he fine or what?"
Roz couldn't spin her girlfriend. "Oh God yes, he's fine girl. Dark skin, slim, and very well groomed: But let me stop, it's not that type of party."
"Yeah right" Carmen sarcastically responded. "You haven't been with a man in a long time."
Roselyn divorced her husband of 17 years, and dated a police sergeant for a year, but broke if off after he proposed to her. She had no desire to be married again, especially to a cop. She wasn't too fond of cops, despite her being one herself. If she didn't have a guaranteed job for life with the Chicago police department, she probably would've become a restaurateur. But because of her injury sustained the second year on the force, she now had a comfortable desk job.
"Yeah, I know," Roselyn said. "But you know I'm taking a break from men right now. I just need to focus on my life, and kids, I don't need no man."
"I feel you girl but, ain't nothing like a lil' dick in yo' life from time to time," Carmen said with a light laughter.
"You crazy, girl." Roz responded. "You a freak."

      Rico was still stretched out on the couch when he realized that he was still at Roselyn's. He could hear Roz talking on the phone, and decided to relieve himself in the bathroom. When he exited, he was met by Roz, holding a bag. "Hey sleepy head, your friend dropped these clothes off for you."
"Thanks, how long have I've been out?" he asked as he grabbed the bag and peeped inside. "About 9 hours, you were sleeping so good, I didn't want to disturb you. My kids are with their father for the weekend so you can change your clothes in Abu's room. I think a lot of your friends are waiting on you outside."

After he got dressed, he looked out the window and seen his guy's scattered all over the block. He knew they were waiting for him to direct them in devising a plan for avenging Kenyatta's death.

"Rico, like I said before I'm not going to get in your business, but I know what's up. Believe me; the police don't care if ya'll kill each other. I'm not going to give you a long speech or preach to you. All I'm going to say is be careful out there, baby! If I can do anything to help let me know. Remember Rico, nothing you do can bring your friend back." He weighed her words, and was tempted to tell her that he didn't know how he was going to go outside and tell his guys that they couldn't retaliate on Kenyatta's killers because of Derk's threat. He opted to just thank her and offered a monetary form of appreciation, in which she declined. "I'll only accept your gratitude, your money is no good here," she said to Rico as he exited her apartment.

****

As soon as he crossed the threshold of Roz's door, the Brothas flooded him with their queries and filled his ears with their frustration.

"Man, Rico, where you been Joe?"

"We heard you got a dome shot,"

"We gotta get dem' bitch ass niggas! What are you talking bout, when you said don't do nothing? Them niggaz changed that Brotha, they gotta pay!"

The angry mob grew larger and louder by the minute, as Rico tried to appear cool as a cucumber. Steve, who had just learned of Kenyatta's death, and was still dressed in his work uniform cried uncontrollably. It was clear that he was drunk, which was not an uncommon sight for the Brothas.

As Rico attempted to explain his strategy to the Brothas, Steve continuously interrupted with his half drunken remarks. "Fuck dat' shit Brotha, dem' niggas out there right now" Steve slurred. "Listen!" Rico said with authority. "We can't hit dem' niggas right now, the police waiting on us, and the D-boys are probably expecting us too. I told ya'll that the police gon' pop me off if one dem' vics gets hurt. I wanna get'em to, but we gotta be smart. We gon' get at dem' niggas on our terms, when everybody least expect it."

While most Brothas listened intensely, Steve sat on a car with his lips twisted, an obvious sign he disagreed with Rico's orders.

"Dis' what I'm talking bout!" Steve blurted our angrily. "Niggas is soft, Rock Island don't get down like that. If somebody does something to one of us we suppose to get down on they ass; not wait around…"

Rico's orders were clear; no one was to act until further notice. "Somebody take Steve home." Rico ordered, before getting in

119

the car with Rio and Head, they all had to go check in with Kenyatta's mother, who everybody knew as Tee-Tee. She was a former Black EEl Sista from back in the day, and had been involved with the streets for most of her 35 years. She struggled most of her life with welfare, and odd jobs. She and Kenyatta were more like sister and brother, than mother and son. So when Kenyatta first became involved with the streets, she schooled him and taught him the game.

After Lil Mikey's arrest, she noticed that her son's involvement in the drug game had deepened. Largely due to his association with Rico, Rio, Myron, and Head. Kenyatta's success in the drug game enabled him to buy his mother 2 cars, and a nice down payment on a house far away from the gang infested streets of the Rock Island area. A house that Kenyatta filled with fine furniture and fine amenities, a house that now will be void of Kenyatta's presence. Tee-Tee was no stranger to grievous lost. Kenyatta's father was also shot and killed on the streets; a week before her 23rd birthday. She had also attended the funerals of a lot of her Eel Brothas. But nothing prepared her for losing her only son. She greeted the Bros at her front door. She hugged each one of them for an extended period of time. Rico handed Tee-Tee an envelope filled with hundred dollar bills. "If you need anything else, just let me know" he said calmly.

"I wanna let you know that your son's death won't be in vain. It's just a lot going on right now." He assured her.

"Yeah I know" Tee-Tee spoke softly. "I spoke with the police and they asked me to encourage ya'll to identify somebody. Did you see who did this to my baby? Because they say you did."

Rico took a deep breath, and watched as Tee-Tee lit a Newport. "Of course I did," Rico responded. "And that's why I'm trying to keep everything on the low, cuz the police don't care about Kenyatta, I do, all of the guys do."

She tried to convince Rico to go to the police and aid her in finding justice for her son. But her pleas were only a formality. "I made a promise to Kenyatta," Rico said, as he hugged Tee-Tee on his way out of the door. "And I plan on keeping it."

****

Meanwhile, Steve had plans of his own, despite Rico's order to postpone the retaliation of Kenyatta's death. He was determined to put in some work. He felt that his friend was wrong about not retaliating. Steve was old school and use to doing things the more traditional way; a way that demanded immediate retribution on anyone that crossed the mob. The Brothas denied him access to all of the

"Nation guns". so he borrowed a MAC-10 sub machine gun from the Black EEls and took matters into his own hands. The shots could be heard 3 blocks away on 76 Street, as the Bros wondered what was going on.

****

Rico was on his way to his Grandmother's house when he received several pages from Quetta- 9-1-1. She routinely paged him in such desperate fashion, so he didn't pay it much mind. He figured she had just heard about the Kenyatta incident and was concerned about him. Rico made a mental note to call her when he arrived at his Grandmother's house. Barbra was sitting on her front porch when her Grandson pulled up with his associates. The Brothas didn't mind accompanying Rico to Barbra's, because Barbra was very hospitable and often cooked festive meals.

Barbra on the other hand, was use to the sight of a few guys accompanying Rico on his visits; although lately he traveled with four or more guys. She wasn't naïve enough to assume that his comrades were merely casual friends as Rico tried to make it appear. She knew her Grandson was of some importance to his peers and didn't regard him as a common thug like his mother. She never accepted the many gifts Rico offered her, claiming that the items were probably stolen or purchased with the devils money. But Barbra accepted every gift Rico bestowed upon her. She didn't pretend not to know where the large bills came from in her change jar on the candy and snowball stand.

Barbra tried to hide her smile from her neighbors that were enjoying the warm weather as well, as the two car motorcade searched for parking spaces. "We came to buy some candy" Rico joked, as he and his crew approached the porch. "Hey, boy." Barbra said, wrinkling her face after noticing the band-aid over Rico right eye brow. "What happen to you?"

"Oh, this ain't nothing, Grandma" Rico replied, trying to down play his near fatal encounter. "Just a lil' accident on the court," he reluctantly lied.

Barbra fed the group some of her deep fried chicken, oven baked Mac & cheese, collard greens, and warm corn-bread. For desert she treated them to her double chocolate cake.

"Man, dis' cake is fye as hell Joe," one Brotha complimented.

"On everything dis'a nuke!"

Barbra enjoyed having a house full of guest, even if they were ill-bred individuals. She hated eating alone. She hated being alone. While Barbra entertained the Brothas with desert, Rico used that opportunity to call Quetta back. He felt bad about not returning her calls, especially since the whole hood probably heard about what he'd been thru by now. He expected to hear her animated disdainful voice, but was shocked to hear an uncharacteristically sober Quetta on the other end.

"Rico you need to come home right now," she said in a serious tone.

"Why, what's going on Quetta?"

"It's Steve! They just shot Steve! He went over there fucking wit' dem' D-boys and they shot him."

It didn't make sense. Rico secretly hoped that Quetta was grossly misinformed. But after a couple more phone calls, his fears were confirmed. Steve attempted a hit on the D-boys on 79th and Carpenter, and during the shoot-out, his weapon jammed. The D-boys returned fire, killing him instantly. Rico knew this revelation would probably alter his plans drastically. So the last call he made before leaving Barbra's was to Vic, and a few other well known killers.

CHAPTER 19

The neighborhood was fairly quiet, as Rico drove towards his home base. News of Steve's death traveled fast, prompting the southside over-seer C-man to meet with Rock Island's Elites. "Fuck dis' shit Joe" Rico said angrily as he drove towards his home base. "Those pigs just gon' have to lock me up, cuz it's on." Two Brothas killed in three days, Rico knew he had to act. As he neared Toby's house he could see the C-man had already arrived, and was speaking to some of the Brothas with rank. Rico told two of the shorties that was ear hustling to post up on security, as he neared the group's proximity. C-man didn't stop his rapid fire conversation as Rico neared. "…So it's about getting this money and progressing, know what I'm sayin'?" C-man said passionately, before acknowledging the presence of Rock Island's young Elite. The two moved away from the crowd of angry and restless Brothas to speak in private.

C-man attempted to sympathize with Rico. "I'm sorry about what happen to dem' Brothas Rico! All this gang-bangin shit is getting played out. We need to get to another level of the game."
Rico listened intensively as C-man gave him a long boring speech about the organization moving forward. But he had to interject when C-man suggested that R.I. not retaliate, because of a so-called understanding the ranking Brothas and the D-boys leaders had in the joint.
"We trying to work out a peaceful solution; C-man concluded."
Rico felt his blood pressure rapidly rising. "With all due respect Brotha I don't give a flying fuck what dem' niggas in the joint are saying or trying to do. Two of our guy's just got changed, and you expect me to go tell them some bullshit story about what niggas tryin' to do in the joint?" Rico knew he was out of line, but he didn't care. He felt disrespected that the organization would even put him in this position. He knew that if he defied C-man's orders that he would be placing himself, as well as others in unfavorable light, and possibly all of his efforts to get the Island back in grace could be in jeopardy. But he also knew he couldn't face his friends with the C-man's plan. *"Ain't no sense in being scared now,"* he thought to himself.
"So what you trying to say, Rico?" asked C-man, in a concerned tone.
"We about to handle our business on dem' niggas, and ain't nothing stopping that," retorted Rico. By now the R.I. Brothas as well as C-Man's personal security could tell that the 2 men were at odds. The R.I. Brothas instinctively started sizing up C-man's crew. "Rico, listen," C-

man said, as calmly as he could while making a threat. "I don't think you wanna do this."
Rico exasperatedly responded. "What da' fuck you mean you don't think I wanna do this?" he shouted. "Dig Joe, ain't none of you niggaz ever lived over here, so ya'll don't know our struggle, how we came up and the sacrifices we made. We been over here for years. None of ya'll put in work, or lifted a finger for our hood. So you think I'm gon' let some niggas that didn't even know we existed a few years ago tell me what's best for our land."
C-man, stood attentive, rubbing his thick goatee, as Rico vented. He knew Rico had a point, but as the overseer he had his own agenda, and law was law. He tried one last attempt to reason with Rico.
"Law governs all events, and what the Old Man and nem' say is law. Rico and the other Brothas in earshot were unmoved.
"Ain't nothing you or anybody else can say right now that's going to save dem' niggas from their fate. Point blank! That's all to it! So if you wanna' put us under fire for that, so be it. But at the end of the day, mutha fuckas gon' know we ain't no hoes."

****

  Meanwhile at the area 2 station, Derk, and his partner received a call from his R.I. informant. By the end of the conversation, they had the names of the 2 shooters in Kenyatta's murder. Derk knew the two D-boys well and he was surprised that the 2 low level crack dealers had elevated to murder. Derk reported to his Captain, while waiting for the warrant to come back.
"How reliable is this **C.I.** of yours?" The bald, heavy set Captain asked.
"Oh, he's very reliable sir," Derk replied. "He's provided us with information that led us to of dozens arrest, and he's out there right now getting more Intel' about the second shooting today. Over there on 79th." The Captain allowed Derk to work out of the box after the death of his partner Quick. "I thought you had the thugs over there on 76 Street sitting on their hands. The Captain asked. Derk didn't like being probed. "I do, this was an isolated incident. The victim was acting on his own accord, according to my C.I."
"I'm not going to ask you how you managed to get those guys over there under some-what control, but keep up the good work."
Derk glowed with pride as he thought of something slick to say in response. *"Don't worry about it Cap, I got this area under control, just trust me."* (He would soon eat those words.)

****

Two Hours later, in area seven police station Roselyn said a silent prayer as she listened to her police radio scanner. The reports of shots fired, and several shootings throughout the 79th street area made her cringe. It was happening, the newly raged war between two street gangs that would only cause more harm than good. As reports of more and more shootings came in, she wondered where the generous young man with the infectious personality was at. She'd left him several messages, but he never returned her calls. *"Fuck that shit,"* she thought briefly. *"He chose that life."* Despite her position, she couldn't keep her mind off him.

****

Meanwhile, Rico, and one of his goons sat in a stolen van outside the house of the young D-boy who had ambushed him and Kenyatta. "You think this nigga coming home anytime soon?" the seasoned killer asked Rico, as they stalked the 2 story home in a residential area about a mile away from R.I.

"I don't know man," he replied. "But it's 2 in the morning, and he ain't came home yet. We can try'n catch this nigga tomorrow."

"Na'll, I got a better idea," the goon said, as he cocked his chrome nine mm back and exited the van. *"What the fuck this nigga doing?"* Rico asked himself, as he got out the van and followed his soon-to-be accomplice up to the dark house. "Just follow my lead, Brotha" he whispered to Rico as he rung the door bell. It took a few minutes before a voice broke the silence. "Who is it?" the young boy said from behind the door.

"It's me" the goon replied.

"Who?" the boy asked again through the door.

"C'mon man, you know who this is stop playing."

Rico couldn't believe how easy it was, when he heard the locks of the door being unlocked. The young boy who couldn't be older than 13 only had the door cracked a couple inches before it hit him in the face with a force that nearly knocked him out.

"Who the fuck here with you?" Rico asked as the goon applied the sleeper technique on the young boy.

With the tip of Rico's weapon in his mouth, he managed to tell him who else was in the house. One by one, they gathered the entire family up and positioned them in the living room. By now they all knew why they were being tied up and held against their will. The two intruders wanted to know the whereabouts of the D-boy that lived there. Once they couldn't provide that information, Rico demanded that one of them call him and urge him to come home.

The problem with that was that the D-boy wasn't available, due to the fact that he was at the area two police station being charged with Kenyatta's murder, along with his partners in crime. Hours went by, before Rico decided to concede that the D-boy wasn't going to return his family's call or come home.

"Let's get the fuck outta here Joe" Rico said to his partner!"

"Aight man, lets' get the fuck outta here!"

Rico was tired, and dawn was approaching, as he carefully looked up and down the quiet block. And if his mind wasn't on getting home and giving his body a much needed rest, he probably would've noticed that his partner wasn't directly behind him. But the gun shots from the house quickly put him on alert. The familiar sound of gun shots urged him to speed up his pace to the van parked a few houses down the street. Rico and his partner drove in complete silence for the duration of the ride.

The next day, two more D-boys were arrested in connection with Steve's murder. It was a mystery to Rico how the police knew exactly who had done the crimes. He started to grow suspicious, but he was oblivious to the fact that a Brotha he interacted with on a daily basis was practically the police himself.

After Rock Island defiantly retaliated on the D-boys, and the news of a D-boys entire family being murdered topped all of news cycles; Rico knew that he had to remain unsuspicious. Derk was probably looking for him, the Brothahood probably wanted answers, and now the entire Family Hood was probably at him too. Head and Toby ran the Island, as Rico laid low in his suburban condominium. Head was the only Brotha allowed to visit him. "Man Joe! Shawntae' been sweatin' the hood like crazy." Head told Rico, as they both sat in front of a large screen plasma TV. "And some Brothas from the 100's been through the land looking for you. They didn't look too friendly either."

"I don't give a fuck" Rico replied in an exhausted tone. "The Brothas just gone have to do what they have to do, cuz dem' niggas had it comin', and I ain't neva having no type of peace treaty wit'dem' vics."

"So what you want to do?" Head asked. "They popped dude and nem' off for Kenyatta and Steve."

"I don't care how many of em' go to jail, I want they asses wiped off the fucking map. Tell the Bros to keep going through there makin' it rain on dem' niggas. As soon as the police and the ambulance leave, hit em' again."

"Alright Brah, I got you," Head said as he did the C's signature handshake, readying himself for what was about to be a long bloody summer. "You just chill Joe and take as much time as you need. You need me to take care of anything else?"

Rico thought about it, and lowered his voice from the prying sonic ears of Quetta, who was in the bedroom pretending to be asleep. "Um-- yeah, there is one more thang I need you to take care of."

Rock Island: A Gangstaz Graveyard   N.U.T.T.Y. "C"

CHAPTER 20

It had been weeks since Roz heard from or seen Rico. Nobody seemed to have any information about their leader who appeared for all intended purposes to be M.I.A. Roz didn't want to put herself out there by inquiring about the crafty Con, to his friends that were still conducting street business. Her daughter said she heard he was out of town. *"Maybe he moved,"* she thought as she parked in front of the house after a long overtime shift. *"That's probably best for him."* Her thoughts immediately detoured, as she noticed something was different about the front of her house. She could not believe her eyes looking at the freshly cut and manicured, lawn. All the broken glass and trash that once littered the sidewalk, and gangway, of her property had been removed.

"They were out here all morning" Mrs. Cox, her heavyset neighbor from across the street yelled from her porch, noticing Roz's bewilderment. "Somebody must'n paid them a pretty penny. Cuz they were out here working their asses off. They did a good job too."

"Um, yeah they did." Roz replied softly still inspecting her property. As she entered her apartment, she noticed a small envelope on the floor. Someone had apparently slid it under the door.

She opened it, it read:

Sometimes people come into your life and you know right away they were meant to be there to serve some sort of purpose, to teach you a lesson, or help you figure out who you are or who you want to become. You never know who those people may be; it could be anybody, even a complete stranger. However, when you lock eyes with them or feel their energy, you know at that very moment that they will affect your life in some profound way.

She read the note repeatedly throughout the rest of the day, finally attaching it to her refrigerator with a magnet. *"No,"* she told her self. *"I can't be feeling like this over a drug dealer,"* she rationalized. But the more she tried to fight them, the more her feelings intensified.

The next day after work, she noticed Head standing in front of the spot and decided to approach him. "Excuse me," she said, as he talked casually into a cell phone. "Do you know where Rico is?" Head concluded his conversation and gave Roz his undivided attention. "I just need to holla at him," she continued.

"Oh yeah, that's what's up, is everything okay?" He asked politely.

"Yeah everything' cool, it's just that… Mmmm, I haven't seen him lately."

She said hoping that she didn't sound too desperate. "Is he okay?" Head let out a light chuckle relieved that Roz was only concerned, and her inquires weren't about nothing else. "Yeah, he aight, you know everybody needs a break from time to time."

"Well if you see him, just tell him I said thanks."

Rico used his time away like a paid vacation from a fortune five hundred company. Work was never far from his thoughts. As hard as he tried to clear his mind, he was overwhelmed with the feeling that something major was going to happen in his life. He couldn't put his finger on it, but he knew it would be one of two things; long-term incarceration or a violent death. He began having nightmares about the family that was executed in cold blood. This prompted him to better his own relationship with his family especially Virginia, his mother. They went on a road trip down south to visit other relatives. Rico hadn't spent much time as an adult with his mother. So when they got to North Carolina, he took full advantage of the opportunity. His mind seemed to be in a different state. He walked around for the first time in years without constantly looking over his shoulders, watching every car as they approached. Nobody tripping about colors or the way that he wore his hat. He felt relaxed within his new environment. "Man, these people got it made down here," he thought.

Virginia noticed her son's efforts, and appreciated the quality time that they were spending together. "Ma, have you ever felt like something bad was about to happen to you?" Rico asked as he sat at an outside café over looking the ocean.

Virginia, never really had her son's attention. Most of the time their conversations were one-sided with her chastising him about his lifestyle. She knew her son was hurting inside, she felt, and she saw it in his eyes and now could hear it in his voice.

"What are you talking about, Rico?" She asked, as she finished her meal.

Rico looked around, inhaled the fresh sea breeze, and fought hard to not let the tears fall from his eyes. "I'm just sayin', ma; it seems like I've made my life so hard and now I can't catch a break. Nothing has come easy for me. Even though I consider myself lucky to be sitting here right now, it seems like this is all leading up to something...I think something bad." Virginia weighed Rico's words, and moved closer to him. She took his hand and squeezed it gently, and looked into her weary son's eyes. *"He was so handsome."* She thought to herself, "Rico, baby, listen to me. Sometimes things happen to you that may seem horrible, painful, and unfair at first; but in reflection, you find that without overcoming those obstacles, you would have never realized your potential, strength, will power, or your heart. Everything happens for a reason; nothing happens by chance or luck, good or bad. Illness, injury, love, lost moments of true greatness, and sheer stupidity all occur to test the limits of your soul. Without these small tests, what ever they may be; life would be like a smoothly paved straight flat road to nowhere. It would be safe and comfortable, but dull. The battles, and little downfalls you experience, they help create who you are and ultimately who you'll become. Even the bad experiences could be learned from, Rico. We all make mistakes, but more often than not, it's how we respond to these mistakes that determines our destiny. God works in mysterious ways, son." Rico listened, as Virginia soothed his soul with inspirational words of wisdom. Rico finally opened up to his mother, telling her everything about his life that she didn't know. They prayed together daily and enjoyed each other's company for another week.

****

  Back in Chicago, the war with the "Family" continued. Darnell was shot and killed as he walked down 79th street with a girlfriend. His brother Chad, (now known as Shorty C), didn't take the news well. He took his grief out on every opposition he could find. His mentality completely changed after Darnell's murder. Some suspected because their father had passed away a year prior, and Mitch, (his older brother) was in prison, Chad felt alone; even in the close knit organization like the Brothas. Despite R.I's policies, Chad dropped out of school, and began selling drugs independently full time; only taking breaks to terrorize the oppositions nearby. He never knew who was responsible for his brother's death; his vengeful ways never provided him with the closure that he needed. The fifteen year old started drinking and smoking blunts every hour of his working day.

  When Rico returned from his hiatus, he received a call from Mitch, asking him to personally look-out for his little brother. Rico assured Mitch that he would. "I've got your brother," Rico told Mitch over the phone. "I'ma cuff shorty, and put him on the team! You just hurry up and get out so you can get some of this money, my nigga. I need you out here Joe! They poppin' the guys off like crazy these days, my whole team is almost gone. It's just me and Head on Carpenter now that Rio and Myron got locked up."

"What they pop Rio and Myron for?" Mitch asked just before his phone time was up. "All I can say, it's that swine ass nigga, Derk" Rico replied.

With Rio, Kenyatta, Myron, and others now out the picture, Derk knew that Rico had to make a move, thus making him come out of hiding to run his Carpenter Street operation. With the aide of his informant, he was able to put cases on all Rock Island's major players. Derk knew to keep his eyes on the new up and comings. Such as Black, Rashad, M-dubb, who were all Bo Oley protégés that mostly hung out on 79th and Peoria or Sangamon. Cornerboys, Reese and Ronald, maintained their positions in the complex. Toby, Qualo, and Jo-Jo held down 77th and Sangamon. The original Rock Island block, 76th and May wasn't as popular as it once was. And new Cornerboy Wacky, stayed posted twenty-four seven, making sure the loyal crack customers still received their product. 75th and Carpenter (Fin and the EEls old block), was occupied by Milton, T.P. and Anthony. It seemed like the Brothas decided to spread- out, and put a little more distance between themselves and their oppositions. The days of fifty to sixty Brothas cluttered on one block were done. This made the oppositions, and the police jobs a lot more difficult.

When Head, T.P., Milton, and Rico arrived on 77th and Carpenter, they noticed Shorty C standing near the gangway with a small caliber pistol already drawn. "Slow down "C", it's just us!" Milton said as they exited the white caddy. "Shit, I didn't recognize the car," Shorty C, said as he greeted his guys with a handshake. "Yeah, that's his new demo," T.P. said pointing to Rico.

"Gotta keep flipping new shit on niggas" Rico boasted. "I can't get complacent in this game." Rico then took the time to inform Shorty C about him and Mitch's conversation. "So you wanna check some real paper with a nigga or what? I'm about to open up a new dope-line out here," Rico said. "We could use a real nigga like you to help us hold shit down over here."

"I'm down for wud ever" Shorty C replied. "The rest of the Brothas scared to get money over here." He muttered, looking directly at T.P. and Milton.

From that day on Shorty C, Head, and Rico were one. Shorty C's bond with Rico was like one he shared with his blood Brothas. He stuck to Rico like glue, and vowed to protect him, with his life. He didn't want to lose another brother.

The Carpenter Street spot didn't take long to produce above average profits again. Jo-Jo was promoted to Chief of Security and Black became First Lieutenant. Rico tried to spread himself out as thinly as possible, only going on Carpenter to pick up money and to make drop offs.

Roz knew he was back around and figured if he wanted to see her, he knew where she was. She wasn't about to sweat no boy almost half her age. The sight of Rico made her stop in her tracks, as she approached her building carrying a bag of groceries. Rico pretended not to notice her intense stare, acting as if she caught him off guard, although he had already peeped her car before she arrived at her destination.

"Nigga, stop playin', and go holla at her," Head said to Rico who was trying too hard to look busy.

"Hey, how you doing?" Rico said as he walked towards Roz casually, noticing that she was still staring at him silently. She wanted to say something cool or sexy, but her brain couldn't function properly as he got close enough for her to get a slight whiff of his mild cologne. She just handed him the bag of groceries and smiled as she made her way back to her apartment. Rico followed, once inside he attempted some damage control. "Alright, I know you mad but..." She cut him off with a passionate kiss, as they both stood in the middle of the kitchen floor. A surprised but elated Rico followed suit by running his fingers through her long black curly hair. They ignored the groceries falling to the floor as they leaned against the countertop locked at the lips. The room filled with no words, just soft moans as their clothes melted away. Her honey colored skin seemed to electrify as Rico gently kissed her neck. She held on for dear life as he entered her for the first time. Since her kids were gone to camp for the summer, she knew that no one would hear her moans and screams of pleasure. Rico seemed to be in a trance as he pumped harder and harder, causing her large breast to jiggle uncontrollably. A shower of guilt flooded her body as she rode her multi-orgasmic wave. "Mmm, Rico, stop, we can't... Oh-- please don't stop, ah, ah, ah, shit!" She screamed as he started hitting her spot. "Rico we can't be doing this" she moaned into his ear, as he went deeper and deeper. "Baby, you making me... cu-cum, oh, ooh..." Rico said nothing; he allowed his body to do all of the talking. Rico, spoke to her all over the kitchen and finally in her soft bed where she watched her young stallion in the mirror, feverishly, yet skillfully drill her from behind. She wanted to tell him to slow down, that he was hurting her, but the pain felt so good. His long member reached areas inside her that hadn't been touched in years. Noone had ever made love to her that way. It was rough but gentle at the same time. She wanted to talk, but every time she attempted to verbalize her pleasure, Rico pumped harder; causing her to scream in more delight. Finally, they both climaxed and collapsed on the bed, both trying hard to catch their breath. Roz in her weakened state managed to issue a light playful slap

133

to Rico's head. "Aw, what was that for?" Rico asked playfully as he enjoyed the view of her naked body.

"For having me worried about you all of this time!" she responded as she got up enough strength to go to the bathroom. "And for what you just did to me," she said with a sheepish grin.

Her walk said it all, as she limped out the room. *"I just beat that pussy up!"* he thought to himself, as he proudly laid back in her queen-sized bed.

After they washed up, they laid in the bed and enjoyed some pillow talk. They stayed there talking another hour or so, then had sex again. Rico never had a lover that he cared to have a deep conversation with. In a way, he felt like he was on his therapist's couch. Roz, did not grow up in the streets, and could not directly relate to Rico's life style; she never associated herself with street- individuals.

Now Roz looked forward to the excitement that a hood figure could provide her otherwise dull and mundane life. Conversely, Rico was thinking as an opportunist. Feelings to the side, he knew Roz could benefit him as well as his organization.

"All of this time we've been next door to you, why you never called the police on us?" Rico asked her as he caressed the side of her face.

"I don't know" she replied. "I just couldn't, especially after I met you," she confessed.

"So, should I feel special?"

"I guess so."

As Roz slept peacefully, Rico laid in the bed wide-awake, thoughts racing, plotting his next move. He thought about North Carolina, and how comfortable he felt down there. Then his thoughts were interrupted by the sound of Roz's doorbell. "Don't look at me," she said half-asleep. "Don't nobody come to my house at this time of night." Rico looked outside; it was Head and Shorty C. He took a deep breath and muttered a few expletives: "Man, "C", we sorry to disturb you, but it's an emergency." Head explained. "Somebody just shot Brandon on 77th and May."

"Whud?" Rico exclaimed. "I just saw that nigga earlier. He told me he was gone chill wit' his girl all day. Is he okay?" The two Brothas just shook their heads. "Who did it?" Rico asked, numbing himself to another murder.

"We think the G-boys from Central City," Head revealed. They waited in the hallway as Rico went back into the apartment to get dressed. "What's wrong baby?" Roz asked sensing that Rico wasn't in his loving mode anymore. "One of my guys just got murked; I got to go

handle some business." Roz already felt like she was Bonnie and he was Clyde. "Is there anything I can do to help?"
"I'll let you know" he replied, then kissed her goodbye.

Rock Island: A Gangstaz Graveyard   N.U.T.T.Y. "C"

CHAPTER 21

The smell of wet pavement filled the air as Rico, Head, and Shorty C got into the Caddy to go investigate the murder of Con member Brandon. First, they toured the area in which he was shot looking for any witnesses that may have seen anything. The police tape was still around the area where Brandon's body once laid. Even at the wee hours of the night, traffic from the residential crack-heads was still high.
"Ay, my man! Let me holla' at cha' " Rico yelled from his car. The dingy faced hype slowed his pace just enough to be recognized as Killa Curt, one of Shorty C's best customers.
"Who dat'?" Curt asked hesitantly as he squinted his eyes in attempt to get a good visual on the occupants of the fancy car. "Man you niggas was about to make me shit in my pants." Killa Curt said.
"Nawl' Killa, we don't want that" Chad said, pulling two rocks out of a pack and handing it to the familiar hype.
"Man thank you, whud dis' fo?"
"We just need some information, Curt" Rico replied.
The group questioned killa Curt for fifteen minutes about what he saw that night. He also led the guys to other hypes that may have pertinent information. A common theme seemed to have emerged in the streets. The guys that ambushed Brandon yelled out Raulo's name. This made sense as far as a motive. Since Raulo started smoking crack, he resorted into all sorts of petty crimes to support his habit. Apparently, he stuck up a well-known G-boys spot. Brandon, his cousin; who he could resemble Raulo on a good day, not to mention a dark rainy night, was more than likely shot due to mistaken identity.

Two hours and ten bags of crack later, the Brothas had seemingly solved a murder, becoming judge, and jury. Leather face-the mid level G-boy whose car was described at the scene of Brandon's shooting, was shot the next day. At Brandon's funeral, Rico consoled his old friend Terry who was planning to make a return to the hood. Terry performed a heart-warming eulogy. Dressed in black and gold, Terry spoke with poise from the podium to the large crowd of mourners. "Brandon, was more than a cousin to me!" He said letting tears roll down his face. "He was like the brother I never had. We were born one week apart…" Rico hugged Terry as he planned to exit the funeral home. "Terry, ya' know Brandon was my nigga too," Rico said assuringingly. "Ima miss him, Joe" Terry said diligently. "I should've been over there wit' him, maybe this shit wouldn't have happened."

"I'm coming back Brotha and I ain't never leaving. Soon as I hit this lick in a few days, Ima be on location, "aight' Brotha?"
"Yeah "C" take yo' time, we'll be waiting on you," Rico replied.

Four days later Terry's body was found in a small alley on the north side, with a gunshot wound to the head. Ironically, the seven days that separated him and Brandon at birth also separated them at death. Terry's murder remained unsolved by the police and the Brothas. Although many suspected that the Jamaicans Terry was dealing with probably was involved.

Shortly after, Wayne got out on bond for his murder. During his two-year incarceration, the overzealous 4-Corner Brotha earned a little rank, and like his mentor, K-Man, he wanted to make his presence felt as soon as he set foot back in his old neighborhood. Playing off his reputation as a fearless killer, he immediately tried to issue directives to every Cornerboy in Rock Island. "I'm the muthafucking Chief over here now!" He told Cornerboy members, Wacky, Co-Co, Al, and the others as they stood on 76th and May. "The 4's betta' get they shit together or else be dealt wit'. They running round listening to them C's! We need to start worrying about ourselves."

Wayne spoke with a treacherous look in his eyes. His position didn't sit well with most of the remaining Corner Brothas, who considered the C's Brothas as well. Besides him being a ranking member of their branch, most of the Brothas tried to distance themselves from Wayne, and his reckless ways. "Ya'll Brothas need to start picking up guns everyday, and putting in work," he said at a Rock Island goal. "It seems to me that everybody just concerned wit' getting money and chasing these chicken head broads."

Rico had to interject "pardon the body Brotha!, but you've been locked up; you don't know what we've been doing. For the record, we have been putting in work, and if we don't get money, we can't buy guns and ammo."

Wayne retorted, "But ya'll playin' games wit' deys Ops out here. Niggas supposed to be feeling the wrath. We suppose to be the Almighty Rock Island, niggaz have died for this thang. Niggaz don' got soft."

Fed up with his remarks, a short-tempered Duke (Bo's little brother), snapped." What you say, nigga?" Duke said angrily as he stepped into the circle to confront Wayne, causing Rico and Black to hold him back. "Who soft, who soft?" Duke continued.

"Alot of ya'll niggas!" Wayne shot back." Ya'll lucky that it wasn't no 4's that got killed, because I'll show ya'll how Rock Island really get down."

"Fuck you!" Rico spat back, contemplating on baring arms against one of his Brothas for the first time.

"The 4's gon' do their own thang from now on," Wayne said, after ordering all the 4-Corner members to follow him out the playground.

"Man, I ain't on that!" Co-Co said sternly. "I'm on some Rock Island unity shit. We need to be together. We all Brothas ain't we?" Wayne retreated with his security and a handful of confused Cornerboys.

With a tirade like the one he had just unfolded, it would seem that Wayne would only want go-getters around him. Instead, most of the Brothas that did follow him, were questionable, to say at the least. Like Tony, a.k.a Swole, he wasn't known for being a gangsta. In fact, he was more known as being a buster, a serial flip-flop. He started off claiming to be a G-Boy, then turned EEl, then turned Con, and now 4-Cornerboy. As soon as he became disenchanted, with one mob, he'd pledge to another. It seemed like he wanted to be on whose ever team that was winning at the time. If he was a female, he'd be what Chicago gangs consider a *"nation hoe"*; a female that runs from hood to hood, usually chasing a guy. To further illustrate this point, Swole's mentors in chronological order were Lil Mikey, Fin, Max, and then K-Man. He was now Wayne's biggest fan. Tomato, another 4 Brotha that had a sleazy reputation wasn't exactly a trusted figure either. So it was extremely baffling why Wayne would choose to target the C's for his verbal warfare.

After the goal, Rico and Toby tried to calm the rest of the Brothas who obviously felt Wayne had just checked them. "On my momma, Joe!" Duke swore, "I'll change that nigga right now for that pussy ass shit he stipulated out his mouth. Who the fuck he think he is? What's his problem?"

"I don't know," responded Toby, "maybe he been around some foul Brothas in the County."

"We gon' have to deal with that nigga." Rico said calmly. "He got a lil' juice and now he feelin' himself. Don't nobody care about that shit." Some of the non defector 4's remained in the park and spoke about their feelings towards the situation. "Man Joe! On da' 4, that nigga crazy if he think we goin' against the grain for him." Co-Co said as he broke down a blunt.

"Hell yeah, that's why niggas be getting changed" Al responded... "Coming home thinking they tough and shit, trying to flex on niggas in da' hood. Why niggas be doing that shit?"

"I don't know," Antwoine said, "but niggas need to start finding something else to do wit' they time when they on lock down other than plot on some take over shit, cuz' I don't know bout' the next guy, but I got heat for muthafuckas like that."

None of the Brothas never fully figured out what Wayne was so disgruntled about, or what influenced his attitude. Despite the company he kept, Wayne was still a threat to anyone on the wrong side of his temperament. While out on bond Wayne continued to "put in work," and divide Rock Island. But fortunately for everybody, he was re-arrested for weapon charges and convicted on the murder, along with Cornerboy Nelson. They both received life sentences. The triplets and T.Y. all plead for lessor charges.

The incident with Wayne reminded Rico of his own standings within the Cons. He knew that the war he sanctioned on the D's was done so in direct defiance. And since he hadn't heard from any of the ranking Brothas in awhile, he figured he was in violation; but in a phase known as the "calm before the storm." (This is where the Brothas put a subject on no-talk, and cut off all interaction before they issue out their punishment. The calm usually allowed the subject to let his guard down. And when the storm came, the helpless victim usually didn't know what hit them.)

CHAPTER 22

Wood, was a high ranking Con, and a close friend to Rico. They met shortly after Rico was released from prison, and quickly realized they shared the same business savvy. After hearing about Rico's defiance, he managed to set up a meeting between Rico and the Old Man. Rico was little nervous being on the other side of the fence that not so long ago confined him. Wood accompanied him on the two hour drive. They obtained phony i.d.'s to enter the prison. (Ex-offenders are not allowed to visit prison inmates). Wood had been through process dozens of times. "Just act natural Brotha" Wood informed Rico as they sat in the waiting area waiting for their names to be called.

The visiting room was full, mostly with women and children. "How did he manage to get in a joint like this?" Rico Asked, referring to the plush minimum security facility, usually reserved for short time offenders.

"Gotta' have that juice card" Wood replied. "All the heavies up in here." Wood went on to point out all the leaders of various organizations. *"Wow!"* Rico thought to himself, *"all of Chicago's main heavy hitters are about to be in one room."* Rico went into a deeper awe, when the 5'10, dark skin, slightly bulky Brotha who they called "The Old Man" entered the visiting room. He expected him to appear menacing, with a mean-mug engraved on his face. But the jolly forty- something year old man was all smiles as he checked in with the guards.

Even more shocking to Rico was the way The Old Man greeted all of the other ranking gang leaders. "Hey Mack, Buddy" Big Larry, the Chief of the G-Boys said as The Old Man walked past his table.

"How's it going?" replied the Old Man. "How's the wife doing? Tell everybody I said hi."

Rico couldn't believe what he was seeing. The fact that the gangs were savagely out there on the streets killing one another in a feuding relationship laced with hatred, and the leaders of these same gangs were incarcerated together on a much friendlier level was baffling.

Rico and Wood stood as they greeted their Chief with a brief hug. Rico remained silent as the Old Man and Wood made small talk. But he took a deep breath when the attention turned to him. "So what's up with you young blood?" The Old Man asked, looking Rico directly in the eye. "You're not honoring what I lay down out there?"

Na'll, it's not like that Brotha," Rico replied. "I'm sure you're aware of the circumstances! Given what happened, I felt inclined to act in an unpopular fashion. In no way was I trying to undermine you or any of the ranking Brothas, I just couldn't allow those dudes to get away with murder. It would have affected the morale of all my guys."

The Old Man did not respond right away, instead he sat in his chair looking off in the distance, and rubbed his cleanly shaven bald head. Then finally, the eerie silence was broken. "So did you retaliate?"

Yeah!" Rico replied proudly.

"So what did you gain from retaliating?"

Rico knew this was a loaded question, and stalled for a couple of seconds before answering.

"Um, respect, I guess" Rico replied.

"So did they get back at ya'll?"

Rico shook his head up and down.

"And you think that's respect?" The Old Man shot back. "How many Brothas have been killed, injured, or imprisoned since then?"

"Quite a few sir" Rico said solemnly.

"That's all part of the game; nation business!?" The Old Man exclaimed; "You think all that reckless shit ya'll out there doing benefitting the Nation?" Readjusting himself, the Old Man moved closer to Rico, not taking his eyes off the young Con, lowering his voice to a whisper. "Give me one good reason why I should allow you to exist after today?"

Rico remained silent. He was tired of going in circles. He knew that no matter what he said, it probably wasn't going to change the outcome. He decided that he wasn't going to sit there in a prison, and beg for his life. In his eyes, that would constitute in him being a punk. Finally, he said. "I was raised by some real Brothas, they taught me how to carry myself in these streets, they taught me how to get money, shoot guns, and even how to get girls. They also taught me pride, and to believe in something bigger than myself. They taught me to love my brother, not to snitch-even on your enemy. They taught me to never waiver, even in threat of death; they taught me to be respectful and to raise my mind. They taught me a lot about this game, but the one thing they didn't have to teach me was loyalty, because I came into this game with that. You can't teach loyalty, it has to already be a part of who you are. I watched one of my Brothas die in my arms, and promised him that I'd avenge his death, not because that's a way of life where we come from, but because I'm a loyal nigga, and I'm proud to be a loyal nigga. I always heard, if you can't live for nothing, you might as well die for something. So if I gotta lose my life, *for my life*, so be it, I'm from Rock Island, I'll be buried a Martyr."

The Old Man sat with his arms folded listening to Rico, glancing up at Wood as if he was saying *"the nerve of this lil' nigga."* "Alright Brotha!" the Old Man said, without showing a hint of emotion in his face. "Let me holla at Wood for a minute, you could wait in the car."

Rico got up and exited the visiting room, realizing that he had possibly condemned himself. *"I hope he felt me,"* he said to himself as he waited in the car. He thought about the family of the D-Boy that killed Kenyatta. Maybe now his own family was in danger.

Wood walked slowly back to the car, noticing that Rico appeared to be extremely calm considering the circumstances. "Man, I didn't even want to know" Rico said as soon as Wood got into the car. "Just take me to the crib, Joe."

After a brief pause, Wood informed Rico that he couldn't do that. "I have orders Rico, the Old Man said for us to go straight to the Argyale Gardens (projects) to meet up with the Brothas on the committee. "Wood, don't do this, my nigga, fuck that shit." Rico pleaded.

"You already know what dem' niggas on Wood, they probably finna' kill me Joe. Just tell them that I got away or something."

"Rico, Rico, Rico, you just talked all that shit about loyalty to the Old Man, and how you'd die for it Now If we don't show up together, that's my ass." Rico knew that he was right, they'd probably do something really drastic to Wood if they didn't show up together. "Aight' dawg, let's go see what these niggas talking about, but first let me grab a burner, just in case, cuz I ain't going out like that."

Armed with a 9MM berretta, Rico prepared to face the music for his actions.

The Argyale Gardens were located on the far south side in the 100's, and the two-story low-income apartments housed all of Chicago's major black gangs. The Cons, occupied blocks one through five, and served as headquarters for the south side. As soon as they entered block one, they were approached by two teenage boys, their guns were visibly present on their waist. Rico and Wood immediately formed a large C with their right hands to put the young thugs on notice. Project security is tighter than the Pentagon. Instinctively, one boy approached the car, while the other stood a few yards away with his hands firmly gripped on his weapon. "Ya'll Cons?" One boy, asked looking into the car with a natural skepticism. "Yeah Brotha, let these Brothas know that Rico from Rock Island and Wood is on location" Wood said.

"Ya'll park over there." the other boy ordered, pointing to a parking space near one of the condemned buildings. After a brief wait, the two boys led them to another building with two older Brothas on security. "What took ya'll so long?" One of the older security detail Brothas asked Wood. "They been waiting on ya'll."
Inside one of the apartments were all of the Brothas with status. *"This was it"* Rico thought, *"as soon as I see one of these niggas flinch, I'ma lace his ass."* The apartment didn't have much furniture, which made it all the more evident that it's intended purpose wasn't for providing shelter. Rico was distrustful of everyone in the apartment, as he greeted the multitude with faux-expressions-of-admiration. He kept an eye on the large handgun sitting on the cocktail table as the Brothas parlayed around the small apartment.

The sound of C Man's phone silenced the chitter chatter of the rambunctious group. All eyes were on C Man as he spoke into the receiver. "Okay, Chief, Mm hm! Yes, sir! Everybody is here." Rico could feel the tension in his chest growing as C Man shot quick glances towards his direction while speaking on the phone. "I'ma put you on speaker phone."
"Greetings, my Brothas" the recognizable voice of the Old Man said. "I gathered you all here today to demonstrate with ya'll about some important issues, one of them being the Brotha Rico. We are all aware of what's supposed to take place right now concerning that Brotha. So what I want to know is if any of you Brothas have any objections to my decision." As the Old Man spoke Rico's anger grew more intense by the moment. *"Pussy mutha fucka!"* he thought to himself as he stared at Wood who was supposed to be his friend. *"Ain't this a bitch?" He won't even speak up for a nigga, that's okay, cuz that nigga can get it too."* Rico could not believe what was happening. No Brothas had any objections. Rico felt the berretta in his jacket pocket. He knew that they'd wait until at least the Old Man discontinued his conversation before they tried anything. But he couldn't be sure. "So it's like that hunh?" Rico said nervously towards the phone. "Yeah, Rico! After what I've been hearing about you and after the conversation that we had earlier, you deserve this. I think a great lesson can be learned today." Rico grabbed the berretta, and was in the process of pulling it out of his jacket, when Wood put his arms around his shoulders and yelled Congratulations Brotha!"
"Congratulations?" Rico said with a puzzled expression.
"You've been promoted, and you're on the committee now" C-Man said, as Rico attempted to make sense of everything.

"We need more Brothas like you," the Old Man said over C Man's speaker phone. Rico was in shock, he bit down on his bottom lip as he usually does when he's anxious, or has a momentary loss of words.

The Old Man changed the entire structure of the south-side committee. No one individual would call all the shots for the south side. Instead, all important decisions will be made as a group. An executive board that'll govern all the sets on the entire south side and south suburbs. The Old Man wanted fresh ideas and faces on the board. So the elder Brothas were reassigned to out-of-town or out of state posts. A lot of the older Brothas didn't mind going out of town, because of their status, they could be the Chief of an entire small City or town, only answering to the Old Man. C-Man was ordered to take over Rockford Illinois, the second largest City in the state. Wood was promoted to a spot that gave him control over all of Central Illinois.

The Old Man was proud of his south side protégés, but he knew that all of their personalities would not mix for long. Everybody wanted to be "the man" and he feared the possibility of "too much power" would corrode the unity of the south-side, much like most of the west-side Brothahood. Considering what he was prepared for, Rico was relieved at what had just happened.

"Man, why the hell you had me thinking I was about to get it my nigga?" Rico asked Wood, as they made their way out of the projects. "Got yo' ass good, didn't I?" Yeah you got me, but you could've got some muthafuckas killed today too.

****

Later that evening the Cons threw a private-party; complete with strippers and a DJ. Rico was allowed to bring a total of 3 guests to the small event. Head, Shorty C, and T.P. came to support Rico's promotion. Brothas with status showed up from all parts of the City, even Big Saw made an appearance. This was a big moment in the lives of a lot of Brothas. Some of them had never been out of Chicago, and now in less than a week they were going to relocate and take over small towns. It was almost certain that those Brothas would gain tremendously in their new positions. Wood never considered going out of town before that day, but he was extremely optimistic. "I'm telling you Rico it's a lot of money in them little towns," he said as they mingled with the crowd. "You should come out there wit' me and help a Brotha out. That's a lot of land to cover. I'll holla at the Old Man for you, it'll be cool we wont have to answer to nobody."

Rico continued to bob his head to the loud music, and had to speak over the blaring bass. "I can't leave right now Joe. R.I. needs me, but you know we're partners so if I can assist you in anyway, I got you Bro but my obligation is to the hood right now."

Wood was disappointed, but he understood nevertheless. "Where the hell the strippers at," Rico said tryin' to change the subject as fast as he could.

"They just came in a few minutes ago" one Con said. "Dem' bitches thicker than some king size snickers Joe!"

"Oh yeah!" Rico said as he ventured in search of the entertainment, that was still in the hallway being screened by security. The ladies attracted a lot of attention from the thirsty ballers waiting for their entrance to the main dance floor. Rico noticed something familiar about one of the ladies, and approached her to get a better view in the dimly lit hallway in the lodge. Standing 5'6, her thick, double jointed, toned legs and shapely round back side covered in a short Coogi dress made her one of the baddest chicks in the building. Her blond wig was not doing a good job concealing her identity. "What the fuck you doing here?" Rico asked with a surprised tone looking her up and down as if he was inspecting her.

An equally surprised Lavada smiled at the sight of her R.I. Brotha. "Man Rico, I'm glad to see you" she confided. "I just started doing this shit wit' my sister, cuz me and the drug game don't mix. I'm still new to this, so don't trip on me out there ok?"

"I got cha' shorty. Does ya' man know about what you doing out here?" "Hell naw' and ya'll can't tell him either. I wanna tell him on my own terms. You know that nigga crazy."

"Aight' ya" secret safe wit me" Rico responded with a sly look on his face...if I can get the first lap dance.

"Boy you crazy", she said laughingly.

"What if I got something better for you?"

By now they were both looking into the crowd that was being entertained by 2 dancers on the main dance floor, and a plethora of lovely females that worked the crowd.

"What you talking bout?" he asked. "I'ma introduce you to my cousin La-La, She's the red bone over there with the black thong on."

The young thick tender-roni could pass as a lighter version of Lavada. "She decent, what she on?"

"She ain't on shit, but when I put her in tune wit' who you are, she'll bust down."

"So you just gone put yo' cousin out there like that huh?"

"Rico she my cousin but I call a spade a spade, and La-La is a bust down" She like niggas that got juice, so if you take her somewhere in one of these rooms, you'll probably git' more than a lap dance."

        30 minutes later: Lavada's predictions came true, much to Rico's delight, as La-La's large round shapely ass bounced up and down on his condom covered man-hood, riding reverse on a small fold chair. The music drowned out the loud moans of the young stripper. The large butterfly tattooed on her ass seemed to flutter as their bodies came together making a clapping noise, Rico briefly wondered how a teenage girl could get to the point in her life where she would be having sex with a stranger in a utility closet.

"I'm leaving with you tonight alright Daddy," she said, breaking his train of thought, as they gathered themselves to go back out to the party. "I wanna show you what else I can do."

"Aight' lil' mama, we'll see, Rico responded as he walked out of the side room, where he immediately seen his R.I Comrades. "Where you been dog?" Head asked as Rico approached them. "You missin' the show, these bitches wildin' out in here."

The small dance floor was surrounded by Brothas as they watched 2 girls tease each other, and do their tricks. The seasoned strippers wooed the crowd by exhibiting their dexterity and ability to make their butt cheeks clap. One girl could shoot ping-pong balls from her body clear across the room. Lavada looked like she had been dancing for years, as she slowly and sensually maneuvered her way around the dance floor, prompting the on lookers to throw balled up bills at the temptress.

"Ya'll better not say nothin," Rico said to his R.I. cohorts as Lavada danced naked in front of them.

"My lips are sealed," responded T.P., who was relishing the moment.

"I ain't go say shit "Shorty C" added. Lavada noticed her Brothas eye ballin' her, and it made her comfortable. She trusted them. B-MAC, the Chief of the Chicago Avenue Out Law Cons, noticed the eye contact between the group and the pretty stripper.

"Ya'll know shawty or something?" B-MAC asked.

"Yeah she from tha' land." Rico said proudly. That's how we getting down out South!"

"Dam, lil' mama is decent" B-MAC admitted, as he tipped her another $20 dollar bill. "I'ma start fuckin' wit' ya'll niggas out here" he said laughingly.

"Yeah my nigga, do that" Rico said.

"You a real nigga and I respect what you doing on the Ave. "The Outlaws always got my support."

B-MAC and Rico had a lot in common, and their meeting would solidify a long standing relationship.

It had been a long day for Rico, so after taking La-La to a motel for a couple of hours to see *what else she could do*, he decided to call it a night and retire at one of his suburban hide-outs.

****

Back in the Island, Al toured the hood looking for his girl as usual. "Ay wacky," he yelled from his raggedy Oldsmobile. Wacky was pulling another all nighter on May, and knew what Al was about to ask. "Na'll man I haven't seen her" he replied sarcastically. "She probably wit' Keisha and nem' at a party or something." Al had already checked wit' Keisha and Lavada was M.I.A. *"Where the fuck dis' bitch at?"* he thought to him self. It was 2 a.m. and she hadn't called or nothing. *"All this shit bout to end, she finna' start staying in the crib and taking care of these shorties."*

CHAPTER 23

Whenever certain Brothas returned home from doing time, it was always a big deal. Ever since the demise of Ed and Max, a lot of Brothas became used to looking forward to R.I.'s next Savior. With Brothas like K-MAN and Wayne coming home with dictatorship mentalities, the buzz surrounding the eventual releases of influential members was great. You could often hear R.I. members speaking about their soon to be released Brothas as if it was dire. "You know dude bout to come home" one would say. "I hope he don't be on no bullshit."
Con Bo-Bo received mixed reviews upon his release from prison. Bo-Bo was a second generation Brotha from R.I. who was arrested just before the fall of Ed and Max.

Some guys welcomed the fact that another older Brotha was going to be back in the fold to assist Rico,Toby,T.P. and other ranking members in bringing back the old glory days. Bo-Bo in his prime was bright, intelligent, and charismatic. His ability to be a thinker and a gangsta exemplified the fact that he was the last of a dying breed. Conversely, others alleged that right before his incarceration, Bo-Bo had been indulging in the taboo affairs that doomed most of his generation. They felt that because of his history, no chances should be taken on him right away. Some Brothas wanted to observe his behavior for awhile, but Rico and Toby gave their friend the benefit of the doubt, placing him in a high position immediately after his release. Although this was a sensitive subject for Rico, he reasoned that even if Bo-Bo was indulging before, the 3 1/2 years he spent in prison was long enough for anybody to get their mind right. He figured the risk was worth the reward. Bo-Bo's leadership skills were surely needed amongst the R.I. elite, especially now that Rico's would be split due to his duties on the south-side committee.

The Hull Brothers and T.Y's release wasn't as controversial as Bo-Bo's, but that didn't stop it from having their own post incarceration agenda. T.Y immediately set back up on May Street, the same block that Wacky dedicated himself to even in its darkest days. Wacky nursed the block back to life after Max and Ed left. Unfortunately Rock Island was free enterprise for all members so the 2 committed Brothas had to coincide. But Wacky didn't seem to mind, he was confident his bigger bags and loyal customers would give him the advantage he needed, no matter how many Brothas flooded the block. T.Y. remained low key, avoiding a lot of Rock Island activities. However the Hull brothers were a bit of a mystery. One could not tell exactly what their agenda was. "We just came from up under some drama" T-fly, the oldest brother said. "And we ain't trying to go back." They seemed a little arrogant at first. Their *"we don't need R.I., they need us"* attitude was starting to get underneath the skin of some members. They weren't overly antagonistic like their rappy Wayne, but they were not exactly saviors of the hood either. They spent a lot of their time chasing women and partying. When Travis came home from the juvenile joint, after doing 3 years for the accidental death of his friend Eric, The Hull Brothas were the first to gravitate to him. For a while it seemed that Travis shared the same attitude as the brothers. He also seemed hesitant on going back to his gang-banging ways. But no matter how hard you try to separate your agenda and do the so called right thing, the inevitability of trouble is ever present, and as Rico and the other Brothas would soon find out doing the right thing and being apart of the street's were an antinomy.

"They shootin'!" They shootin'!" exclaimed Paulette-the skinny Sista who hung with most of the 3rd generation Brothas.
The group of Brothas sitting on Anthony's stoop on 75th and Carpenter had to calm her down. "Who shootin'?" asked Lawrence aka Lil Law. Paulette, was out of breath, but she managed to get her message out. "Them D's on Throop Street just shot at T-Fly and nem'!"
Like a 5 alarm fire warning the Brothas sprang to life, ready to go aid and assist their guys. "You got dat' heat Brotha?" Black asked Lil Law. "Hell yeah, let's go!"
They ran as fast as they could toward Racine, where they met T-Fly and his brothers, who almost drove right past them. "Dem' bitch ass niggas just shot my brother car up Joe," T-Fly yelled out the driver's side window of his van.
The shooting was a big deal because the D- boys on 77th and Throop Street were mostly former Brothas from Rock island, and for years poised no significant threat. Some Brothas even considered them to be cool and spared them during the war. Lil law and Black got in the van and just like that The Hull brothers were back in the mix.

"I told ya'll we should've been took dem' vics off da' map" Rico shouted into his cell phone, after hearing what happen. "Yeah, Yeah, make it rain on dem' niggas, tell Anthony to give ya'll the chopper and go handle that!"
Roz sat in the passenger seat and listened to her man handle his *"nation business"* on the phone as they drove down Western Avenue en route back to the hood. Her large.38 sat on her lap per Ricos instruction as they bought the large shipment of Heroine back from the West side.

She was all in now, assisting him with transporting, manufacturing, and distributing. She even allowed him to use one of her apartments as a night spot. *"Look at my man,"* she thought to herself, glancing at him out the corner of her eye. *"We like Bonnie and Clyde. I don't care what Carmen say, I aint giving my position as his Queen up."*
She was well aware how useful she was to the young hustlers operation and prided herself in providing confidential police information and tactics to Rico. She didn't know how things got to this point. She didn't need Rico, she didn't have to do the things she was doing, but yet he somehow possessed the ability to bring out the best or worst in people, depending on which ever one benefited him the most. He made Roz feel like she was part of something much bigger than herself. In her eyes she was just as important to Rock Island as Rico was. She never felt more alive in her life. Her distorted sense of purpose allowed her to take risk that could cost her, her job, her kids, and her life.

****

As one couple was solidifying their bond, another was on the verge of a tragic end. Lavada and Al stood in the middle of the apartment toe to toe, arguing. "You can't tell me what to do!" Lavada screamed, in response to Al's decision to keep her from stripping.
"You gon' stay in the house and take care of these kids and stop being a hoe in dem' streets."
"I ain't doin' shit, as a matter of fact it's over, I'll just take my kids and move back with my Grandmother."
Her words enraged Al; the thought of Lavada leaving him was too much to bear. "Bitch! You ain't goin' no where" he said as Lavada jetted in the bedroom to begin packing. She had planned on leaving Al anyway, but she was trying to save enough money to get a nice house for her and her kids. "I hate you Al, you stupid mutha'fucka, you can't control a bitch like me. I was taking care of yo' ass. Niggas have offered me tons of money just to eat my pussy. I could have any nigga I want, you ain't on shit."
Her rant continued until Al slapped her with an open hand. Lavada fought back fearlessly giving Al a run for his money. In the end she was no match, he over powered her and slammed her on the bed holding her hands down. "You hate me huh?" He said angrily. "You ain't goin' no where. You think you just gone leave me and run off with some nigga?" "I'm gon' have the Brothas fuck yo' ass up for this shit Al!" she cried. "Get off me!"
Al finally freed Lavada and allowed her to gather her things and take them to the car. He sat on the bed crying, as Lavada dressed the kids in preparation to leave. Lavada didn't notice the 9MM in his hand as she

entered the bedroom to grab the last of her belongings. By the time she did it was too late. The thunderous shots startled the kids in the next room. Lavada's daughter opened the door to find her Mother with 4 bullet wounds in her chest, and her Father with one self inflicted wound to the head. Lavada was 20 and Al was 24.

Rico was in bed when he received the news of Rock Island's first murder-suicide. He sat silently on the side of Roselyn's bed still holding the phone in his hand long after La-La called and informed him of what happened. He was tired of going to Funerals, which seemed to be prerequisite for him and his peers. Silently he cursed Al for taking one of his Sistas. *"How could he do that?"* he thought to himself. *"Yeah maybe it's best that you killed yourself my nigga' cuz if I would've got a hold to you...."*

Like Rico, many of the Brothas didn't attend Al's funeral held at the South side's premiere funeral home, Gatling's Chapel on 101st and Halsted. Casper, Al's younger brother offered several of the guys a ride. While some of Al's close associates paid their last respects, others protested. Al was a Brotha that never denied one of his guys anything and he put in his fair share of work in the hood, but now his legacy was forever marred. Although he demonstrated the capacity to commit murder, the suicide pondered many of those who were close to him. Leaving many questions to be answered. *Can love drive a seemingly normal man to murder, then suicide? Can a woman's prowess alter the psychodynamic and cognitive behavior of a man?*

Lavada's homecoming was exceptionally different from that of Al's. Her funeral was held at a family owned funeral home located on 79th Street between Carpenter and Morgan, walking distance from her house and most members. However, 79th and Carpenter was headquarters to the once dormant and now notoriously violent D-boy's, R.I's new arch rivals. So a lot of pressure was on the Chief of Security for both mobs, as every member of the Cons and 4 Corners made their way to the funeral home. A lot of guys simply walked boldly down 79th, ignoring the possible threat of their enemies. For Rico, more precautions had to be administered. He couldn't take any chances. "Be careful bay" Roz said as he strapped on his bullet proof vest. "You can over heat in these things." She armed herself with a 13 shot semi-automatic hand gun. She checked Rico's weapon of the day, a lemon squeeze hair trigger .45 automatic. "And this thing don't have a safety bay, so be careful on that too."

Even with Roz's house only 2 blocks away, for security purposes Rico was driven and escorted to the funeral home. Just as expected the D's were on point across the street from the funeral home, apparently guarding the front entrance of their block.

    Only a busy 2 lane street separated R.I.'s security detail and the D-boy's. Lil Law leaned on a mailbox facing his enemies, sporting a specially made jacket that concealed several weapons. Shorty "C" finally got his hands on one of the 50 shot M.P.5 automatics that he'd been anxious to shoot. New Brothas Justin, Wild "C" and Willie (from the complex) stood flanked along the inside doors of the funeral home. Swole arrived with the Hull brothers by car. The D'boy's security seemed a little anxious as Rico got out his car to enter the small funeral home. Cold stares were exchanged. "Wet dem' niggas up if they even act like they wanna do something crazy" Rico said to Lil Law and Shorty "C" loud enough for all to hear.

    Lavada's funeral was packed way beyond the building's capacity limit. There were more standing than there was sitting in the seats. Her family seemed to be in awe, as the crowd of young people poured in to get one last look at the pretty face they grew to love. Kesha had to be carried out twice as she broke down at the sight of her Con Sista and best friend. Sporadic outburst of friends and family echoed the room as one of her cousins sang *'it's so hard to say goodbye.'* One of R.I.'s more emotional Brotha Milton paced back and forth with tears in his eyes. Seeing that he was about to go into one of his emotional prances, several Brothas escorted him outside to vent, where the growing crowd on both sides of the street lingered. "What da' fuck ya'll niggas lookin' at!?" Milton angrily yelled in the direction of the group of D' boys on security detail.

"Come on man, respect the dead Brotha," Jo-Jo said tryin' to calm his temperamental friend down.

"Na'll man, I'm cool, but I'm just sayin', we up here trying to show our respects to one of the Sistas and these bitch ass niggas mean-mugging over here like they wanna kick it off, or something."

"Just be cool Brotha, we on they set, they suppose to act like that, it's a lot of innocent people out here and they're respecting us just by not shootin' this place up."

Despite all of the ill feelings and hardware, Lavada's funeral ended peacefully. Al's brother Casper was offended by the lack of love and commitment the Brothas showed his brother, renounced his allegiance to R.I, and flipped to a D'boy shortly after.

Rock Island: A Gangstaz Graveyard   N.U.T.T.Y. "C"

CHAPTER 24

The D-boy's seemed to adopt an open door policy, excepting any and everybody, even former enemies. In addition to that they recruited heavily, targeting mostly young males. However there were some well known street vets approached by the D's and offered large sums of money or drugs to flip. They seemed determined to build an army and takeover by any means necessary. They completely lost their *"less is better"* attitude. Taking a clue from the D's Rico decided that R.I. needed to go on a recruiting spree of its own. The block of 78th and Sangamon was full of young impressionable boys that could potentially become future Brothas. "Ay Yo!" Rico yelled out the driver's side window to the crowd of kids playing nerf football in the streets. "What ya'll lil' niggas out here doin'?"

The crowd looked dumb founded, as Rico got out of his car. "Ya'll niggas can't be out here like this. This is Rock Island if you ain't no Brotha, it ain't no hanging out on this block."

The group of teens knew not to oppose, and by the time Rico worked his mojo, the young block dwellers were convinced that Rock Island was their home. "You see, you might as well be Brothas cuz if some ops come over here on some bullshit they gon' shoot you to.

Kenny, Tim, and Drew all became Brothas in the following weeks. Not all Brothas were forced into the gang, some actively sought out the Brothas, as is in the case with Swan and his crew from the other side of the tracks-on 74th Street, home to the defunct 7-4 boys. Swan was recommended by Anthony who went to school with the Con hopeful. "Why you wanna be a Brotha?" Rico asked Swan, as if he was doing a job interview. "Man, I remember when I was a shorty; you use to have dem' guys on my block spooked."

Rico pressed on. "Yeah, but what that gotta do wit' what's happnin' right now?"

Swan's right hand man Buster spoke up. "Man we could be anything else but we wanna be different, and da' Brothas is different."

Rico looked at the group trying to spot potential weaknesses. "So all dem' niggas want to be Brothas to huh?" Rico asked.

"Yep!" replied Swan.

Rico looked at Anthony with concern. "You know dem' niggas too?"

"Um na'll, not really" Anthony replied.

"Man they down!" Swan interjected. "And we ready for war, we got our own guns over there." That statement caught Rico's attention. "Your own guns huh? What kinda heat you got over there?"

155

"All types of shit" Swan boasted. Rico then sent Lil Law and Jo-Jo with Buster to verify their claim. 30 mins later, Rico got a call. "C," *these niggas is holdin' heat,"* Jo-Jo said into his cell phone. "They got AK's, Macs, Shot guns it's like a candy store over here."

It was a highlight that Rico would cherish for quit awhile. He got lucky, not only was he able to acquire one of his well known foes territory, but the new Brothas came bearing gifts.

Swan and his crew were blessed after they went on a couple of missions. 74th and Racine was now Brotha territory, and Rico felt good about the fact that none of the high powered weapons would be used on his guy's. Furthermore Rico also did something that he'd never done before; he delegated Swan to an acting Chief, giving him authority over his crew and block. He could recruit and bless Brothas on his own. Only a few select Brothas knew of this development. Rico was becoming distrustful of his entire circle. In light of the string of arrest around the hood, he developed an uncanny feeling that the code of silence was being compromised within the ranks. *"The police can't be getting that lucky"* he reasoned. His decision to make Swan's 74th Street crew of Cons a separate entity was one out of precaution. He wanted to protect the young Cons, at least until he could clean up his own back yard.

Rock Island seemed to be blossoming with new Brothas everywhere. Dank was the "auto boy" of the hood. The hazel eyed young criminal had a reputation for acquiring any auto body part you needed within 48 hours. Rico blessed him, in hopes that his hustling ways could be converted into running 75th and Carpenter. Anthony, Lamelle, T.P, Dank and Milton kept the money flowing on 75th while the new Brothas on 78th and Sangamon prepared for war.

With membership at an all time high, Rico knew it was going to be hard to please everyone. He was aware that a lot of the Brothas were starting to become jealous of the new up and comings like Dank. "The haters" Rico called them, "will always exist, that's their job. You just gotta be aware of them and do yours."

"Straight up!" Shorty C" said with a blunt in his mouth. "Niggas don't got nothing better to do." Shorty "C" could've have been arguably the most hated on young Brotha in the hood. The 15 year old self proclaimed "pretty boy" , who just months prior was a reckless, trigger happy, loner, was now deemed as Rico's pet who could do no wrong in the eyes' of his mentor. Shorty "C"'s ability to attract some of the finest women also kept the haters on their job. They'd often travel to the hood looking for him.

"Ya'll seen Chad?" one of the Ladies shouted out the Lexus S.U.V, to a small group of Brothas standing on the corner.
"Na'll we ain't seen that nigga," one of the Brothas that was doing his job said in response,"
"What ya'll grown ass want with that lil' boy anyway? Ya'll need to fuck wit' some grown dick."
The ladies in truck all looked at each other and burst into laughter.
"Fuck you nigga, wit' yo' dusty ass, you need to get a real job, cuz this hustlin' shit don't look like it's working out for you!"

The ladies weren't the only thing Shorty "C" was being hated on for. At 15, and no rank, he was making more money than a lot of the older Brothas with status. Dank seemed to have this same problem, but the difference between the 2 young hustlers was Dank was much more reserved and Shorty "C" seemed to relish in the fact that he was envied by his peers. He was starting to take advantage of his relationship with Rico. It wasn't a well kept secret that Rico showed favoritism to Shorty "C" most Brothas were just afraid to say it, everyone that is except Dollar Bill (a Bo Oley protégé) who always had an input on the various happenings in the hood. "You need to holla at cha boy Rico, the streets is talking and niggas is tired of playin' games with shawty. We told that Brotha to stop comin' to goals off his square (drunk or high), but he think he above the law, ya' fell me?"

Rico knew Dollar Bill was right, it was forbidden to come to any of the meetings drunk or high, and Shorty "C" could often be seen smoking blunts before the goals. If it were any one else they would've been violated or fined. "I'ma holla' at him Dollar," Rico assured. "Nobody's above the law. I know the Brothas have warned him, so I'ma holla at him"

"Man fuck dem' niggas!" Shorty "C" said, in his bravado voice while blowin' a thick could of smoke in the air. "Dem' niggas just jealous cuz a nigga shinin' harder than nem! On my momma these niggas startin' to act like some hoez. You need to do something about that shit!"
Rico was hoping that Shorty "C" wouldn't respond in a fashion that would force his hand. He had grown fond of Shorty "C", but he sensed that he needed to be firmer. "What da' fuck you mean, I need to do something....?" He shot back in a serious tone. "You need to follow the fuckin' rules. I'm tired of saving yo' ass. The law is the law, you can't keep frontin' me off like that. You see dem' niggas out to get you, why give them a reason? You keep playin' games and watch what happen, they gon' fuck yo' ass up!!" Despite the serious tone in his voice,

Shorty "C" seemed to find Rico's words amusing. "I wish one of dem' niggas would try to put their hands on me......."
Rico just remained silent as Shorty "C" went on talking like a gangsta. "I know you ain't gon' let that happen anyway."
Rico just hoped his favorite shorty didn't have to find out the hard way.

CHAPTER 25

Gang wars are often started over money, turf, and pride. Many wars are started over females. Many gang members have lost their lives over females. As a precaution some sets prohibit female membership. But not Rock Island and most EEl sets in close proximity. Brothaville, Nation, Foster Park, 8-tray, and Duck Town all have Sistas. Ironically, despite an occasional feud between male members of these sets, quite a few R.I. Brothas had girlfriends that were EEL Sistas. On the contrary R.I. Sistas seemed to favor EEl Brothas. However the female members themselves never really got along with one another. The Sistas constantly feuded over what most Brothas called trivial bullshit. "We gon' have to fuck dem' bitches up!" Java said to a group of Brothas. "They (the EEl Sistas) jumped on one of the Sistas for no reason." But the guys knew better than that, they knew that more than likely the altercation arrived from one of the R.I Sista's involvement with one of the Black EEls. "And dem' EEl dudes acted like they wanted to jump too," Gina, another Sista said disingenuously, trying to put cables on their male counterparts.

"Man, this is why I don't like having Sistas. Theses bitches will send a nigga off," Waverly said in response to the news.

"Hold fast Brotha" Rico responded. "Don't call dem' Sistas bitches: You know how these hoes get down," he said laughingly.

But all jokes aside, Rico wasn't interested in a beef with the Black EEl's. He had long standings with a lot off the Black EEL Generals, and decided to take a diplomatic approach. He decided to arrange a Sista fight between the 2 gangs.

"That's a good idea," Toby said in response. "It'll be better than a Tyson fight."

"I might be able to get some money off this mutha' fucka," said Dollar Bill. So it was agreed, the Sistas from Rock Island would go at it with the Sistas from Nation and 8-tray.

"It ain't no sense in fighting over no pussy, "said Ceno the Black EEl General from Nation, who Rico had known for 15 years.

"Yeah, I'ma bring popcorn" Rico replied. "My Chief of Security will rotate with yours and work out the details, but for the record, Your guys know that we're not getting in it no matter the out come right?"

"Yeah the EEl's know what's happening. " The news of the brawl was on the tongues of everyone in the Island in the preceding days leading up to fight day. Cynthia (Bo Oley's Sista) seemed the most animated as she pep talked all the Sistas. "Anything goes, ya'll can stomp dem' bitches heads to the ground if ya'll want. Ya'll better not run or else ya'll gon' get dealt with when we get back."

Erika a skinny Con, Sista who probably had the most experience out of the vogue Sistas looked as if she was going to a break dancing contest rather than a bloody fight, adorned in blue jeans with patches and bandanas. Every Sista that ever claimed R.I showed up for the fight even the one's who hadn't been around in months, including Boonie, "I wasn't about to miss this for the world," she told Rico as he began a head count of the Sistas. Mary Ann, Ruthie, Java, Vicka, and Paulette all arrived together, looking their worst, obviously dressed in expendable clothing. The Oley building on 79th and Green was the meet up for everyone just before the fight. A large jar of Vaseline was passed around to the Sistas, all jewelry, or head garments that could distract or get in the way were removed. "Everybody meet back up here when it's over," Duke yelled to the 42 Sistas as they marched out the door. The fight itself would be held on EEl territory just 2 blocks east on 79th and Emerald St, in a large vacant lot behind the bus barn. Rico, for obvious reasons didn't disclose the location of the fight until the last moment.

"Alright, everybody remember what we talked about," Rico said to the Brothas that remained in the apartment." "Everybody just be cool, we ain't on nothing, let's go see some weave and titties fly".

By the time Rico arrived on Emerald at least 150 people were on location. The Sistas waited patiently as EEls and R.I members made small talk w/one another. Rico approached the General who had planned the event. "Where yo' Sistas at"? Rico asked with a grin painted on his face. The General looked down the street squinting his eyes, noticing the second large crowd; "here they come now." As the Con Sistas turned the corner, several car loads of EELs from other locations such as Rack City, The Terrace, Duck town, and others pulled up to witness.

Then Rico noticed that a lot of the EEl Sistas were carrying bats, golf clubs, and small sticks w/nails in them. "Ay Brotha,, you said no weapons," Rico informed the General.

"Oh yeah, I was talking about the Brothas not the Sistas", the General replied sarcastically. "

"Hell naw', we ain't going like that, tell them bitches to put those weapons down and knuckle up like we agreed" Rico said sternly.

"Ay Homie" another EEl Brotha interjected looking at Rico, "look where the fuck you at, this Black EEl hood, we make the rules over here, and dem' Sistas bout to handle they business. And if anybody jump in it, then we ALL gon' be fighting!"

Rock Island: A Gangstaz Graveyard

Rico looked around, he knew that he and his guys were out numbered at least 5 to 1, and he wouldn't stand a chance in a brawl, but with the EEl Sistas armed with weapons, R.I Sistas was just as dire. Four Brothas came to Rico's side to secure him more tightly, as Rico bit down on his bottom lip looking side to side. "So it's like that?" Rico asked his soon to be former friend.

"I guess so my nigga, I'm riding with mine all day."

"Aight then," Rico said shaking his head as if he was agreeing with the EEl Brotha, taking small steps backward.

He felt like he had no choice, he was glad he was prepared. He looked towards the corner and nodded his head toward Lil Law who was calmly leaning on the mail box as if he didn't have a worry in the world. Shorty C, directly across the street from law sat inconspicuously. "**ROCK ISLAND**"! Rico shouted to his crew. **"Put this bitch under arrest!" "Up dem' thangz!"** Instantly Law opened his jacket as Shorty C ran over to him to grab one of the 50 shot MP.5's, and a 9MM to hand to Jo-Jo. Law walked towards his mentor with 2 nickel plated .38's in each hand, a Brotha who stood away from the action on the other end of the block quickly dialed the number to the Oley building where Duke and 5 more Brothas sat and waited with 2 Mac11's, a tech 9MM, and 2 AK'S. Law handed his Chief one of the 38's and Milton the other, keeping the other MP5 pointed at the crowd of EELs. "Act like you wanna flinch nigga," Shorty C yelled at one of the EEl's, pointing the MP5 at his car. 30 seconds later, the van with duke and the other Brothas pulled up on the curb next to the stunned EEl's, "I just seen a couple of dem niggas running down the alley Joe, probably going to get some heat," Duke said, as he exited the van with one of the Mac's in hand. "So unless you wanna make this a massacre "C," I suggest we git' the fuck outta here." Rico tucked his weapon in his waistband and approached the slick talking EEl Brotha from moments earlier, and administered a vicious open-hand slap across his face. Head was on point with his .38 as Rico vented. "The next time you fix yo' mutha' fuckin mouth to say some bogus ass shit, you better know who the fuck you talking to nigga, I'm Rico mutha' fuckin' C, from Rock Island and we don't follow nobody's rules; bitch ass nigga!" By now the only Brothas that remained were the ones with weapons, which were approximately 20 in total. "Let's get the fuck outta here', Rico said to Head as the crowd started dispersing. But reinforcement had arrived for the EEls. **Tat, tat, tat, tat!** The crowd of Brothas and EEls scattered as they exchanged gun fire. "**Plow, Plow, Plow!**"

"**Tat, tat, tat, tat, tat,**"

"**Plow, plow, plow, plow**...."

"This is what I'm talking bout' right here!" Duke said as he, Rico, and a Brotha called 2pac ran further into the hood chasing and shooting at the EEls. They could hear the sound of the AK's rapid gun fire on the next block. Lil Law shot up all the cars of the visiting EEl's to obstruct escape.

"Where the fuck these niggas run to?' Duke said excitedly, as they walked up Union Street, the block of Rico's girl (Quetta). Rico had already told Quetta to go out of town day's before the fight, and she reluctantly obliged.

"There go some of them niggas right there on the porch," Rico said as he put more shells in his gun, with a quick loader, noticing a large crowd trying to run for the safety in the hallway of the 2 story brick home. The Brothas opened fire on them, **"tat, tat, tat, tat, Boom, Boom, Boom, Boom, Plow, Plow, Plow, Plow!"** The Brothas split into groups of 4 or 5 and flooded the few blocks of the EEl's, leaving bullet holes in several cars, houses and bodies of their former allies and new adversary.

CHAPTER 26

Every neighborhood has one nosey neighbor or resident that knows everybody's business. Rock Island was no different. Her name was Nikki AKA "Da Mouth of the South'. Nikki lived on Morgan Street and went to C.V.S with T.P, Milton, and Head. The chocolate brown skin, pleasantly plump teen was R.I.'s super information highway. If it happened on the south-side, she could find out about it, no matter who or what it was Nikki was always on point. She knew who got pregnant and when, who was copping keys versus who was getting ozs. Nikki who no one ever seen or heard about having a man, hung wit some of the finest and most sought after females out South, which made her even more popular. Although she was never affiliated with any organizations, she grew up w/ the members of R.I. and most of them considered her a play sister. She often played the role of match maker to a lot of the Brothas and her friends. The Brothas loved Nikki for a variety of reasons. Her mother's house was always open to the Brothas. Nikki's sister Tameka and her friend Da-Da were two wanna be G-girls who the Brothas considered harmless, often pranced around tryin' to act grown when the R.I. heavy hitters came thru.

"Ya'll niggas is crazy as hell!" Nikki yelled from her porch as she seen the two car loads of Brothas pull up in front of her house about to park. Rico, T P, Shorty C, and Head all exited their vessel, and could hear Nikki's big mouth yappin' away on her cordless phone, holding up her index finger indicating for the Brothas to wait. "Straight up girl?" she yakked into the phone. "Ok, mm hm…yeah I know…so you mean to tell me that she….? Hold up girl, let me call you back, I got company".

"Dam Nikki" said Head, "You always running yo' mouth on the phone."

"Shut up boy," she replied hastily. "Don't try to change the subject, ya'll niggas is wild as hell, I heard about that shit that happen over there in the Nation. Ya'll niggas is the talk of the town right now. And you Mister Rico "C", you are fuckin' nuts."

"Who me?" Rico replied coyly. "What I do?"

"Yeah right nigga," Nikki replied. "They say you slapped the shit out one of them shorties."

The group all laughed, everyone except Rico who only replied even more coyishly, "I don't know what you talking bout'." But what dem' niggas talking bout' anyway?" Rico asked Nikki.

"They ain't talking bout shit right now," Nikki responded. "But I heard this EEl Sista named Cako is one of the people who got shot and she supposed to have indentified somebody."
"What?" Rico asked surprisingly. "Hell na'll, the Black EEls don't get down like that, they ain't no rats or stool pigeons." But as usual Nikki was right; 2pac was arrested after Cako recognized him as one of the shooters. She also recognized Rico as her next door neighbors on-again off-again man and opted to spare him to avoid conflict with her EEl Sista. Rico who hadn't visited Nikki in awhile decided to milk Nikki for everything she knew. "So what's up wit' dem' ops?" Rico asked, knowing she couldn't hold water. "Oh yeah!" Nikki said as she cracked sunflower seeds in her mouth. "I heard dem' d-boyz suppose to be paying one of the Brothas to go to court and testify on their guy's behalf, sayin' that they weren't the shooters for Kenyatta's murder."
"Straight up?" head asked
"When you hear this?" T.P. cut in.
"The other day," Nikki replied.
"What you been hearing about the G's?" Rico asked.
Before Nikki could answer, the loud mouths of Da-Da and Tameka could be heard coming down the stairs. "Whud, did I hear somebody say something bout some G's?" Tameka asked as she squeezed past the crowd of Brothas. "Cuz we G-girls over here and all ya'll stupid ops gotta get off my porch, except Shorty "C" cuz he cute"
"Bitch, how the hell you a G-girl, when you been living over here all your life and you cant barely come of the porch?" Rico said to his fake enemy.
"Don't worry bout it nigga," you just mad cuz I ain't no Sista," Tameka replied.
"I ain't worried bout it cuz you ain't no real G-girl either," Rico said laughingly.
"How you gon' tell me what the fuck I am?"
"Cuz I know," Rico shot back.
"How?" Tameka snapped.
"Cuz you still a virgin, that's how."
     Rolling her eyes, Tameka just said "so what," as she motioned towards the bottom of the stairs with Da-Da in tow, hoping for a swift escape from what she knew Rico was capable of doing; embarrassing her. But he wasn't about to let her slide that easy. "If you was a real G-girl, niggas would've been dug that lil' merch out," Rico stated. "You gotta give that merch up through the door." You phony as hell Tameka, last month you was claiming you a g-girl from the low end somewhere,

now you saying you from Killa Ward. Wherever Da-Da boyfriend is at the time that's where you from."

"Um, excuse me," Da-Da said provokingly. "I didn't say nothing to you, that's ya'll conversation, why you put me in it?" Da-Da stood about chest high to Rico and had to look up when she spoke, the light skin young vixen favored a young Salt (from the female hip-hop group) *Salt-N-Peppa*. "Na'll I'm just sayin' Da-da, I think you a real G-girl, cuz ain't none of my guys hit that or I would've hard about it", Rico said as he walked down the stairs with her. "Look at you, on the "C," you getting thick as hell, I know somebody hittin' that lil' phat ass back there." Da-Da smacked her lips: "Boy please my whole family G's, so I was born into this", she said smilingly as she walked around Rico to catch up with Tameka who started walking toward 79th. "Ay Tameka" Rico yelled, "You better be back before the street lights come on or I'ma get Ms. Richmond to beat that ass out here again like she did last year."

With the Black EEls not being much of a threat at the present moment, R.I focused most of their attention on their real enemies, the ops. "If I find out who it is, it's curtains," T.P., R.I's enforcer said in a goal.
"We heard the D-boys paying somebody over here to help one of them niggas get outta jail," Head explained to the multitude of Brothas that stood in a 360' circle. Rico looked at his watch, it was 7:05 pm, Shorty C' was officially late. "Probably get a mouth shot" Rico thought to himself. "7:15pm time to take attendance," Toby said.
"Whoever ain't here is in violation," Bo-Bo stated.
Shorty 'C' wasn't the only one missing, there had to be at least a dozen no-shows, and T.P was frustrated.
"This don't make no sense, Brothas know they supposed to be here, they act like they ain't tryin' to hear nothing."
"Whoever ain't here, we giving them a S.O.S (serve on sight) violation were not waiting till next Friday."

Rico felt all eyes on him, knowing what this meant for Shorty 'C'. He knew what the Brothas was thinking: That he would overrule them and find some way to allow his protégé to escape unscathed. But those days were over, and he had to set an example for the growing young Brothas in the organization. "I'm cool wit' that", Rico said into the circle. "Everybody has had their fair share of reprimands and warnings."
"Remember, although it's a S.O.S, the same violation rules apply, don't put your feet on a Brotha," Milton added.

When the goal ended the mob of charged up Bros took to the streets of R.I looking for any unsuspecting absentee members that assumed their actions were probationary, and caught most of them before the night was over. But nobody saw Shorty 'C'.

****

Mean while Rico had to high tail it to a Committee meeting that was being held at Mr. G's lodge on 87th street. Today was important because it was mandatory that Cheives from each South Side set attend to give their quarterly reports. Toby, Bo-Bo, and Milton represented for Rock Island since Rico now sat on the board. The board members sat at the long table with their backs against a wall and the others sat in folding chairs faced in their direction, usually in groups that were members of the same area. "I think in order to take the organization to a new plateau. We need to focus on legitimizing a lot of areas within the organization," Chico from the wild 100's said to the crowd of Cons. "Maybe start buying property, opening up businesses and stuff like that."

"I agree with you 'C', said Baby 'C' from the 100's, but we have too many things working against us, what ever level we get on."

"I agree with Chico, interrupted Rico, legitimizing is the way to longevity; however, I also feel what Baby 'C' is trying to say."

"In my opinion, we need to take cues from every other organization around us, every group of influential people. The reason they're successful is because they have people in positions to help them out. I simply suggest that we do the same."

"So, what are you proposing Brotha, that we start bribing police and other government officials?" Wood asked as he leaned back in his chair.

"Na'll," Rico replied as he stood up, demanding the attention. I'm proposing that some of us become police and government officials." The room sporadically filled with what's and *hunhs* from the light chatter. "Hold up let him finish!" Tank yelled from the table. Rico continued to explain: "Not every member of this organization is a big drug dealer or gun slanger. We have some very smart and intelligent Brothas and Sistas. Imagine if we had Con members on the police force working as council members and state representatives. Could you imagine the Nation having its very own lawyers, and maybe judges?

If you study other organizations from the Mafia to the Klan, to the free Masons, they always had people in high places to help them out in some sort of fashion." I propose that each Chief from every set take a count of their members who have no criminal records to get their

G.E.D's, finish school or college and apply to jobs in various police departments, the Cook County Sheriffs Office, and the Department of Corrections. That should be easy, these entities are always looking for fresh new bodies; and their presence will give us the advantage we need on the criminal side of things. Their jobs would be to take care of the incarcerated members and provide us aid and assistance on the streets with the drug trade. Now, secondly I propose that we use Nation funds to pay the full tuitions of interested members with no criminal background. We need to send people to school for business, politics, and law. With Business managers, accountants, and legal aides at our disposal, we will be a force in our communities." Starting with Wood and then Chico, Rico received a standing ovation from the crowd of 'C's for his proposal. The enthusiastic, prolonged applause surprised even Rico whom wasn't sure of the reaction he'd receive for his first proposal.

"Damn Joe!" Wood said to Rico as he shook his hand after the meeting. "I didn't know that you were able to think that deeply; what made you think about all of that." Not knowing if he should be offended or flattered by his partner's comment, Rico simply stated, "I've just been doing a lot of thinking lately."

"Yeah well, whatever you on, I'm up wit it too Brotha" Wood stated as they walked to the parking lot of the lodge. "I'm just tired of this shit," Rico said in a frustrated tone. I'm ready to do something different."

"Whud?" Wood shot back. What you saying, you don't wanna be a Brotha no more?"

"Stop playin', Rico quickly answered. You know I'm going to the grave being one of the guys. It's just all this other bullshit, I'm growing tired of; mainly this drug shit, it's like I'm addicted to the game more than the crack heads."

"Yeah man, but you getting ugly money Rico, said Wood. You shouldn't be complaining about shit."

"Yeah man, I know Rico responded. How long this shit gon' last? I know a gang of niggas that was getting much more paper than me, and they locked up doing natural balls or fifty years Fed time, because they was getting money, and stayed in the game too long. Those niggas was addicted to the shit and as long as you've known me, I've neva been addicted to shit. That proposal that I just laid down, that ain't finna happen over night, so until then, the odds are against us. If I go to jail for life, it's going to be for pushing one of these niggas shit back, not for getting money. It's too many ways to do that without the risk."

Alright my nigga, what you saying?" Wood concluded.

"I'm glad you asked, Rico responded. I'm not saying that we fall outta the game right away, that'll be impossible. However, I got a decent amount of money that I'm ready to invest into something legit. We got this bogus production company; I figured we could use it for more than just a front. Maybe even start a record label and be on some Chi-town Death row type of shit. We got a lot of talent in the Chi." Wood sat in his sports car listening to Rico with one foot hanging out the side of the door.

"I'll tell you what dawg, let me handle this business down state and get shit in order down there for a few months and then we can do the damn thang."

"Aight Brotha, it's a done deal then." Rico said smiling as he got into his own car. The next day (Saturday morning), the Bros were up and running on 77th and Sangamon where Toby and Qualo and sometimes their cousin Juan lived. Toby wanted the Bros out early to finish issuing out the last few violations to the no show Brothas of the previous night's goal. He sent word for the remaining Bros to come on 77th, without revealing the reason. Unsuspectingly, Brothas were attacked and punched immediately as they arrived on the block.

Rico stood near the corner of the block away from the large crowd of bone crushers talking to Dollar Bill, "who the fuck you is, L.L or something?" Rico joked with Dollar who seemed to love walking around with his shirt off. "Na'll nigga, I'm Dollar "Cool" Bill; I stands to be the coldest ya' dig!" Dollar said as he admired himself thru the reflection of a car window. "Aight man, whatever," Rico said shaking his head, noticing the familiar car slowing down just in front of him, and the familiar voice hollering out the window; "wud up Joe?" Shorty 'C' said leaning over his girlfriend and Rock Island Sista Twin. "What dem' niggas on down here? Talkin' bout they wanna holla and shit." Rico looked at his buddy, knowing that he couldn't feel any empathy for him and said: "I don't know, go down there, and see."

"Brotha you bogus, where you been?" Dollar interrupted.

"Shut the fuck up Dollar" Rico snapped back cutting him off. "Don't pay this nigga no mind, he just a lil' drunk" Rico assured as he moved Dollar Bill to the side. "Aight right then, what we on today?" Shorty C asked as he continued to lean over a seemingly annoyed Twin. "Oh, Roz, her buddy and me got to go to the gun store today and reup on some ammo, so I'll get up wit you then.

"Bet," he said as he slowly drove down the block to see what the crowd of Brothas wanted.

Unbeknownst to the Bros, Shorty C had been warned by his girlfriend whose twin also was the steady girlfriend of Toby. Still Chad didn't really think that Rico would let anything happen to him.

"Ay C," let a nigga holla' at cha' for a minute bout' some business," Toby said to Shorty 'C', who remained in his car. Shorty 'C' then got out of the car, only to reach back in the window and grab the 9MM glock Twin had sitting on her lap and deliberately tucked it into his waistband. "What up?" Shorty 'C' asked again, throwing his hands in the air. Um, um, 'C' put the gun down Joe, one Brotha said as he approached the crowd. In light of the fact that Shorty was armed, the S.O.S couldn't be carried out as planned.

"You in violation Brotha put that burner down or we gon' take it as you bearing arms against the Bros." Qualo said as he stepped back.

"Violation?" Shorty C exclaimed. "What the fuck these niggas talking about?" Shorty C yelled down the street to Rico, who was trying to pretend he was engaged in deep conversation with a female resident of the building that he was standing in front of.

Rico with his signature devilish grin just looked in the direction of the crowd and threw his hands in the air. Just in time for one of the Bros to grab Shorty C from behind and place him in a tight bear hug, allowing another Brotha to disarm him.

"Rico, you knew what the fuck these niggas was on?" Shorty C yelled as they carried him kicking and screaming to Toby's garage and issued a beat down. Twin jumped out of the car, "yawl stop, yawl stop," she yelled.

But the beat down was swift and Chad was the first to appear out of the gangway, visibly upset and disenchanted. Looking in Rico's direction, he yelled with blood running from his nose and mouth; "you let these niggas do this to me?"

"You did it to yourself," Rico yelled back.

The 5'7 Con had a lot of heart as he cursed at his friend and leader. "Fuck you then nigga." Prompting the group to grab him again and rough him up some more for his disrespect. "Fuck you Rico," he screamed as the boys punched him repeatedly.

"Let'em go ya'll" Rico said as he walked towards the crowd.

Shorty 'C' slowly got up and began dusting himself off. "Ya'll niggas didn't even fuck up the crease in my pants," he said as he started laughing wickedly, making his way back to his car with Twin now in the driver's seat. "Ya'll keep that gun, but I know one thing, ya'll better not be out here when I get back." Twin hit the gas on the cutlass and screeched off, down Sangamon. As Rico stood there in front of Toby's house watching the large crowd dwindle, probably not wanting to take

169

any chances that Shorty 'C' was serious about his threat. He thought to himself, **THIS IS JUST WHAT THE HATERS WANT!**

CHAPTER 27

The news of Rico and Chad's separation seemed to be on the tongues of everybody affiliated with Rock Island and if they were not talking about it, Rico knew that's what they were thinking as he and his other right hand man Head, entered Lenzy's for a quick pit stop. They made small talk as they waited on their order.
Head: Man Joe, guess who I hit last night.
Rico: Who nigga?
Head: Gina's thick ass,
Rico: Who you talkin' bout', our Gina, the C-Sista?
Head: Hell yeah, nigga. Me and T.P. was kickin' it wit' some of the Sistas and the next thing you know, she get to asking me if I gotta big dick and shit, talkin' freaky. So I took her to the crib, and nailed her ass. I ain't going to even lie 'C', she got a nuke. That pussy in my top five now.
Rico: Hell nawl, nigga, I can't believe you fucked Gina. I thought she fuck wit' dat' nigga Duke.
Head: Man, she don' fucked all dem' Bros over there that be on Sangamon: Toby, Juan, Qualo, M. Dub; too many niggas.
Rico: Straight up, damn, I can't be fucking with them Sistas across Sangamon. They burnt up, if I had to choose a Sista or two, it'll be a Vogue Sista. One of them chicks that be with Kesha and em'.
Head: I heard Kesha be bustin' hoez down these days, straight eating the Sistas pussy.
Rico: (laughing) shit why not nigga, fuck it. If there's one Sistas pussy I would've ate, it would've been Bubba's before she moved down south; all pussy ain't good pussy.
Head: Ew, nigga you bogus. The Brothas don't eat no pussy!
Rico: Shit, you crazy as hell, niggas be eating, they just keep that shit on the low.
   (Back in the car)
Head: Speaking on the low my nigga, we about to drive through the complex, I know you den hit some of these young hoez.
Rico: Uh, na'll..All right man, you got me, I fucked that lil' bitch Stephany last week. I hope that bitch ain't put my business out there, cuz I ain't tryin' to burn my name up with them bitches in the complex.
Head: What that bitch Stephany working with?
Rico: Her stuff was decent, but it ain't all that. I hit her in the back seat and dropped her off over her friends crib; she didn't wanna go home and wash her pussy or nothing.

Head: She a nasty ass-trifling hoe...
Rico: Damn, there go some of they ass right there.

The complex was home to some of the finest females. As Rico exited his car noticing, Angie, Tiffany, Shamone, Shavone and Tasha he wondered why he never approached them about being Sistas. Tasha, a medium brown skin, skinny teen, with thick full lips that even a succubus would envy seemed to be their leader. Her tomboyish ways and no nonsense attitude made her seem unapproachable. Derricka, a young chocolate goddess with model looks was the stuck up one who always bragged about a boyfriend who didn't live in the area. Shamone was a carbon copy of her oldest sister Shelia (Wayne's baby momma).
"Hey, what's to it?" Rico greeted the girls that were talking about him under their breath as he approached.
"What's up with you and Shorty 'C'? We heard ya'll beefin"; Angie, the youngest out the crew asked.
"Don't believe everything you hear in the streets shawty," Rico replied as he walked up on the cool sexy one of the crew, to take care of some unfinished business.
"What's up Tiffany?" Rico said to the light-skinned seventeen year old. "Long time no see."
"Whose fault is that?" She asked smiling at Rico seductively, with vivid memories of the last time they were together still freshly implanted on her mind.
"Yeah, I've been busy" Rico added. "But why the hell you didn't tell me you fuck with my man Reese?"
"It wasn't that serious back then," Tiffany replied. "One week we together one week we not, and you just so happen to catch me when we wasn't. "And besides," Tiffany said raising her voice so her nosey friends could hear, "it ain't like we actually did something."
"Yeah, you right, Rico responded licking his lips looking Tiffany up and down, it ain't like we did something."
"What's that all about?" Head asked as they turned the corner of the complex, walking towards Corner boy Ronald's apartment.
"Nothing, my nigga everything ain't for the streets Rico replied. Ron, who was hanging out of his apartment's second floor window, noticed the two Brothas as they approached. "What's up fool? Rock Island nigga" he yelled. Ronald, who was obviously impaired from several substances, opened his apartment to the Bros to smoke and hang out with frequently. "Rock Island" Head and Rico, responded from the ground. "Who all up there?" Head asked.

"Uh, Uh, Um...Oh yeah, everybody up in here, the triplets, Lil Willie, Shorty 'C'" Head looked at Rico, not sure of what he would say."
"Man, C'mon get off that bullshit with Shorty C" Head pleaded.
"It's cool Joe," Rico said smoothly; gone head and enjoy yourself up there. That ain't my type of scene anyway, I don't get high or drink."
"You sure?" Head asked.
"Yeah" Rico assured. "I'll be on Carpenter if you wanna find me."
"Bet it up homie," Head said as he did the Bros signature handshake with Rico and entered Ronald's smoke house.

  Rico passed Tasha and her girls again as he walked back to his car. *"That's the type of Sistas we need,"* he thought to himself. But Rock Islands Sistas were in disarray as the three groups all distanced themselves from one another. Keshia fell back after Lavada's death. So Mary Ann had her crew and Cynthia had hers. They all hated on each other whenever given the opportunity. *"The future ain't looking good for the Sistas right now"* Rico thought as he drove out of the complex and headed towards Carpenter St. deciding to go give Roz some much needed sexual attention. *"She always complaining that I don't spend enough time with her"* he said to himself as put the key into her lock of her apartment door, hearing the loud radio blasting from her bed room. *"Good, the kids ain't here,"* he noticed as he passed their perfectly cleaned rooms. Roselyn's door was cracked about five inches, enough for Rico to notice the large round ass cheeks of the china doll faced, red bone Carmen on her stomach servicing Roselyn with some seemingly good tongue action. Roselyn so busy moaning and tryin' to gyrate her hairy nest into Carmen's face she didn't notice as Rico opened the door wider to get a better view. Carmen jumped and screamed in fear when she saw Rico in the room. Both women leaped from the bed, but Carmen grabbed the largest garment she could find in attempt to cover herself, as Rico turned off the loud music. "Rico Rico, I... I... Uh, uh... I'm sorry baby, I just... " Roselyn continued to stamper.

  "So this what ya'll be doing when I'm not around hunh?" Rico asked the two sweat drenched lovers. Carmen remained silent, as she fought hard to hold, her D cup sized breast with the brown saucer areolas In her arms and put on her panties at the same time. "Is this why you've been hatin' on me all of this time?" Rico asked Carmen.

"Baby please listen to me" a teary-eyed Roselyn, pleaded from the bed not bothering to cover her shapely body; "I wanted to tell you, but..."
"But what?" Rico cut in, as he paced the large bedroom back and forth.
"So what you tryin' to say, that ya'll been doing this shit before I came into the picture?"

The two women looked at each other and shook their heads up and down slowly. "Unh hunh."
"So I guess that practically makes ya'll a couple hunh," said Rico as he sat down on the bed beside Roselyn. "What I wanna know is, where I fit into all of this? "
"Baby I'm sure we can work something out," Roselyn cooed. "I don't wanna loose you over this."
"I should slap the fuck out of you for keeping secrets from me," Rico added. "What else are you keeping from me?"
"Nothing baby, I promise" Roselyn said in her girlish voice. "I promise, I'll never keep nothing else from you Rico."
"Well you gotta a lot of making up to do" Rico said feeling that he had to assert his dominance.
"Me and Carmen can try and make it up to you if that's what you want" Roselyn added, as she grabbed Carmen by the arm indicating her to sit on the bed.
"Oh yeah"? Rico asked as he began taking off his shirt. "How ya'll planning on doing that?" Carmen, still half dressed from her escape attempt began to shed her clothing. The thirty-seven year old mother of three still had the body of a twenty year old.
"It's been awhile, so bare with me" Carmen said as she unzipped Rico's pants and went down slowly.
"Feels good doesn't it boo," Roz whispered into his ear in between one of her wet kisses.
"Hell yeah," Rico replied, as the vet made his toes curl. The three of them had sex every which way possible, for the rest of the evening. It was the most incredible sexual experience Rico had ever had. The two older women drained the young deviant.

  Roselyn couldn't have been happier, now that she had both of her lovers together; it was a perfect world for her. This wasn't Carmen's first three-way encounter, but after being in an abusive relationship for five years and hating men for two, her sex drive was at full throttle and she was intent on satisfying all of her sexual desires. She always wanted to get with Rico from the first moment Roz bragged about their aggressive first sexual experience. *"Damn Roz wasn't lying,"* she thought to herself, as she laid naked in one of Rico's arms. *"That boy sho' can work it."* For Rico, Carmen wasn't just another sexual guest. *"I gotta cuff this chick,"* he thought, as he stared into the darkness of the night. *"She work at Cook County Jail, and she got good credit. She's going to be real useful."*

The next morning Rico wanted to see the two women get it on before he left and Roz and Carmen were doing just that, when the phone rang. "It's for you baby" Roz said, handing Rico the phone.
Rico: It better be important.
Head: Yeah man it's me dawg.
Rico: Oh, what's up nigga?
Head: Man Ima' kill that bitch...
Rico: Hold up Brotha, who you talking about.
Head: That bitch Gina man.
Rico: What about her?
Head: Man that nasty Bitch burnt me.
Rico: What you talkin' bout', she stole some money from you or something?
Head: Na'll, that bitch gave me the claps.
Rico: Oh shit, you fo' real Joe?
Head: Hell yeah man. I just woke up this morning and all this green shit...
Rico: All right, all right, Brotha, you can keep those details.
Head: Man Rico, I need you to come, get me, and take me to the clinic. I can't be walking around like this.
Rico: Aight "C." I got you, just give me a minute. I kinda got my hands full right now.
Head: What you doin' nigga?
Rico: (laughing) I'll tell you later.

Rock Island: A Gangstaz Graveyard   N.U.T.T.Y. "C"

CHAPTER 28

Meanwhile at 26th & California-Cook County Court room 101.,"It says here in your affidavit that you were present during the shooting incident that left the victim dead, is that correct sir?" The Latina trial lawyer asked as the former Con member sat on the stand. "Yes Ma'am, I seen everything." Raulo lied. After testifying that the two guys weren't the shooters. The judge gave a direct verdict and ordered the two-gang members to be released. A dozen or so D's and family members cheered when the judge banged her gavel.

"Aye man." Raulo nervously said as he approached the group of high-ranking D's outside of the courthouse. "Ya'll still gone keep ya'll end of the bargain right?" The elated D-boys, were still in disbelief that they were able to get a Brotha, let alone someone of Raulo's caliber to work for them and betray his Nation for five thousand dollars and a quarter kilo of cocaine. Raulo told them that he was the one actually calling the shots in Rock Island, not Rico as everyone thought. "Yeah, we got you on that." One of the Ministers for the D's said laughing. "We appreciate that man, straight up."
"I'll call you later and let you know where you could get the rest of that cake at."
"All right Joe, remember to keep this on the low." Raulo said as he walked off.
"Man niggas would do anything for money." One D-boy said as he stared at Raulo from a distance.
"I wonder what he gone do wit' that little coke we gave him." Another one asked.
"I know if he got rank like that, that lil' shit ain't nothing to him."
"Maybe the Bros got some bullshit work over there."
"I don't know and I don't give a fuck, I'm just glad that my mans an nem' bout' to come to the crib today."
"Them bitch ass niggas in Rock Island getting all of the guys locked up with they stool pigeon asses."
"Now we gotta try to pay these niggas not to come to court, what part of the game is that?"
"I'm tired of them niggas."
"Fuck dat' shit fam, the next time anyone of those niggas do anything, call the fucking police on they ass!" Their leader said.
"Get some of their asses locked up," another said.
"We gon' show them that two could play that game."

"And when the guys go to trial, we'll always have a bargaining chip."
"Hell yeah!" They all agreed.

****

"Man, I can't believe that bitch burnt you Joe," said Rico as him and Head drove back from Englewood clinic.
"Why you keep bringing that shit up?" Head asked in his fake hostile voice. "I remember when that broad from over east popped you off wit' the drippy dick, and you were crying and shit."
"Oh, it's like that hunh?" Rico asked with a smirk on his face.
"Yeah, these chicks out here nasty, you gotta strap up these days."
"I hate using rubbers," Head added.
"Me too" Rico replied, "but I hate getting burnt even worst."
"Ay dog you think Gina got that shit?" Head asked with a look of fear and resentment in his face.
"Aids?" Rico asked rhetorically. "I don't know, but if she do, the Ops should recruit her cuz half of Rock Island will be dead in a few years," Rico said as he pulled his cell phone from his belt to answer a call. "Who dis?" Rico breathed into the flip phone. "What?... When?... Is he still there?... O.K., I'm on my way. That was Shorty C's momma," Rico explained to Head. "This lil' nigga at the crib wildin' out."

When Rico arrived at C's house, he could hear C's unmistakable and mid-puberty voice: "Shut the fuck up," Rico knew to use the side door where the spare key was hidden beneath a brick. Once inside, Shorty 'C' with two semi automatic weapons in each hand, paced back and forth waving the weapons at his apparent hostages; his girl Twin, his two cousins, stepfather and friend of the family. Chad's mother met Head and Rico at the door. "Please do something, talk to him, I don't want to call the police", she pleaded. "Wud cha' call dem' fo' hunh?" Chad asked as he noticed his mother and friends enter the living room. "They can't tell me nothing," this is my house, and I pay the bills up in here. My brothers are gone, my daddy is gone, and I'm the man of this house."
"Chad, what's up Brotha?" Rico greeted, speaking directly at him for the first time in weeks. "What's all this about?"
"What the fuck you care?" Chad snapped back. "You don't care bout' a nigga."
"That ain't true,"Rico answered. "You know you still my lil' homie, I was just givin' you a little time to get yo' mind right."
Chad seemed relieved at that point but quickly re-focused his attention back on his hostages. "Na'll man, one of these muthafuckaz stole my

shit, and I wanna know which one it was, so till one of they ass tell or fess up ain't nobody going nowhere."
"Look man, this ain't the way to do this" Rico said as he approached his friend and put his arm around him. Let's talk about this outside, in the fresh air."And just like that Rico managed to talk Chad down and more importantly put him back on the team.
"Niggas was talkin' all type of crazy shit behind yo' back," Chad confessed as he sat in the back seat of Rico's car. "They thought it was a wrap for me and you, so all them bitch ass hatin' niggas tried to cuff me. But I'm a real nigga 'C', I ain't neva go cross you even if I am mad at you." You taught me that loyalty is everything."I was just tryin' to see how far those niggas was going to take it."
"It's cool my nigga" replied Rico who sat in the passenger seat counting large bills as Head drove.
"We can get them niggas," Chad said emphatically.
"Na'll" said Rico, holding up the bundle of money, "this is all we need to worry about getting right now." Them type of niggas will always exist as long as there's a nigga like me around, they're like flies, they only be around for a season, and if they don't get killed or something, they'll just die off later.
"Yeah" Head agreed. "And there's always some maggot ass niggas in the process of getting their wings." They all laughed, as they pulled in front of the mini-mansion of one of Rico's cocaine connects. Head and Chad waited in the car with the money and guns as Rico negotiated a price for the drugs. The two admired the beautiful landscape and immaculate exterior of the multimillion dollar home. "Man, I need to get me a crib like this" Head stated.
"As a matter of fact, I'd have too many hoez with this joint" Chad concluded.
"Hell na'll", Head said condescendingly, "this is what you cop to do the family thang, wifey and kids.
"Fuck that, I'm throwing parties in my shit," Chad said dreamingly as Rico got back into the car.
"What's wrong Brotha?" Head asked, noticing disenchantment on Rico's face. "This is some bullshit," an angry Rico said, as he drove off. "Everybody talking bout it's a drought on the coke in the city." None of the people got no weight and the one dude I do know that always has work wants to charge thirty a brick. I ain't paying no thirty for a kilo of cocaine, that's ridiculous."
"I don't know Rico, we only got about two days worth of work left, and that's only if we make the bags smaller. This drought is gon' hit the

streets hard by tonight and everybody gone get tight with they shit," Head reasoned.

"You could send Roz back out to Cali to get some work from your cousins again" Chad added thoughtfully.

"Yeah that's a good idea; I can have her fly out there with postal money orders, and drive the birds back. I can get em' for about ten out there. I'll make a killing out here during this drought," Rico said.

"But we gotta find something in the meantime cuz that'll take about a week total, and what's up with postal money orders?" Head added.

"Oh yeah, it's less bulkier than cash, you can put twenty to thirty money orders worth thousands of dollars each in an envelope and it wont be detected. As long as the envelope is sealed, the police can't even open it," Rico stated.

****

"The family (Ops) keeps work during droughts; we got to find a way to rub some of that." Rico thought aloud.

"Candace!" Roz said to Rico as if she had just found the cure for cancer. "Candace aka Scandalous G, Roselyn's step-daughter from her ex-hubby was the first lady of a local infamous G-boy set. Roselyn still spoke to her and helped her out even after the divorce.

"Hell fucking No!" Rico exclaimed. "I ain't fucking with that snake ass G-girl bitch. You know I can't stand her ass, and even if I could trust her, she wouldn't fuck with me anyway from what happened the last time that we saw each other."

"Alright Rico, Roselyn said suit yourself, all I'm saying is that she may know someone, and she owes me a favor anyway."

Rico exhaled deeply shaking his head looking at Chad and Head who were emotionlessly sitting on the couch.

"Aight," Rico said reluctantly. "But I swear to God, if that bitch say anything crazy or try to pull any stunts, I'ma choke her ass out again, this time I'll finish, I promise you, so you betta holla at her ass".

So Roz set up the meeting with the notorious G-girl. Candace and Rico talked for about an hour mainly about Candace, he wanted as much information as he could possibly get, before exposing his intentions. The slightly stout built young woman didn't seem as defiant as he remembered her, in fact even with a new born, she seemed down on her luck and depressed.

"So what exactly do you want from me Rico?"

"I need you to use your G-girl juice card to hook me up with some weight," he revealed.

"First of all," she replied, I'm G-girl to the heart, but right now I ain't fuckin' wit' niggas. Secondly, you know it's a drought, so my guys' ain't got nothing but that Nation work, and last but not least, what makes you think I would fuck with you on some shit like that anyway?"

"Well, I'm glad you asked that" Rico said cunningly, always prepared to retort. "First of all, you don't have to convince me of whose side you're on, but I was under the impression that you liked money too. Yeah, I'm aware it's a drought, but I'm also aware of the facts, that like my Brothas on the west side with the heroine, your guys out here have an endless supply of cocaine. I'm also aware that your baby's father Gary got his hood on lock and he the man over there, which would make him have the sole responsibility of supplying all the G's in his area with work."

Candace arched her eyebrows, indicating that she was impressed at the man who had choked her for disrespecting him over the phone. "Yeah, you right about all that, but I don't fuck wit' my punk ass baby daddy. Dude might as well be dead to me." She continued to tell Rico how she and Gary were engaged in a heated battle over the custody of their child, and that he even had her beat up by some more G-girls. Rico allowed her to vent, while he ran ideas though his mind.

"Well since you don't give a fuck bout' him, why don't you give me some info on how to get close to the nigga?"

****

Meanwhile near 76th and Racine: Wacky, Milton, wild C, and T.P. were standing near the game room when several cars full of gang members pulled up, jumped out, and fearlessly opened fire. BLAM! BLAM! BLAM! "Oh shit!" T.P. said, as they ducked for cover. BLAM! BLAM! BLAM!BLAM!... TAT-TAT-TAT-TAT-TAT-TAT... BOOM-BOOM-BOOM! As T-fly and Travis exited the complex, they heard the commotion and drove faster to the scene. Travis armed with a German nine-millimeter caught the unsuspecting assailants by surprise. POP! POP! POP! POP! "Dem niggas is everywhere," Travis said as he unloaded his clips towards the Ops.

Lil Law was on 75th and Carpenter when Milton and Wild C ran past with the Ops clear on their trail. "On dem' Ops! On dem' Ops!" Milton yelled as he passed.

Armed with a forty-caliber handgun Lil Law shot back, BOOM! BOOM! BOOM! PACUB, PACUB, PACUB, PACUB, TAT-TAT-TAT-TAT-TAT-TAT-! "Watch them gangways" Travis said to Brothas as he walked 77th and May where some of the Ops fled on foot, with his gun drawn like it was the wild, wild, west. The guns Wacky had stashed on May came in handy, as he armed himself with two weapons, and gave T.P. a three fifty seven magnum. "On this car!" T.P. said as a mini van slowly drove down May. POW! POW! POW!

They shot holes in the vehicle before the Ops could react. "Who the fuck is these niggas?" Wacky asked after firing a few more shots at the Ops.

"I don't know T.P. replied, but who ever they are, they mean business." On 75th and Carpenter, Lil Law managed to come out on the fair end of the shoot out, but Wild C took a bullet to the leg.

"Where dem' niggas at?" Jo-Jo said as he arrived with a car full of Brothas with guns.

"They gon'," Lil Law replied.

"I know one of them niggas," Milton said, causing all the attention to be diverted to him. "Man that was dude and'em from KILLAWARD."

"KILLAWARD!" exclaimed Jo-Jo. "What killa ward niggas coming all the way over here for shooting at us like that? We never had no beef with them like that." Jo-Jo knew he could find out by eliciting some information out of his oldest brother, who was a low ranking G-boy.

Later that evening: The emerald green Lexus coupe sat in front of the Dolton Illinois apartment complex, with its cabin full of weed smoke. "Man Joe, this bitch talkin' bout' she met me at the club a couple months ago, I'm bout to see what dis' bitch on." The two occupants passed the blunt back and forth. "So I asked the bitch, what club she talking bout, cuz you know how I do, and the she say the fifty yard line. At first, I'm thinking this bitch on some bullshit trying to set me up or something. But she told me what I had on that night, what whip I was driving, even what kinda cologne I was wearing, and everything. She had a little nigga at the time, but I've been on her mind every since. I don't know what's taking this bitch so long to get down here, she got a mutha fucka waiting on her, and this bitch betta be raw as hell. Here come somebody now."

As the female neared the car, she could hear one of the occupants saying "Damn, this bitch is popped!"

The girl, who approached the car, was far from the type of females that the high-ranking gang member was use to. Even his strong faced personal security man looked baffled as the girl spoke to them through the passenger side window. She was smiling from ear to ear. "Um, which one of ya'll is Curtis?" The bewildered passenger sat up in his seat to get a better look at the mystery girl. She was supposed to be meeting his guy not him. "How do you know my na...?" BLAM!

BLAM! BLAM! Three shots to the head at the point blank range sent pieces of his skull and brain flying onto Gary. The recently released Sheeky remained calm as she did on her first mission years earlier.

Gary could feel a drip of urine starting to exit his body, as Sheeky commanded him not to move. "I wouldn't reach for that gun if I were you" she said to Gary, as the stolen Delta eighty-eight pulled up right beside the drivers side window with a Mac eleven pointed out the window.

"Let me see yo' hands," one of the masked men in the car, demanded as two other armed figures jumped out and removed the scared G-boy from his new ride. Gary was blindfolded and duck taped before being searched and placed in the trunk of the stolen car. Cocktail bombs exploded inside the Lexus with Curtis still inside. Gary was driven to a nearby abandoned warehouse. His captures informed him of why he had been kidnapped. "Now we go ask you one more time where that shit at if you keep bullshitting us, you gon' end up like your man," one of the masked men said.

Gary couldn't believe this was happening to him, he never thought that anyone could catch him slipping like this.
"Alright Joe" said the shaken G-boy. "I can get you some money, just don't kill me, please don't kill me. I can get you whatever you want."
"We want ten of them thangs" a voice said.
"Man, you know it's a drought, I don't got it like that."
"Well you about to join your man in the Lexus nigga! You had better think of something.
Call yo' baby momma and tell that bitch where the shit at, so you can live."
"Man, I don't even fuck wit' my baby momma, I swear to God Joe. I can call one of my guys."
"Hell na'll! We running da' show, you get one call, and if you don't tell her where that shit at so she can drop it off at the drop off point, we go blow you muthafuckin brains out. Gary had no choice, he had to call Candace and tell her where his stash was. He didn't suspect that she had anything to do with it, a mortally dangerous underestimation. After receiving the large quantity of drugs, Rico ordered the release of Gary. Rico knew that the G-boy probably had access to more, because the G's would never have all of their Nation work in one safe house, but he was satisfied with what he had. This was more than enough to get him through the drought, and probably lay the ground works for an early departure out of the game for good.

CHAPTER 29

Rock Island's Minister of Information (Milton) and Chief of security (Jo-Jo) informed the Brothas that KILLAWARDS attack was spurred on by an incident involving some of the Black EEls from **Brothaville**. According to the information they got off the street, a couple of the EEls beat and robbed a fourteen-year-old boy, on 76th and Racine. The boy turned out to be the nephew of a high rank G-boy from Killaward. "What the fuck the EEls doing over here robbing muthafuckas and shit for?" Black said.

"Them niggas bogus" replied Wacky, who nearly lost his life as a result. They didn't inform us or nothing. Rock Island didn't have a standing beef with the Eels from Brothaville. The history between the two sets was quite cordial since the Eels that originated from Rock Island relocated three blocks north.

But a lot of pressure was on the young Eels who like Rock Island underwent structural changes. Most of the older Eels were either locked up or non-active. The young fifth generation Eels were in charge now. Their generals Lampty, Dae-Dae, and Frank were all under twenty-one. The Brothaville EEls were under a lot of pressure from their cohorts from other sets, who were at the odds with Rock Island. Places like the local schools and parties were microcosmic locations for the two gangs to bump heads. And the EEls from Brothaville were forced to ride with their brethren from other locations, who didn't like Rock Island's Cons and Corner boys. The beefs were miner compared to those of their natural enemies, but Rico knew all too well, how relatively small beefs could turn full-scale wars. Lampty and Dae-Dae were cool with Rico and arranged a meeting between the leaders.

"Ya'll need to holla at them shorties." Rico said to the two Generals.
"Them lil' niggas be startin' a lot of bullshit with my shorties."
Lampty, a light-skinned Brotha with long cornrowed hair spoke first.
"Yes sir, ones go rotate and demonstrate wit' da' multitude and exercise that measure Brotha. But draw off this, ones can't be omni present. Some of the key soldiers are not in tune with the ancient relations that our hoods both share, and by Rock Island not seeing eye to eye with other Brothas from other locations, they are only inclined to gravitate towards their name sake."
Sometimes it was difficult to decipher Lampty's EEL lingo, but his colorful commentary was....entertaining to say the least. Da-Da was a little more practical in his linguistic delivery.

"The little young Brothas are wild as hell, Dae-Dae interjected but like the Brotha said, we can't be everywhere at all times. But on da' strength of our respect for you, we'll try to curb any overzealousness on the part of the key soldiers (shorties). So, is everything all well with us?"

"Fo' sho", everything all good for now" Rico replied. "We always gon' be all good, no matter what, cuz yawl some real niggas. But I know at the end of the day, yawl gon' ride wit' yo' own, and believe me, I ain't into the business of giving out passes."

So the group all agreed that if the two hoods ever went to war, they had diplomatic immunity.

But not every EEl close to Rico shared the sentiments.

"We got to talk," said the EEl Princess Quetta, into the phone of Rico.

Rico: What's up now Quetta?

Quetta: "Um, me and you, that's what's up"

Rico: What the hell you talking about?

Quetta: Did you know that some of the EEl's approached me about settin' you up?

Rico: What? Who? I'll go murk dem' bitch ass studs right now!

Quetta: All that doesn't matters Rico, you already know they ain't feeling none of yawl Rock Island niggas right now anyway.

Rico: So what you tell dem' niggas?

Quetta: What the fuck you think I said? I cussed they ass out. I'll neva do no pussy ass shit like that, c'mon now Rico. I feel disrespected because muthafuckas know I love yo' black ass." (The phone went silent for a few seconds, as Rico paused to retort.)

Rico: Love? So when did that happen, you'n caught feelings? I thought we had an understanding, we suppose to be just friends. I ain't with that boyfriend/girlfriend shit right now.

Quetta: You make me sick Rico, this how you gon do me? After all that we've been through. I got your name tattooed on me. I love you, and we can't be just friends. I know about that old bitch you got, and dem' buss down hoez over there. I'm tired of you treatin' me like I'm just one of your hoes or something. So you need to make up your mind right now. I'll drop all this shit right now and become your woman.

Rico: So what are you tryin to say?

Quetta: I'm trying to say either you go be my man or my enemy.

Rico: Oh, it's like that hunh? You think you can just call me and give me ultimatums. Bitch, you got me fucked up, I don't give a fuck about you or none of them EEl niggas you run with! So if you wanna be my enemy, so be it, get in line. (click)

Rico uncharacteristically allowed his emotions to get the best of him. In hindsight Quetta was his only eyes and ears into the potential threat of the EEls. The odds now were in their favor. With Quetta armed with a wealth of information about him, she herself was a potential threat. *"I should've just told that bitch what she wanted to hear,"* he reasoned. *"Fuck it, it is what it is."*

The EEls from neighboring sets continued having minor altercations with Rock Island. Dembo's a popular neighborhood liquor store that both Eels and Rock Island members could go to and purchase liquor without an I.D. or the threat of Ops, was becoming a clashing site for the allies. Located at 79th and Halsted the two groups often traveled to Dembo's in large numbers for security purposes. Fights were common outside of Dembo's. The twenty- four hour store even had an attached bar.

The rap group "Dayton Family", even made a song about their experience on 79th and Halsted. The song titled: *"79th and Halsted"* illustrated the dangers of coming to Dembo's and how quickly the Brothas would assemble to assault unwanted guests in their territory. The group who had just finished a concert traveled to Dembo's where members of the EEls, Cons, and 4,s were about to engage in a brawl. The group of Brothas temporarily put their differences aside and banned together to beat and assault the unsuspecting rappers, who were believed to be affiliated with the G-boys.

But even after their brief union, the EEls and Rock Island continued to have run-ins at Dembo's. Driving down Halsted, Rico could see one such altercation in its pre-stages, and decided to stop and see what was up. "What up Joe?" Rico yelled from his car with Shorty, Candace, and Head inside.

"These niggas act like they want some trouble," Jo-Jo replied from outside the store. Rico parked his car and headed towards the crowd of EEls and his guys. "Fuck this shit, what's all this wolfin' for? Rico exclaimed as he approached the crowd.

"You niggas wanna do something?"

The EEls responded by throwing the first punch. A big fight ensued, prompting the police to be called. Some of the members continued fighting, even after the police arrived. Some fled, eluding capture including Rico who left his car parked near the scene. A small crowd of spectators that included some of the EEl Sistas gathered around as the police rounded up the gang members.

After waiting fifteen minutes, Rico decided to go back to his car and get away. All of the Brothas were lined up against the wall of a store still in the process of being searched for contraband. Several

paddy wagons arrived and waited for their passengers. The police were so busy gathering up the fighters, that Rico made it all the way to his car unnoticed. *"Man, that was a close call"* he thought to himself as he pulled his keys from his pocket. But little did he know, his presence didn't go totally unnoticed.
"That's one of them right there officer" the loud female voice yelled from the crowd of spectators. "He's the main one, he started it all"! Rico didn't want to look back, as the familiar voice kept shouting, "get him, that's one of the ones that started it."
Rico was halfway in the car when a young looking white officer approached him. "Excuse me sir," the officer said. "You mind stepping out of the car."
"Fuck" Rico muttered under his breath, knowing the gig was up. As soon as the officer seen his gang tattoos, he was placed in handcuffs. It was then he saw the face of the voice that was all too familiar to him.

Quetta stuck out her tongue when Rico made eye contact with her on his way to the paddy wagon. Rico was furious. "That bitch gon' get it," he told himself on his way to the station. "I swear she gon' regret this," Rico and several other Brothas were charged with disorderly conduct and mob action.Since Rico was on parole, he was sent back to prison, pending a hearing with the prison review board.

In his absence, several events took place that would alter the course of Rock Island. The inevitable war between Rock Island and Brothaville took place. EEls, such as Villian, Shadow, and Lil Moe gave the young guns of the Island a run for their money. But Brothas like the newly released light-skinned, Con, Moosie and 4 corner boy, Co-Co proved to be a force to be reckoned with. Co-Co was arrested for attempted murder on one of the Black EEls after an altercation on 75th and May. Moosie's reputation grew because of him getting shot, and coming right back on the block. The EEls and the Family tried several times unsuccessfully, to kill the menacing Con. But Moosie just kept coming.

Besides all of the warring, some members of the EEls still resided in what was considered Rock Island territory and some of the Brothas felt it was time for them to go. As a result, they took to the streets and threw firebombs into the house of every EEl that resided in Rock Island. The only exception was Rock Island's barber and Rico's neighbor Lamelle, who decided to denounce his affiliation to the EEls and flip to a Con. Even the female EEls were banned from the Island.

Rico wanted to send a message of his own. Four Rock Island Sistas assaulted Quetta on 79th as she exited a department store. The attack left her hospitalized where she discovered she had had suffered a miscarriage. Rico allowed his anger to kill his own child. The trauma from losing her first child and her first love was too much for Quetta. She renounced her affiliation to her gang, but not her love/hate feelings for Rico. She tattooed R.I.P over his name on her arm. When asked why she did it, she simply said it was for his unborn child.

After a while, Rock Island was forced to disregard the Black Eels as a prominent threat, and focus all of their attention on their natural rivals-"The Family". Toby's house looked like a block of Swiss cheese from all of the bullet holes that it endured over the years. As the new shorties on 78th and Sangamon made names for themselves, their block became more and more popular, leaving less Brothas on 76th street. Not all Brothas migrated to Sangamon.

"Man, I ain't neva fuckin' with Sangamon" Dank said as he sat on Anthony's stoop on 75th and Carpenter, with Lamelle. "All them Brothas crowded on one block, fuck that shit,"

Dank and Anthony parlayed on 75th and Carpenter to a lucrative spot. Swan and his new crew on 74th and Racine were also making a name for themselves by aggressively going at the G-boys near 72nd and Ada, where many 7-4 boys relocated. Swan managed to develop his guys in the absence of Rico and without the help of Rock Island; just as Rico planned it.

Rock Island: A Gangstaz Graveyard   N.U.T.T.Y. "C"

CHAPTER 30

Rico was released after ninety days for the violation of his parole. It was business as usual as soon as his feet touched the ground. One of the first things he did was throw a party, but not for himself. On Kenyatta's birthday, the Brothas surprised his mother at her home on the east side. Tee-Tee seemed as elated as the small crowd of Brothas entered her house. They bought an assortment of alcoholic beverages and a large quantity of weed, as well as chicken and ribs from *Leon's B.B.Q.* "It's so nice to see yawl" Tee-Tee announced as she played hostess to the Brothas. "Nobody hardly comes by anymore since…" Tee-Tee was almost teary eyed.

"Yeah I know Tee-Tee, but we just wanted to let you know that we still love our homey," Rico said.

"I miss my nigga," Head added.

"I miss him too" said Rico.

Tee-Tee informed the Brothas about Raulo coming to court and testifying on the behalf of the D-boys. The Brothas were heated and the news almost spoiled their festive mood. "That's some pussy ass shit," stated T.P as he passed the half smoked blunt to Qualo.

"Hell yeah!" Qualo replied, "That nigga out of order."

"Don't trip," said Rico, who already had the wheels turning in his head.

"I'm tired of that nigga Raulo," Anthony cried, "he stay on some bullshit in da' hood. Last week, he robbed two of the shorties at a dice game."

"And that nigga been tryin to steal packs from the spot," Shorty 'C' added.

"We should go head and fuck dat' nigga up and run his ass off."

"Hold up yawl" Rico interjected. "I've known Raulo longer than any of yawl. He has had his ass whipped plenty of times. Any and everything that we could've possibly done has been done to him. Right now, we here for Kenyatta, don't worry about Raulo. The wrath has no statue of limitations." Rico knew what had to be done to Raulo but the right hand couldn't know what the left hand was doing, until both could be trusted.

****

Officer Derk was eyeing the young gang-banger as he sat in an interview room from behind a two-way mirror. "This lil' high yellow mutha-fucka doesn't appear to be a killer," his partner said.

"None of them do these days," replied Derk in a condescending tone. Moosie sat in the chair and tried to mask his nervousness, as Derk entered the room and pulled up a chair next to him. "You wanna square?"

"No thanks" replied Moosie. Derk sat and eye balled Moosie for a few more minutes before speaking, a tactic he'd played for years.

"Seems like you've been a busy young man," Derk finally said as he looked in a file.

"I ain't did nothing" Moosie shot back. "Look I'ma tell you like this, I've got evidence to lock you up for at least twenty of em'. I've got witnesses from every mob out there that are willing to testify on you" Derk lied. "Before you get to lying to me and disrespecting me, I want to make you a nice proposition."

It only took twenty minutes for the veteran officer to flip another one of Rock Island's trusted members. Derk almost felt it was too easy.

But nothing was easy when it came to shutting down one of the south side's most notorious groups of criminals. Rico was still on his shit list, but his other prized informant had been unable to link him to any of Rock Island's major crimes. Derk suspected that Rico might have grown suspicious. But who would suspect one of Rock Island's most dangerous characters of being a snitch. Armed with two snitches, Derk felt the ball was back in his court.

For Moosie, he didn't initially consider himself a snitch. He thought Derk was foolish for giving him a get out of jail free card, which would enable him to do as he pleased on the street. Moosie and others like him would eventually change gang warfare. He would shoot up his rivals in a relentless manner, but if or when they retaliated, he would have them arrested. Other gangs began to slowly mimic these actions. For Rock Island, they didn't understand why their rivals suddenly added the police to their warfare arsenal. But the trend was proving to be effective and successful. Instead of acting out violently towards potential threats, members would often fabricate crimes against them knowing they'd be arrested.

"You see this hoe ass shit," Black angrily said, as the police cars turned the corner after shaking them down. "I know dem' D's sent Chantae over here."

"Hell yeah!" Milton said, "Them niggas are some stool pigeons."

They were unaware of their own guy's transgressions with the law, like Toby and M. Dubb, who both cooperated and testified against Cat Eyes-the D-boy who was charged with the shooting death of Derk's partner, Quick. Cat Eyes was convicted and given one hundred years for the crime.

However, not all of the Brothas transgressions went undetected. Tomato's cooperation with the law was discovered by Roz at her job. Rico didn't bother to go through the proper channels of bringing the rat up on charges. *"Times had changed,"* Rico thought to himself as he and his goon squad drove across the state line with Tomato in the trunk. "We got to nip this problem in the bud" Rico said to the car's other occupants. "Niggas think it's cool to work wit' dem' people these days; like its part of the game or something."

"I don't like this nigga anyway" Lil Law said. Indicating with his right thumb pointed to the back of the car, "bitch ass nigga was up wit' dat' bullshit wit' Wayne back in the day."

"We gotta make an example outta dis' nigga" said Rico. Little did Rico know, his stance might have been too little, too late.

****

Roz's step-daughter Candace was becoming extremely popular amongst the young Brothas. Assisting Roz with the day-to-day operations involved in running the Carpenter street spot, Candace, once a hated enemy, was able to befriend many of the Brothas. She became the new-bust-down of the hood and quickly gained a reputation for her oral skills.

"Man Joe, that bitch Candace gotta nuke on the head" said Wacky, who was sprung on the G-girl. "I see why she was the top bitch over there in Boys Town.

Candace enjoyed her newfound celebrity, as well as the money Rico allowed her to make. But, he was growing tired of her presence, and only allowed her to hang around because of the stain with Gary.

After Gary was killed by some of his own guys, Rico figured that she was no longer a liability. "I'm tired of this broad," Rico said to Roz and Carmen, while lyin' in the bed with both of them. "I don't trust that bitch as far as I can throw her."

"But she's helping us make a lot of money boo," replied Roz.

"Yeah Rico leave that girl alone" added Carmen. "She's harmless."

But Rico knew better than that. *"Bitches like that are never harmless,"* he said to himself as Carmen attempted to please him with her mouth. *"They're just waiting on the perfect opportunity."* Nevertheless, with two naked women in the bed with him, he was in no position to debate.

Despite Candace's popularity, not all of the Brothas held her in high esteem. Rock Island's number one bust down was without a doubt Keda from 78th and Sangamon. Keda was one of the most desirable young women in the hood. She was the epitome of sexy; light brown flawless skin, long silky black hair that always looked as if she just came from a beauty salon, five foot six, one hundred forty-five pounds, with all of the curves in the right places. Rico and a slew of other second generation Brothas pursued Keda endlessly back in the day, to no avail. She just wouldn't deal with street dudes. But now-a-days, it would be hard to find a young Brotha who hadn't slept with the former good girl.

"I remember when a female like Keda wouldn't even give a Brotha the time of day," Toby said, after getting his turn in the train line that consisted of four other Brothas. But after experimenting with heroine and cocaine, her addiction consumed her and the once respectable college bound young woman used what she had to feed her addiction. After getting out of rehab for a heroine addiction, she moved in a building on 78th and Sangamon where the new Cons set up shop with Rico's crack.

She first began smoking crack-laced cigarettes and managed to work and be functional for months, but after losing her job, she began doing "favors" for young Brothas that worked outside of her building. The word of Keda's liberal ways spread like wildfire. Eventually, the Brothas would take over her apartment and Keda's legacy would be cemented in the hood, as the #1 Bust down.

Rico hated going on Sangamon to drop off work. It was always something that enabled him to leave the block in a timely fashion. A dice game, a lecture, hood rats, etc. Keda and a few of her hype girlfriends mingled in front of the building, as Rico, Shorty 'C', and Head pulled up. "Keda! Go get one of the Brothas and tell'em come and get this shit" Rico said out the window. Keda, instructed one of her girlfriends to do the lowly task. "Ay, Rico?" Keda said as she approached the car, "why you ain't got none of this fye ass pussy yet?" Rico looked at Keda with mild contempt. He couldn't believe how far from grace she had fallen. She still had it going on. The crack hadn't destroyed her killer body and looks. She'd definitely trick an unsuspecting lame who wasn't aware of her lifestyle. Nevertheless, Rico knew better. "They haven't invented the type of condom that would allow me to fuck wit' you Keda", he shot back, with a toothy smile.

"Nigga, you just scared I'll have yo' ass sprung" she replied.
"You better ask yo' boy Shorty 'C' about this." Rico just shook his head as Tim ran out to get the work for the rest of the day. Tim was a new Con that Rico pursued to oversee Keda's building. "This shit is some butter Joe" Tim said of the product he received.

"Hypes love this shit." Tim handed Rico the profits from his last pack, and quickly descended back into the building.

"Shorty 'C' you bogus" Rico said teasingly, referring to Keda's comment. "You fuck wit' dat' nasty bitch?"

"Man I was on some thirsty shit one night." Chad responded. "She do got a nuke though, you should see what it do..."

"I ain't going at gun point" Rico argued. "I wouldn't fuck that broad with killa Curt's dick. She'll do anything for a bag. This crack shit is powerful."

"So which one do you think is the most powerful Joe?" Head asked breaking his silence. "Crack or this right here," holding up a large roll of money. Rico pondered the question for a few seconds and then added, "Man it's hard to say, I ain't never did a drug a day in my life, but this other shit got me hooked. I ain't no better than Keda. Just like she'll do anything for that rock, some people will do anything for the money. At the end of the day, we all addicted to something."

CHAPTER 31

Driving down Sangamon, Rico seen a familiar face; it was Silo, the first generation Con who introduced Toby to Rock Island. He seemed to be doing well for himself, standing next to a shiny new range rover, blasting rap music. "Oooh shit!" Rico exclaimed as he exited his car to greet his old Conrad. "Damn Brotha, you hit the lotto or something?" Silo smiled proudly with all his jewelry glistening in the dusk lit sun.
"Na'll man I've been up there in Minnesota getting money with that nigga Lil Ed."
"Lil Ed?" asked Rico surprisingly.
"Hell yeah, Lil Ed" replied Silo. "That Brotha back on his square, he is as clean as a whistle. We doing big thangs up there in Minnesota. We were moving a little something, but we bout' to get into this real estate game and make it happen."
"That's good to hear," said Rico as they made their way to Silo's mother's porch. "What you doing back in da' hood then? You came to stunt on us?"(They both laughed)
"Man you still crazy as hell Rico. It looks like you're doing well for yo' self. I came back to pick up Marco, he just got out."
Rico remembered taking pictures of the Brothas back in the day to send to Marco, who caught a case for Rock Island. "Damn, I forgot all about that nigga." Rico said. "Why didn't he come to the hood when he got out?"
"Man, he ain't fuckin' wit' the Brothas like that no more, especially after what happened to Ed. He been gone so long, he don't even know none of these guys over here. His Rock Island days are over with Rico, we're on some improved shit right now. Some shit that's bigger than the hood, bigger than the organization, and all the shit ya'll see everyday."
"What you talking bout?" asked Rico.
"I'm talking bout life Joe; Rico, you just don't understand. The way the game is now, the odds ain't in our favor. The haters, the police, the snitches, even some of the guys are all forces against you. Real talk, niggas don't give a fuck about Rock Island, none of the Chiefs, even the Old Man himself. You think you on something cuz you got these lil Brothas out here risking their freedom and life selling packs, and the Brothas got you copping from them, and they copping from the Old Man's connect. It's trickled down pimpin'. Niggas at the top pimp the niggas under them."

Rico, Head, Shorty C, all listened as Silo went on philosophizing. "I ain't neva looked at it like that "said Rico.

The conversation with Silo reminded Rico of how disdainful he was becoming with the drug game. And he decided to expedite his plans to go legit. He and Wood started a production company. The goal was to find raw talent in the Chicago area, and turn them into stars.
"I'm telling you Rico, there's a lot of talent in the hood," Wood said, to Rico over the phone. "We just gotta get them off the block and into a studio." As business partners, Wood and Rico created a bond that was slightly different from those in the gang life. All affairs were done with a handshake. "Man if anything happens to me; make sure my peeps are cool" said Rico to his partner.
"Nigga, why you always talking like that Bro? Ain't nothing bout' to happen to you." Nigga, I'm a realist, Rico said sternly. I know it's a possibility that something could happen to anybody in my position."
"Brotha you just paranoid, stop worrying about shit like that" Wood finally retorted.
"I ain't worried, I'm just ready."
****

Meanwhile on 75th and Carpenter....

Lil Ron, Anthony, and Lemelle sat on the stoop taking turns selling rocks to the steady flow of customers. "What's taking Dank so long to come thru wit' dat' weed?" Anthony said blatantly, as he counted out his profits for the day.
"I don't know, but here come that nigga Raulo," Lemelle said "Put that money up, you know that nigga be on bullshit."
Raulo had been M.I.A for a couple of weeks, enjoying the fruits of his labor, provided by the D-boys. After smoking the entire "quarter kilo" of crack with his brother Calvin, and blowing the $5,000 on cheap hood rats, he was back in his usual thirsty mode. The young Bros deemed Raulo Rock Island's *Deebo* (from the movie Friday). "What ya'll lil' niggas on?" He asked trying to sound cool.
"Shit,"
"Nothing,"
"Just chillin," they all replied without making eye contact.
"What dey' hitting for on da' dice," said Raulo as he pulled out a pair of red dice and began shaking them in the palm of his hand?
"Man I ain't on nothing" Anthony began lying, "I ain't got no money, I'm popped Joe."

"Yeah I'm leaking too" followed Lil Ron. But Raulo wasn't about to be put off that easily. "Man ain't ya'll Brothas out here getting money?" He replied, sizing Anthony new gold chain up.
"Damn Brotha! You doin' it hard wit' dis' slick chain lil' homie."
"You wanna sell this?"
Anthony was nervous as Raulo hands began to search for the clamp to unhook it. "I'll hit you wit' something descent for this."
"Unh, unh, na'll I just got it man. I'm straight," Anthony said in an attempt to stand his ground. "Alright then" Raulo finally said. "Let me just try it on, see how I look, for when I go cop one." Anthony didn't have much of a choice, with Raulo already removing the chain from over his head, and putting it around his neck with one solid motion. "Hell yeah, this me right here" Raulo cooed at his reflection in the glass of a parked car, "I like this piece. This me Joe?" He asked, seemingly looking for appeasing responses.
"Um yeah,"
"You cool,"
"That's you," they all responded nervously.
"Aight then, I'll holla. Raulo said as he began walking toward 76th street. Anthony was far from gangsta, but his honor was on the line. "Man Raulo stop playin' Joe," Anthony pleaded as he followed the disgraced Con down the street.
Raulo turned around and grabbed Anthony. "Nigga don't be runnin up on me like you bout to do something! You gave me this muthafuckin chain, you said it was me nigga, you better get the fuck out my face before I beat yo' lil' ass." He promptly threw his victim to the ground.
"Man Joe, I'm just sayin..." Anthony whined pathetically as Lemelle and Lil Ron watched in fear.
When Rico got the news of the incident, he didn't respond. He wanted to distance himself from the soon to be doomed pest. *"I got plans for that nigga"* he thought to himself.

****

The annual end of summer/back to school bash at Mr. G's on 87th Street was a much-anticipated event. Located in the heart of EEl territory, Rock Island knew that they had to attend the party in great numbers. For security purposes, a mandate was put out for all Brothas, to attend. But for most Brothas, they didn't have to be told to attend; they wouldn't have missed it for the world. The Brothas prepared all day, going shopping for new outfits and getting groomed. All of the Sistas, especially the *vogues* planned for the event as well. Vicka, Java, Ruthie, Paulette, and Mary Ann all dressed in their come-get-me outfits. Black and Duke took a count of all the Brothas before they left the set. By ten o'clock p.m., Rock Island's blocks were empty, not a Con or Corner boy in sight. Moosie, Duke, and Jo-Jo drove up to Mr. G's early to stash all of the weapons in various locations across the street from the club. Even though beef with most of the EEls sets had died down some what, history wasn't in favor of the Brothas from Rock Island.

****

The D-boys on 79th Street knew that the Brothas would be attending the party, but they didn't expect the entire hood to vanish. This only meant more customers would come their way.

And Killa Curt was geeking hard, as he discovered his favorite crack dealer Wacky had abandoned his post. "Damn, where deyz guys at?" He said to the group of dirty looking hypes and dope fiends that began lingering on the block. They had been all over Rock Island looking for the poisonous product.

"They got big ba... ba... bags on sssseven, seventy ni... ni... ninth..." A stuttering foul smelling clucker said to the crowd.

Like zombies in search of fresh meat, the starving crack heads all started walking towards 79th where the newly released D-boys were making a nice profit in the absence of competition. D-boys leaders let the newly released D-boys work the block and pocket all of the night's profits as a welcome home gift. "Damn, it's jukin' out here," one D said to another.

"Hell yeah, we getting hypes from everywhere."

The crack heads came so deep that the D's had to make them form lines. "If you want rocks get in that line, if ya'll want some heroine get in this line," the loud voice yelled near the alley of 79th & Carpenter.

"Let me, get-get-get..."

"C'mon man, spit it out" the D-boy said to the stuttering customer who'd traveled several blocks to purchase the elusive work.

"Let me get-get-get... two," he finally said.

"Damn man, yo' nasty ass stank" the D-boy said, as he bent over to get change for a fifty dollar bill, and noticed that the hype had on a pair of brand new *Air Jordans. Hypes don't usually wear brand new Air Jordans.* In the time that it took his mind to process the situation, his fate had been sealed. *"We never forget,"* said the bum, who now held a 9MM with an extended clip in his hand. But the first shot came from the other, as he shot the other D-boy in the face at point blank range, killing him instantly. His Comrade had no time to react, and received the same treatment. Plow! Plow! Plow! The rest of the hypes scattered in different directions, and the assailants got away undetected.

The police were dispatched immediately to canvass the area, under the assumption that Rock Island was responsible for the double homicide. But to their surprise, not one Brotha from the Island graced the streets that night. Only the same lowly hypes and dope fiends could be seen scurrying about.

Derk was forced to work overtime as a result of his captain chewing him out.

"Fuck that," the angry police Captain told Derk and his partner. "You said you had that area under control. There has been at least a dozen shootings and reports of reckless behavior this month; now another double homicide? I don't believe for one second that some bums pulled off and orchestrated a hit like that. I want some answers, and I want somebody in custody for this crime as soon as possible."

Derk was heated. He knew that he was being out smarted. It wasn't a coincidence that the two victims were once suspects for Kenyatta's murder. "This stinks" Derk told his partner, as they both looked over the crime scene photos. "There's only one muthafucka over there that has the capacity to pull this shit off, Rico Love."

CHAPTER 32

Meanwhile: Rico and the rest of Rock Island were at Mr. G's enjoying themselves. The venue was filled to capacity, with the **Terror Town, Duck Town, Foster Park, Fin Town,** and **8-Tray EEls,** as well as the **Machete Ville, fifth City, Trigger Town, Cottage Mob,** and **Rock Island's Brothas.**

"I'm tipping on the numbers," Toby yelled into the ear of Jo-Jo, who had bet that he'd get more girls phone numbers than anyone else. "Nigga, I got these hoez locked in here" Jo-Jo responded as they searched the crowd for their next prize.

Swole, Head, and T.P. were busy dancing with three sexy teenaged looking girls, when the hip-hop classic *"Lay it Down"* by: 8-ball and MJG began blaring through the speakers. The crowd went wild as the classic charged them up. *"Lay it down, lay it down, you hoes lay it down"* the crowd yelled in tune with the song. Some members from Terror Town's Eels opted to add their own lyrics, by replacing the word *hoes* with 4's, in reference to the Corner boys that they were feuding with near their east side set. They raged a war with the 4's after one of them killed a high ranking EEl earlier that summer. But there wasn't any of those East side 4's present, only 4's from Rock Island who felt disrespected.

"Man, we about to go check these niggas temperature over here" Reese from the complex said to Rico.

Rico was in a dark corner bobbing his head up and down to the music, as a pretty dark skinned female grinded her supple back side into his pelvic area. "Man check that shit out, and let me know what's up" responded Rico, who was more interested in getting his groove on than beefin' with a bunch of hard legs. But he knew that it would only be a matter of time before his brief moment of pleasure would be interrupted by duty. "What's yo' name lil' momma?" He said into the gyrating young lady's ear.

"China" she yelled back.

"Where you from?"

"I stay out west in K-Town she replied. " I'm out here with my cousin Tweety."

"I know Tweety," Rico replied. "That's my home girl; just ask her about me, my name is..."

She finished his sentence, "Rico. I heard about you."

"Aight then," Rico said, feeling himself. Just slide me your number and we can make this official like a referee with a whistle." But China's attention was quickly diverted, as she looked over Rico's shoulder. "Um, I think it's something going on over there wit' your guys," she said, noticing a small crowd of Brothas and EEls confronting each other.

"Shit!" Rico said in disgust, anticipating what was about to happen.

Lil Law quickly came to his Chief's side. "These niggas talking crazy 'C', I think you better go over there before it gets out of hand."

Most of the Brothas were still unaware of what was going on as Rico made his way through the crowd of party goers.

Swole was standing between a small group of Rock Island members and Terror Town EEls. He often considered himself as a diplomat, probably because of his past affiliations with almost every gang. "Man Joe, we just tryin' to have fun in this bitch, ain't no need for all that disrespect." But Black wasn't the talking type and he threw the first punch, causing the crowd to part like the Red Sea, with EEls on one side and the Brothahood on the other.

Some of the EEls from other locations were unaware of what the nature of the confusion was about, but instinctively prepared for battle. The small skirmish turned into a full fledged brawl. Luckily, for Rock Island as the security attempted to regain control and the fight spilled unto 87th Street, all of EEls sets weren't seeing eye to eye and chose not to fight. This allowed some of the Brothas to escape and obtain the hidden weapons outside in some nearby bushes.

But **Duck Town** didn't appreciate the action of all the gangs on their set, and promptly called for armed back up, that had to be less than a block away. The crowd scattered as shots rang out from the EEls tech nine. TAT-TAT-TAT-TAT-TAT-TAT-TAT-TAT! The crowd of Cons and 4's were forced to retreat into the blocks of 86th Street, as Duck Town bombarded them with gunfire. The bullets could be heard slicing through the air, illustrating why the eels on 87th street called the hood Duck Town. "What the fuck, they shootin'?" A frustrated Lil Law asked as he ducked behind a parked car to avoid the seemingly stream of bullets. With no shooters in sight and only armed with small handguns, the group decided not to try to out shoot the EEls, opting to save their ammo for what they knew was going to be a long walk home.

Rico, Moosie, Shorty 'C', and Head managed to escape in one of his cars. "Oh shit, that was crazy Jo!" Shorty 'C' said excitedly as he sat in the passenger seat.

"Hell yeah that shit was off the chain" Head agreed. But their excitement quickly turned into nervousness, as they noticed the police car closing in on them from behind.

"Damn man it's Chantae!" Rico said looking into his rear view mirror. "Give me the heat, let me put in da' stash." The police flashed their lights, and Rico pulled over. "Damn, what these bitches pulling me over for? Everybody be cool and don't say shit." The two uniformed officers stepped out of their car with their guns pointed at the gang members. "We have the subject in custody," one of them said into his radio.

They were all taken into custody for questioning. Everybody was released except Rico, who remained in the interview room for three extra hours until his alibi checked out. Good thing for him that he managed to go back and get China's number, who vouched for him being with her the entire night.

Derk didn't know what to do; his reputation was on the line as the brass began losing faith in his abilities. "It's only a matter of time" Derk said, as he exited the interview room. "I swear to God, I'm going to get yo' ass, and put you away for a long time." But Rico was unmoved by the burnt-out officer.

"Yeah, you keep fuckin' around and you gon' end up like your old partner." This enraged Derk, causing him to lunge at Rico violently, while other officers and his Lt. ran into the room to restrain him. "You son-of-a-bitch, cock-sucking-mutha-fucka, I swear you're going to regret that!" Derk had to be carried out of the room, as Rico prepared to exit the station.

Rock Island: A Gangstaz Graveyard   N.U.T.T.Y. "C"

CHAPTER 33

Surprisingly the D-boys didn't retaliate as expected after the murders. Some think it was due to the fact that they didn't know who to retaliate against, the police still had no leads after three weeks, and began focusing their attention on more recent cases. Still Rico wasn't taking any chances. He decided to spend less time in the hood, and focus on his new business ventures. He and Wood were at a studio with a group called "Concrete Mob", laying down tracks, when he noticed a familiar face walk past the studio. He made his way to the next studio where some other local producers were listening to the rapid fire flow of the girl who once gave Rico her virginity, Yoshawn. He couldn't believe his ears as she spit the bars:

I send shots yo' way 4 threw yo' Jersy cuz' I'm super thirsty/I got shit that'll lay down Suge Knight/catch you at a red light, and make it a lead fight/Bullets hit yo' left side and come out yo' dead right/The flo' so tight, straight fo' da' relevance/I'm from a gang infested heritage/If you live to see 21 you considered a veteran/Name me a chick that I ain't better than/My proximity is the epitome of scandalous conspiracies/Knock noodles out yo' dome like yo' name was Kennedy/If I can't steal yo' identity/I'll settle fo' yo' infiniti/Fuck loyalty, money is the only friend to me/Fo' da' right price I'll set up yo 'enemies/Only fuck with heavies, ain't got no time for no soldiers/Break up with that bitch,I'll bring you closure...

"*Wow!*" Rico thought to himself as Yoshawn exited the vocal booth for a break. The two ex-lovers' eyes met and they both smiled. "Damn shawty you gettin' down like that now huh?" Rico said to the transformed Yoshawn, who seemingly shedded her good girl image for a rough rapper persona. He remembered her hardly ever wearing any make up and being smoke free. Now Yoshawn wore shiny lip gloss, heavy foundation, and eye-liner. "I didn't know you had skills like that." She lit a stuffed blunt. "I had good motivation. You turned me out with all your prison poems."

After several minutes of small talk, the two went their separate ways. But Yoshawn would remain on Rico's mind, as he thought about his grandmother's words: *"Rico you are special, you are going to be a leader, people will listen when you talk, and your ability to influence people will become one of your greatest assets."* He was only fifteen when he heard those words but the affect that it had on his adult life was anew. Yoshawn was later signed to a major record deal, and would later become one of the industries hottest female rappers. Despite his influence, he never took credit for Yoshawn's persona; he barely even spoke of her, even after her career took off.

Ironically, his own induldgement into the entertainment business was a little less fruitful. Him and Wood found themselves right back in the drug game where most of their capital was generated. "This shit ain't as easy as I thought would be," Rico said to Wood, as they sat in the dark studio listening to demos. "Yeah, I know but this is what you wanted C. Slow money but fo' sho' money."

"Yeah, it's too slow" Rico said as he remembered all of the obligations he had with his illegal businesses, besides maintaining a life style and an image that was a prerequisite for someone of his status. The drug money enabled him to initiate his own plan to pay for the tuitions of several members that were planning to go to college, and study selected courses. He also helped members financially who were waiting to get certain jobs, so they wouldn't have to be in the streets hustling, risking arrest. He needed the profits from his drug business; he rationalized, for he simply had too many responsibilities.

Back in the hood:

Paulette and the twins were chilling as a car full of D-boys rode down 77th and Aberdeen and spotted them. "Ay fam, ain't that some of them Rock Island bitches right there?"
"Hell yeah, that's some of them hoez. We need to start fucking dem' bitches up too." The D-boys, who had been relatively quiet for several weeks decided that enough was enough; they implemented a plan to really stick it to their enemies. Their reputation was on the line, and in a cut throat city like Chicago a sign of weakness could be critical to your survival. So on a morning in late March, the D's attempted to let the world know that they were still a factor in the streets.

But Rico was already one step ahead of the D-boys, due to his involvement with two D-girls. Tanya and Lil Bit' kept him informed on matters such as security, weapons, and personal information about the everyday operations of the ranking members. Tanya, a short haired, skinny, dark-skinned seventeen year old, was the most useful because her brother and baby's father were both deeply involved with the D-boys. Lil Bit, at nineteen she still had her girlish looks, and bubbly demeanor. Rico first met Lil Bit when she was fifteen at a party. She lived in the heart of D-boy hood and that made it difficult for him to rotate with her. He used her disdainment towards the D-boys to his advantage. He groomed her to join the D-boys organization for the sole purpose of being a spy.

  Jo-Jo, Milton, and a few other Brothas were loitering in front of Anthony's building when Paulette and the twins approached them. Paulette was holding her hand over her left brow. At fifteen, Paulette had proved herself to be one of Rock Island's most respectable Sistas. "Somebody give me a fucking gun!" She said to the group of Brothas who didn't notice the abrasion on her face.

"What's up Sista?" Jo-Jo asked concerned. "What you need a banger fo'?" Paulette showed the group her scar.

"Some pussy ass "Family" muthafuckas jumped on me!"

"Who, some females?" Milton asked.

"Hell nawl, some dudes."

As Paulette explained her incident to the Brothas, more and more people began to assemble on the block, which wasn't too unusual on a Friday. What was unusual was the amount of reported attacks coming in from everyone, including non-members. "I told them I wasn't in a gang" one nerdy looking kid said as he walked by the Brothas shell shocked. "They said I'd better move then."

The grievances just kept coming in as the Brothas tried to figure out what was going on. Hypes weren't even spared. "Dem' muthafuckas crazy over there man, they'n went up side my head and everything, fo' no reason," Killa Curt explained animatedly "Talkin bout' some Rock something, Rock Island, I don't know nothing bout no Rock Island. The only rock I know about is the one I put in my pipe. Now let me get one of dem' thangs man, I just took an ass whoopin' fo' you niggas. I need something to get my mind right."

  "They said that they jumping on anybody that lives in Rock Island territory" Tonya said to Rico over the phone. "They don't have that many guns right now, but some of the D-boys from 100's suppose to loan them some tonight to take care of business on ya'll." Lil Bit sat comfortably next to Rico behind the tinted windows of his car. After giving him an earful of useful information, he dropped her off four blocks away from the hood to avoid detection. "Be careful shorty," Rico said to his spy. "

"Don't worry I'm good," Lil Bit said with a smile as she walked away.

  Rico drove back to 75th and Carpenter, where Shorty C, Head, Toby, Milton, and Jo-Jo awaited a plan. Swole and the Hull Brothers arrived at the same time as Rico. "We got to hit all the schools and pick

up all the Bros." Rico said as soon as he got out of his car. "Make sure everybody get home safe."
Jo-Jo- pulled Rico to the side to speak with him briefly, "Rico, we can handle this, you know you kinda hot right now, why don't you go chill some where and we'll go get the shorties from the schools and handle the business on dem' niggas."

It was a noble suggestion by the Chief-of-Security, but Rico wasn't the type of leader to lead from a distance. He wanted to be in the trenches with his soldiers. Rico had a plan, a plan that if successful would bring a hault to some of his nuisances. "I'm riding wit' ya'll on this one Brotha." Rico replied. He chose to go to Simeon high school to pick up Bubbs, Swan, and Anthony, but as with a lot of things that Rico did, he did so with a double motive. A new recruit by the name of Eddie who was one of Rico's neighbors had been savagely beaten near Simeon, and Simeon was in G-boy territory, a set called Boys Town. "And when we get up here, we gon' see what's up wit' these Boys Town niggas."
"Alright Chief," Jo-Jo responded as different Brothas decided what car was going to what school.
"Shorty 'C', c'mon man, you ridin' wit' me", Rico said. "You got yo heat?"
Shorty 'C' looked offended that someone would even ask him that question. "No doubt nigga, never leave home without it" he said as he brandished a large 44 magnum.
"Damn nigga, what the hell you finna' do wit' dat'?" Head jokingly asked as Shorty 'C' got in the car.
"Dis' fo' dem' big niggas that get out they body, ya' feel me?"
They made it to Simeon fifteen minutes later, just as school was letting out, hoping to quickly spot one of their guys. Instead they only saw G-boys and EEls. "Man, these niggas better c'mon, before we have to put some lead in one of these niggas," Shorty 'C' said anxiously.
Anthony spotted Rico's car and made his way towards Vincennes Street, where the Sedan was parked. "Where dem' niggas at that jumped on Eddie?" Rico yelled from the driver's side window.
"They round here somewhere" Anthony said, as he jumped in the back seat. Anthony wasn't in favor of doing any reckless acts, but he didn't have much of a choice once he got in the car with his guys.

Milton, Jo-Jo, and other Brothas followed in their car. "We can ride thru there right now, they hood only a block away," Head suggested. The car drove to look for Ops near Simeon high school to retaliate on the g-boys that attacked a member. Suddenly they found

themselves in the heart of Boys Town; one of the south sides's most feared G-boy sets.
"Stop the car! Stop the car" Shorty 'C' exclaimed, as he spotted some of his rivals. He jumped out of the car as if it were on fire. **BOOM! BOOM! BOOM! BOOM!** "Rock Island bitch!" Shorty 'C' screamed at the top of his lungs. "I think I got one of dem' niggas."
"Let's get the fuck outta here" Jo-Jo yelled from the car, as he pulled up on the side of Rico's car. The group was headed back to their home turf when Rico informed them of his plan. "Fuck this shit, Joe them niggas talking bout' they finna' snap out tonight, we bout' to beat dem' to the punch."
"Yeah, and we can catch one of dem' niggas that jumped on Paulette" Shorty 'C' added. Anthony wanted so bad to tell Rico to drop him off at home, but he didn't want to appear soft.
The two vehicles drove straight west down 79th Street, where they met up with Swole and the Hull Brothas.
"Man Joe, we bout' to ride on these niggas" one of the Brothas said from inside their mini-van.
"Tell the Brothas we're not having goal today, clear the hood, we're on code yellow," Rico said. "Get at the D-boys on 79th, and then clear the hood."
"Alright Brotha, some of the guys are on their way to get down now" Toby said. **POP! POP! POP! POP! BAM! BAM! BAM!** The sounds of the Brothas gun fire could be heard several blocks away. "That's the Brothas, let's go!" Rico said. As the cars filled with Rock Island gang members and they approached 79th and Racine, the chaos was obvious. Some Brothas were on foot chasing the "Family" members, others were shooting at the homes of suspected oppositions. Nearly fifty Cons and 4 Corner boys flooded 79th. One of the Ops made the critical error of trying to detour down 78th and Aberdeen. Rico arrived just as some of the Brothas were administering a severe assault on the young D-boy. "What the fuck are they doing?" He asked noticing the large crowd of Brothas in the gang way throwing punches and kicks. He thought they were fighting a group of oppositions the way that they were packed between the houses. His instincts told him to aid and assist his guys, and before he knew it, he was in the middle of the crowd swinging away. But there was only one victim, and Rico knew it didn't take ten guys to beat one, and was about to express his frustration when, **BLAM! BLAM! BLAM!** Three shots were fired. **BLAM! BLAM! BLAM!** Three more shots were fired.

Rock Island: A Gangstaz Graveyard   N.U.T.T.Y. "C"

CHAPTER 34
(THE WRATH…)

Meanwhile on 76th street, Raulo was on his way to Carpenter, to rob another one of the money getting Brothas. But nobody seemed to be out. The Island seemed to be deserted. *"Where da' hell everybody at?"* Raulo wondered as he searched the blocks for vulnerable prey. But in an eerie twist of fate, Raulo found himself being in the unfamiliar role of the prey himself. The Chevy Caprice Classic that rolled down on 76th street lurked in the distance as its occupants contemplated the mission. As they neared Raulo's location, they jumped out and opened fire on the unsuspecting menace. **BLAM! BLAM! BLAM!** Raulo managed to run in an alley near his home where he collapsed.

Even though Rico was growing weary of the life he once swore allegiance to, he still possessed a distorted rationale, which in turn made it easy for him to approve of the hit on Raulo, a once highly respected Brotha that he looked up to. The evacuation made it easy for the young would be killers on 74th to come handle what Rico said was important nation business.

T.P. was at home when he heard the shootings and decided to go outside and investigate. As he got to 77th, he saw Rico's car speeding down Aberdeen and flagged him down. When he got in the car he knew something had gone down. "What da' hell going on?" T.P. asked the group of Brothas that were still breathing heavy from their escape. Shorty 'C' was the first to break down the entire days events. "We been mashing on niggas all day!" Shorty 'C' bragged. "And I think one of dem' niggas just got changed."
"We need to get outta' the hood," Rico interrupted. "We all should split up, Shorty 'C' I'm taking you and Anthony home, ya'll get rid of the guns just in case one of dem' dudes did get changed."

Rico planned on going to Evergreen Plaza and doing some shopping, and then high tail it to one of his suburban apartments. "I'm rolling wit' ya'll", T.P. said. It's my birthday so we might as well kick it." Head agreed to stay with his friends too.
"Aight then" Rico said, "I gotta change cars, just in case somebody put out a description of my shit."
He quickly drove to Roz's house and switched cars. But the news of the shootings had already mobilized Derk and his squad of Rock Island haters were already on the case. Rico's arrival on the block played right into the hands of the police, who had set up a perimeter around the

area. They didn't make it to the corner before the unmarked cars cut them off ambush style. Rico recognized Derk's gritty face right away as the two made eye contact. "Don't nobody say shit" Rico ordered. "They don't have anything on us." Derk's mouth seemed to salivate as Head, T.P., and Rico were placed in cuffs. "Let me escort this one" Derk said in his pseudo professional voice, as he grabbed Rico by the arm.

As Rico sat quietly in the back of Derk's car, he looked at the scenery that he passed every day.

"Yeah get a good look at your old neighborhood" Derk said, sarcastically."Cuz it'll probably be the last time you'll ever see it again."

Usually Rico would have gladly taken Derk's comment as an open invitation to respond in one of his infamous sarcastic retorts. But he remained silent, which even surprised Derk.

He knew that he had Rico and his gang this time, but somehow it didn't quite give him the satisfaction that he thought it would. As he looked at Rico through his rear view mirror, he couldn't help but feel a sense of admiration for the young man that he'd practically seen grow up in the streets. Rico was one of the smartest criminals he had ever met, and Derk wondered what kind of life he would've had if he hadn't chose the streets.

Rico couldn't help but feel a sense of irony as he viewed 79th Street from the back seat of the unmarked police car. It had been 10 years prior when he first witnessed a murder committed by his would be Brethren on 79th street. The act of violence solidified his introduction to the street life. And now as fate would have it; the same block would see another victim of a senseless murder by the hands of Rico's peers, only this time Rico wouldn't be making a swift detour home.

Back at the station:

All of the suspects were separated. Derk let homicide take over the investigation; he didn't want to interfere with the case on Rico. He knew that Rico wouldn't talk, but unbeknownst to Rico, Derk held the trump card. And unfortunately that trump card was sitting right in the next interview room making a seasoned statement against Rico, Head, and Shorty 'C'. Derk allowed the State's Attorney to interview his informant. Although he wasn't present at the scene of the incident, he gave his account of how they bragged about taking care of business on an opposition on 78th and Aberdeen.

Rico knew his friend hadn't had much experience with jail, but figured that Head would be fine, and only offered a minimum response. "We gon' be aight Brotha, just get yo' mind right, this ain't the place to be distracted."
After being processed Rico and Head received the good news that they were being housed in division nine, division nine was a maximum security part of the jail, well known for being violent and unstable. But Head was just content that he didn't get separated from his best friend. Rico was happy that he was being housed in Division nine for other reasons.

Rico's imprisonment was immediately noticeable in the hood, as the remaining elites attempted to maintain order. Toby, Milton, and the Hull brothers tried to keep the morale of the Brothas in tact. Toby positioned himself on Sangamon, Milton on 76th, and the Hull Brothers in the complex. Rumors placed Bo-Bo back on his crack horse. The weekly goals weren't being held, and all of the Nation funds dried up. Some excitement did surround the releases of Brothas such as Rio, Mitch, Myron, and Parish. Despite coming home with good intentions to get the hood in order, with the exception of Mitch, none of them possessed the organizational fortitude that Rico had. Personal wealth soon trumped any attempts to unify and restructure Rock Island.

Mitch did try to step up and get things together, but his efforts were met with little fan fare. His tactics were viewed as old fashion, and the elites did not back him. Instead they galvanized themselves around Brothas like Myron, Parish, and Rio, who had all the drugs and money. The despondency of Mitch and other Brothas began to divide the once tight knit organization. While the moneymakers were idolized and worshipped, other ranking members became novelty elites.

Some Brothas did maintain the fruitful teachings of Rico. "I'm telling you C, shit crazy out here Rico," Lil Law said on a phone call to his mentor. "Shit just ain't right. All dem' old niggas is just competing with each other, trying to see who can floss the hardest."
Rico knew that most of Rock Island's problems couldn't be solved with him sitting in jail, but he tried to at least appear to be in charge. "Look man, let my niggas know that I'm bout' to beat this shit and come home. Until then I want you to go on 74th and fuck wit dem Brothas over there, they could use a Brotha like yourself. Let Dank know to hold 75th down and he's got my support on anything."

"Alright 'C', but there is alot of crazy shit happening in the hood, that nigga Raulo didn't die from his ordeal, and now he's going around saying that the Brothas had something to do wit' it. Myron and'nem beat his ass real good the other day on Sangamon." Rico

exhaled deeply and shook his head as Lil Law put him in tune with the current events of the hood.
"You straight in nere' right?" Lil Law asked.
"Yeah, I'm straight my nigga, I'm super cool."
    Indeed Rico was straight in the county, largely due to Carmen supplying him with most of the comforts of home, like cell phones, drugs to sell, fast food, and even an occasional sexual encounter.In addition to that, with his elite status, he'd now be recognized by his peers and even depended upon to call shots. Carmen became his liaison to Roz and Wood, who kept his 77th street enterprise going to help pay for his legal fees.
    Wood kept his word and remained loyal by supplying Roz with what she needed to take care of his business. Candace assisted her in selling the product, and continued to be a bust down favorite for the Brothas.
    Parish was sitting in his truck getting some lip service when he noticed the stocky built Brotha with a lot of jewelry dip into Roz's building. "Who dat' nigga driving that Yukon?" Parish asked.
"Oh, that's Wood" Candace replied. She went on to tell Parish how Wood supplied them with the product necessary to keep the spot running.
"That nigga got it like that hunh?" Candace knew a fellow snake when she seen one.
"Hell yeah, that nigga holding."
Parish rubbed his chin for a moment as if he was in a semi-deep thought. "You gon' have to plug me wit' dude, I need a good connect." Candace knew the game all too well, and she knew that Parish didn't need a connect, but agreed under one condition, "you gon' have to cut me in!"

CHAPTER 35

Meanwhile at the police station, one of Derk's informants led him to Swole, in connection with Rico and the others. "I'm telling you sir, you have me mixed up with somebody else," Swole said to the homicide detective.
"Why would someone lie on you?" The black, Montell Williams looking detective asked harshly. "Your name is Tony ain't it? You fit the description. You caught; you might as well tell us everything."
Tony didn't want to go down for a murder, especially one he didn't commit. Rico, Head, and Shorty 'C' had been locked up for several months; Swole wondered how they could be just now coming to get him. "Um, I'm not the only Tony in the hood," he said to the detective. An hour later, Rock Island member and cousin of Swole, Anthony was put in the holding cell. Anthony was just as scared as his cousin. "Man Joe, what's dis' shit about a murder?" Anthony asked nervously.
Tony didn't expect to see his cousin in the same holding cell and his questioning caught him off guard. "How tha' fuck these people know my name and where I stay at?"
Tony knew that he couldn't tell his cousin that he provided them with that information. "Man, it must be Rico and nem' in the county running dey' mouth. They probably are trying to take us down with them."
"Why would they do something like that?" Anthony asked.
"I don't know, but we gotta come from under this, cuz I can't do no time fo' no bull shit." Swole replied. Swole then convinced his cousin to cooperate with the detective's and the State's Attorney. "Just follow my lead, and we should be outta this bitch. We might as well put all this shit on Rico and nem', cuz dem niggas aint neva coming home anyway."
They both made matching statements giving the details of the day of the crime. Unfortunately, for them, they didn't realize that in giving their statements they implicated themselves as accessories to the crime. So instead of being released, they were charged as co-conspirators.
Back in Cook County Jail:
Carmen pulled some strings to get Head and Rico in the same cell.
"I can't believe they popped Ant and Swole for this pussy ass shit." Head said from the top bunk, as Rico penned one of his jailhouse poems on the bottom bunk.

"Yeah, I wonder how they got knocked. Maybe somebody told on them, you know how that nigga Swole be running his mouth around dem hoes."

"I don't know Brotha, but something ain't right." Rico said as he put the finishing touches on his written expressions. "Check this out," Rico said handing the piece of paper up to Head.

"Damn Joe," Head said after reading the words on the paper. "I wish I had skills like this. You need to let me copy this and send it to my girl."

"Gon' head my nigga, Rico said, feeling satisfied.

"Man Rico, you got skills my nigga, this ain't no place for you."

"Yeah, I know this ain't no place for none of us. Man, I just want to say that I'm sorry for getting you in this mess. I feel like it's my fault. I could've left and let the Brothas gon' and do they thang."

"Man, don't start getting all soft on me now nigga, I know I didn't join the boy scouts when I got into this shit. But when I started fuckin' wit' you, my whole mind set changed. You changed the game Rico, and you made me proud to be one of the guys. That's why I stuck by your side all of this time. You one of the realest and smartest niggas I know, but you got one flaw; you give a fuck about niggas that don't give a fuck about you. Now look at you."

"Its all part of the game Head," Rico said. "You know how this shit goes."

"Hell nawl!" Head shot back. "What part of the game is this? We stuck in this bitch for a bogus 9-1 and you think niggas give a fuck. One of them niggas probably ran their mouth to get us in this position. And now we got two more potential witnesses against us. C'mon man, wake up Brotha, it's a wrap, it's over Rico. Shit'll never go back to how it was. I waited by your side cuz I thought that you would've been out tha game by now. I don't love this shit like you do and I never really understood why you did. I'm not mad about catching this case with you nigga; I would've died for you, so doing this time ain't nothing. I just want you to know that it's over." Head's words haunted Rico for the rest of the night.

The next morning Rico called for an outside investigation on Rock Island to see if any members were involved with cooperating with the police. Although T.P.'s name came up, nothing was found by the Brothas that could link him to snitching. Rico's attorney proved to be a little bit more resourceful in obtaining the statements from Anthony and Swole, whom both were released with low bonds.

"Those niggas bogus!" Rico yelled into the phone that had Myron on the other line. "I want them niggas dealt wit!" Myron, Rock Island's new acting Chief agreed to handle it. Myron was extremely close to Swole and Anthony and violating them weren't on his list of priorities. Some suspect said that Anthony paid Myron off, which would've made sense for the young hustler. The 75th and Carpenter spot had become extremely lucrative and even while out on bond, Anthony continued to get money.

Shorty 'C' and Rico went to trial, where several D-boys testified that Rico's car was involved in the crime. Although no one identified any of the defendants as a shooter, T.P.'s statement convinced the judge that Rico was accountable for the death of the victim. Rico was recognized as the head of a criminal organization and was sentenced to serve 45years in prison. Shorty 'C' was sentenced to serve thirty years.

Head pled guilty to a lesser charge and was sentenced to serve twelve years. Anthony and Swole remained out on bond.

Shortly after Rico's conviction, Wood was robbed in front of Roz's house at gunpoint for a large sum of cocaine and money. It turned out to be Nation work and the Old Man was furious. Although Rico had been gone for quite some time, the fact that this robbery occurred in front of his girl's house made him liable. If the Brothahood suspected that, he had anything to do with the stick up, his life would be in danger in prison. Roz knew that she'd also be targeted and quickly arranged a visit with the Old Man, in attempt to do some damage control. With Candace missing in action, Roz knew that Rico's suspicions were probably accurate. She had no choice but to inform the Old Man about her stepdaughter's potential role in the robbery. Because of all of the non-violent talk that the Old Man preached to some of his followers, it would seem that a peaceful solution would be construed from the ordeal. Candace would find out just how much the contradictions of the Old Man would cost her, after being caught and kidnapped by the Brothas. Ironically, she suffered the same exact fate as her baby's father, but not before giving up her accomplice.

The committee members called an emergency goal with Rock Island elites. Myron was told to attend. He didn't know what to expect, but he knew one thing was for sure. He wasn't going to give up his Brotha.

"We heard that they call him Parish," Timbo from the 100's said to Myron who felt like he was being questioned by a congressional committee, rather than some mid level gang elites. We know that he a

219

4-Cornerboy from your hood, so by you being in charge over there we holdin' you responsible.

We want you to produce either this Brotha or the Nation work in one week.

"Do you know who he is?" asked Tank from 75th and Cottage Grove. "Na'll," Myron lied. I'll find out and get back to you. Myron left the meeting with no intentions on conforming to either of the Brothas demands. In fact, he already reaped benefits from the robbery. "Fuck that shit," Myron, told one Brotha. "If they want that shit, they gon' have to come get it like Tyson got his title."

CHAPTER 36

"Baby I can't do this anymore," Roz said to Rico as they sat in the visiting room of Menard Correctional maximum-security prison. I'm scared for my children. Your friends have abandoned the block and the D-boys are taking over. I miss you, but I'm not getting any younger. If you don't get out on appeal, you'll have to do twenty years straight."

Roz's words seemed to fade and become indistinguishable as Rico let his mind wonder: *This punk bitch, after all, I've done for her, she about to break bad on me. I should just reach over this table and slap the taste outta her mouth.*

"Rico, Rico, Rico," are you listening to me?"

"Um, yeah...yeah... I heard everything you said. And usually I'll have something to say, but what can I say?"

"I guess you can tell me how you feel."

"Roz, with me telling you how I feel right now, would it change the outcome?"

Roz just sat there quietly with tears in her eyes.

"Rico, I'm so sorry baby... I just need to move on with my life." Although life in prison proved to be difficult for Rico, especially without his main woman, he adjusted to the volatile environment. The gang-bangin', drugs, violence, and turmoil had not eluded him in his incarceration. When Mitch came down on a parole violation, he was happy to see his old friend. Despite his disenchantment with Rock Island, he knew that he and Mitch shared a common grievance.

"That bitch ass nigga T.P. got down on us," Rico told Mitch as they walked the yard. "They used his statement against us."

"Don't even trip I got that nigga when I get back out," Mitch said. Mitch was released three weeks later. He caught T.P. exiting a local liquor store and proceeded to open fire with a semi-automatic handgun, a shoot-out ensued, and when the smoke cleared, T.P. emerged unscratched. Unfortunately, the same could not be said for the helpless little girl who caught one of the stray bullets in the chest. Mitch was arrested and charged with murder, T.P. remained free, due largely to his testimony against Mitch.

In the months to come things would only get worst for Rock Island, Anthony was shot in the head as he exited his best friend's apartment. The next day Corner boy Travis was ambushed on 76th and Racine, and shot thirteen times; his Kevlar vest did little to protect him from the assault. Swole was found guilty after a long trial. His statements proved to do more harm than help. He was sentenced to thirty years, and entered protective custody once he reached Menard penitentiary. Tim, one of the 78th and Sangamon kids Rico recruited just before Rico left was killed in a shoot out with the Black EEls. A young Corner boy name Cisco was murdered on 78th and Morgan by the D-Boys.

A couple of months later, Myron, his brother Shawn, and (Corner boy) Antoine was found dead in Myron's truck near Boys Town, all shot to death. Myron's body appeared to have been tortured before his untimely death. The triple murder baffled the Brothas and rumors of a motive were on the tongues of everyone. Some believed that Shawn was not the intended target, and the killers executed Myron's wrong brother. And to further add to the mystery, two weeks after the triple murder, two more Brothas were found in a car trunk shot to death, only three blocks from where Myron's truck was found.

Art and Ne-Ne's death seemed to have further added to the confusion and anxiety that Rock Island endured in the two years of Rico's absence. The rumors continued amid the uncertainty. Parish would go on to bury one of the biggest mysteries in his neighborhood's history with his older brothers Shawn and Myron. Their murders remain unsolved. Oppositions dubbed R.I., "Tha' Graveyard", as more and more Brothas met their untimely fate.

Rico sat on his small bed in the maximum-security prison reading a letter from one of his last loyalist, Dank, who often kept him in tune with everything concerning the hood. Dank managed to stay clear of a lot of nonsense that would put him in the same position as his mentor. But he often struggled writing Rico; it seemed that he never had any good news. This letter contained another obituary. Lil Law shot and killed on his birthday. As he looked down at his "Rock Island" tattoo, he cracked a nervous smile; he remembered what he once told Head: *"This is just part of the game."* He went to his desk and began writing. He dedicated his piece to all people like Dank, who never been to prison, and wondered what his life was like. He called it KAOS.

Enter my world of KAOS, full of crooks, murders and playas, livin' a forced life that some crooked judge gave us, trapped in cages, with different races, and different ages, no misdemeanors only felony cases. What could be worst than being stuck in the concrete hearse, praying for lady freedom but she only flirts, leaving you hurt. Most of my foes carry knives, and you'll never know what's on their minds, can't get caught slipping, got to stay in line, cuz it could go up at anytime. I used to pray to God to erase the fears or embrace my peers, but sometimes I think he'd be scared to show his face up in here. I seen a nigga get murdered and another get raped last year and my momma thinks that her baby is safe up in here. Amongst this KAOS, and hostile situations, my life's been on the line on many occasions, only if you been incarcerated, you can feel what I'm saying, if not there's only one way to explain it; IT'S KAOS!

Virginia and the rest of his family supported Rico, after he seemingly lost everything. They still encouraged him to change his life despite his circumstances. "It's never too late to change," Virginia would say in her conversations to her weary son.
"God would never forgive me" he responded over the phone. "I've done too much damage. I've personally ruined the lives of countless others. This is where I belong. My whole life has led me to this day, this moment, and what is to come."
"You are talking crazy Rico, what's going on in there? You must first forgive yourself son. Ask God to forgive you, and then you can atone for your actions." The days of Virginia trying to promote her own ideologies towards her son were long over as he hung up the phone, he looked around at his surroundings and back to the Kaos;

They wanna know what It's like in here, if these police treat us right in here, do I know Brothas wit life in here? They asking me is it real in here, do we kill in here,
Deep down what do I feel in here? Who do we trust in here, do niggas really get fucked in here, do the gun towers really bust in here? Niggas get stuffed in here, are we able to show the love in here, why do they call us bugs in here? What makes us tick in here? We all sick in here, inmates or convicts in here. They ask me do we feel pain in here, do we bang in here, are we still down with our gangs in here? Subconsciously awake in here, anticipating out dates in here. All the snakes in here, the real niggas and the fakes in here; they wondering do we ever find time to pray in here, do our minds ever wonder away in here? I tell'em, everyday in here. Do we plot suicide in here, and if I'm so smart then why am I in here? I guess I only have one reply in here... It's KAOS...

After Wood was robbed in Rock Island, he distanced himself from Rico, and continued his production company endeavor. Rico wasn't too perturbed by his actions and chalked it up as one of the elements of his incarceration. "I can't believe this broad got a block on her phone!" Rico exclaimed after trying to call a female friend. "Everybody got blocks on they shit. I was taking care of these muthafuckas."

You'll neva understand what it's like, till you're locked up for some years of yo' life, to lose everything, your kids and your wife.
Friends will deceive you; family will leave you, to fend for yourself amongst these forces of evil.
And that girl you had, she'll ride for a minute, but once her peoples get in the business, you're done, you're finished.
They'll start planting seeds about the time she spends, and every dime she sends as if messing with you is a crime to them.
Your money orders will go from a hundred down to twenty, and years from that, you're lucky if yo' ass get any, when you was in the world it seemed like the cash was plenty, but when you locked up you gotta kiss ass for pennies.
You're letters get no response, you mad as ever..
you thinkin; "son of a bitch" this shit won't last forever
you muthafuckaz can't treat me like trash forever, and now that I caught this case for yall you can't appreciate me standing tall….
 Can't even get you to except a collect call
While I'm stuck in here wit' these rats they ready to snitch (to the police) right in yo face'n shyt fruits in tight clothes wearing makeup and shyt
You can barely breathe or escape in this bitch!
And the C/O's walk around here with their personal grudges,
 Actin like they don't like us, writing bogus tickets for nothing when they really mad at their wife or their husband or whoever they fuckin; but they come to work and take it out on us,
And throw our ass in seg for months
 Where the tact police wear orange jump suits, and we call em' the "orange crush" cuz if you get out of pocket, they'll throw you in cuffs and leave you wit' some decent bruises and bumps, and if that aint enough…They'll fuck wit' cha' for no reason, spray you on the face with chemicals to fuck wit' yo' breathin'
That's why I grabbed the broom and began slingin' and even though my eyes were burning and my nose was bleedin' I heard my peers yellin' "whatever you do nigga don't stop swinging", Becuz at the end of the day this is our home, even if we gotta do this time alone. In this Kaos and hostile situation, my life's been on the line on many

occasions, only if you've been incarcerated you can you feel what I'm sayin', if not then I'm tired of explainin', it's just…….. KAOS

The Chaos of prison was taking its toll on the strong willed thug. For his disciplinary behavior, he was ordered to take anger management classes, which allowed him to see a Psychologist twice a month. While some inmates frowned at the idea of getting any mental health assistance, Rico relished the therapy. He looked forward to his regular visits to the prison psychologist for a variety of reasons. The time out of his cell provided temporary relief from Chaos. The psychologist, Ms. Burns small office often provided her inmate patients with a homely atmosphere, and the fact that she wasn't bad on the eyes didn't hurt either. The forty something year old white suburbanite interviewed and counseled some of the state's most dangerous criminals. She had been seeing Rico for six months, trying to treat him for cognitive behavior modification. Rico had really opened up to her, but she found it challenging to provide adequate therapy to many inmates like Rico. After hearing some of Rico's confessions, she questioned her qualifications.

"Mr. Love, I find your life to be very interesting, and I'm not saying that's good or bad, I'm just curious as to the complexity of your life style. Most people in here believe that they were forced into the "street life," but it seems that this case boils down to a matter of choice. Regardless of what you've done, where you come from, or what the results of your choices are, you cannot progress if you remain in the past mentally. How do you feel about the choices you've made?"

Rico sat in the comfortable chair searching for an answer, but flashes of Ms. Burns naked body stained his brain. He reached over, grabbed the attractive psychologist by the arm, and began kissing her. She didn't resist as he unbuttoned her blouse and removed her ample breast from her bra. Her perfume intoxicated him as he removed her panties from underneath her skirt. He hadn't been with a woman in years and his hardness throbbed as it entered her. *"MM, Oh, Mr. Love... Mr. Love... Oh Mr. Love... Mr. Love...* I asked you a question," she asked sitting behind her desk, bringing Rico back to reality.

"Oh, um, I don't really feel anything."

"You must feel something Mr. Love."

"I write most of my feelings down," he confessed.

"That's good, keep writing your feelings down and don't let the past dictate the way you view the future. Despite your situation Mr. Love, you still have a choice."

Days after his session with Ms. Burns, Rico received the news that Barbra had lost her long battle with cancer. He sat in the cell starring at the brick wall for hours, paralyzed with grief unable to shed a tear due to the chaos that surrounded him. So he pondered Ms. Burns last session, mulling over the last conversation he had with his mother. After awhile, he made up his mind. He got down on his knees and prayed: *"God, please forgive me, I'm so sorry for what I've done and where my life has taken me. I know that I don't deserve your mercy, but I seek it with a hardened heart."* After praying, Rico thought about the choice that he was about to make, and sat at his small desk to the only thing that provided him relief- he wrote. The writing tablet was nearly full, but it didn't matter to Rico, in fact, it was quite fitting since it was his last words.

Consumed, and I assume I will eventually resume. Where is God? Because I need him, everything is fleeting, and my heart is bleeding. All of this is overwhelming; the outcome looks grim. How can I look forward to a future so dim? With a past that was suppose to be so bright, and a present illuminated by black lights? Roads built by blind men who cannot see past your needs, motivated by the desires of your heart's pride and greed. Rejected by the faithful and embraced by the infidels, slowly emotionlessly, I feel my eyes swell. I was taught by the ignorant and shunned by the wise, while some try to convince me that there's hope by saying that "God stores every tear ever cried." But the rivers that flow from this soul are icy cold, creating icy roads, while dealing with intimate foes. Demons that have known me from birth call me by my earthy name leaving my will chained and my heart maimed. Pieces of my life lay tattered and scattered, while my mind feels beaten and battered. Disturbed by a whirlwind of turmoil, dancing before my eyes, like a gang of fall leaves... dead... dying. Resurrected each day to torment me again with guilt and shame no escaping this stigma, permanently engraved in my brain. Like thirty lashes to flesh, welts and wounds horrific to sight, painful to touch, infected, swollen, and ready to bust. Is there no healing from damaged emotions?
Is there no silence to the noise as I go thru the motions?
I'm feeling vexed, knowing I was destined to be great, but failed the test, I'm sorry everybody, I'm tired, I need a rest...

After re-reading what he wrote, he imagined what his funeral would look like. *"I bet everybody gon' be there"* he thought. A sudden overwhelming feeling invaded his body, and his thoughts were interrupted as the guard called his name. "Love, you in there?" He asked not bothering to look up from the pile of mail in his hand. "Um, yeah that's me," Rico said as he repeated his prison i.d. number (a requirement for all inmates upon receiving mail). He wasn't expecting any mail and he hoped the guard hadn't noticed the torn sheets that lay across the small bed. Receiving mail usually would be a highlight of a prisoner's day, but Rico's mind was already somewhere else. He didn't recognize the senders name on the envelope at first but he recognized the photo right away.

Cherry was only seventeen when he approached her with a proposition; a proposition that would lead her to going to college. For the first time in years, Rico cried as he read her letter.

Dear Rico,
I hope you remember me. I'm sorry about not getting up with you sooner. I followed your case on the news and the newspapers. I know it's been a long time since you took me off the streets and paid my tuition for me to go to college. At first, I didn't understand why out of all the Sistas you chose me. I have to admit I was too busy having fun to care. You told me that one day I'd thank you, and I guess that day has come. More importantly, I realize why you chose me to attend college. Not only did you potentially save my life, I don't think I would've graduated law school without your vision. But that was what was so special about you, your ability to make people believe. And for that reason, I'm here to let you know that I still believe, I believe in your vision, and I still believe in you. I know that many may have probably given up on you, but you once told me that "loyalty endures all," and my loyalty has not faltered. Like I said, I just finished law school, and I'm about to take the bar exam. I feel like I'm in a great position to help you and some of the other Brothas. I owe you my life, so allow me to help you get yours back. The choice is yours. Let me know how to proceed.

The letter remained on the bunk, as Rico mulled over the choices that were now before him. This would turn out to be the biggest choice of his life. He looked at his tablet, turned the page to the last words he had written and scribbled down one more line, took a deep breath and made his choice.

THE END

Rock Island: A Gangstaz Graveyard   N.U.T.T.Y. "C"

THANKYOUS/ACKNOWLEDGEMENTS

My Mother- Thank you for your unconditional love and support through the ups and down, especially the downs. I don't know where I'd be without you. You are and will forever be my hero.
My Brothers and Sisters: **Tony (R.I.P), Ramon, Kevin, my Diva Sister Cherry, and Dre'**
My Lovely Nieces: **Cherry-Leah** and **Alexa Rae'** (who would've killed me if I didn't mention her name).
My Nephews: **Eric** and **Damian**, you've lived in my shadows long enough, it's time to learn from my mistakes and become the men God intended *you* to be.
Tori A. Starks for introducing me to Bookstand Publishing, "Good lookin' out, Big Homie!"

SPECIAL ACKNOWLEDGEMENTS

Erika my first and still favorite niece and **Cecelia** my big head sister. Without you this book would have never gotten published. You both worked tirelessly and dedicated a large portion of your life to see this in print. Thank you for all the hard work; my success is your success.
THA REAL ROCK ISLAND: "For you my Brothas, my love began at birth......"(you know the rest)! I could've written my first book about anything or anyplace. But I wanted to tell a story about a neighborhood many of ya'll love and call home. To the masses this book is just entertainment, but it is my hope that this book provides a source of inspiration for those of you who can read between the lines.

TO ALL THE BROS ON LOCKDOWN: **Patrick, Rio, Jo-Jo, Yella**(Mitch) and **Nelson**. Keep your head up and remember to serve your time constructively.

KC and **Bo:** ya'll the last of a dyin' breed, therefore change is possible through ya'll.
Lil' Mikey D: I could've made this entire book about you and your impact on the hood. **Lil' Ed Max, Lil' George, Marco, Silo, Parish, Rodney, Bo-Bo, Tommy Joe, Calvin, Vick, Yogi, Teda, feather, Toby, Wayne, Tarche, Antwoine, Latwoine, Teeny, Mario(4), Sony, Co-Co, T.y.** and **Others** made it possible for most of ya'll to walk down 76th Street, remember that!

EVERYBODY FROM DA COMPLEX: **Reese, Lil'Walter, Ronald, Tay, Lil' Willie, Marcus** and all the new **Lil' Bros.** (I can't think of ya'll names right now).
Tiffany, Stephany, Angela, Shamone, Sheila and of course **The O.G. Tasha**, thanx for showin' the hood "U ain't gotta be a bust down 2 B down."

OTHER BROS: **Dolla Bill, Lil' Michael** & **Wacky**: They may have taken yo' legs but nobody can take yo' heart. **Milton-** I still remember the night you got shot in the hand…**Rashaad, Drew, John-John, Cody, Lil' Kenny, Black, Duke, Wavery, Qualo, Juan, Lil'Ron, D.J., Q.P., Joe, Toby….everybody** on **Sangamon, Peoria** and **74th** & **Racine**

SISTAS: **Boonie, Keisha, Gina, Erica, Samantha, The twins, Bubba, Java, Ruthie, Mary Ann,** even you **Paulette**. (I always honored ya'll)

CRUCIAL ACKNOWLEDGEMENTS:

Chad and Yatta: Don't allow time and distance to erode the bond we established back in the day. This aint got nothing to do with the hood, and everything to do with friendship. Ya'll still my niggas!!!

Aaron Rich(Red).. Tha Islands first success story. Thanx for inspiring me, now it's time to inspire others.
Kirby, Brice, Lamell, & Justin: R.I's legit ballers. Continue to show **Da Bros** that we don't have to get money in the street to eat.

Everybody that ever sent me a money order, accepted a call, sent a letter of support, pictures, or even a card. THANK YOU!!!!!!!

Mahogony Wilson: Thanx for coming in my life when you did and leaving when you did. You taught me a lot about myself in your presence, but even more in your absence. There will always be a special place in my heart for you.

To Every Woman: that ever took that epic journey to be a part of a man's life during one of the lowest moments (incarceration)...I salute you. Continue to be a light in a world of darkness.

Friends of the Island: **77th Winchester, Trigger town, Cottage MOB (75th), 89th & Cottage, 60th Winchester, (J-Town), 54th Winchester(5th Ward)** What up **Shorty "C"** and **G.B., Macheteville, the 3 B's, Deathrow, Lordsville,** and all the **Bro's** from the **Wild 100's**.

Notable Areas: **Brothaville, Nation, 8-Trey, Foster Park, Duck Town, Fin Town , Rack City, Killa ward, Boys Town, Central City, 7-deuce, G-ville, Smashville, 9-0, Georgetown** and **Trey Town**. No matter where you come from at the end of the day, we **ALL** share the **SAME** struggles. It took the microcosm of Prison to see that our so called differences ain't all that different. Learn who your real enemy is!

Everybody that's part of the **R.N.A.**, YOU WILL HAVE AN IMPACT!

And last but not least….to the whole **City of Chicago, Englewood, Tha Low-end, The Wild 100's, North side , West side** and the **East side**…..**Nobody Got Swagger like US!!!!!!**

R.I.P. All Da Bros in the Graveyard

To contact the author, please e-mail him at:

realityallah31@gmail.com

CPSIA information can be obtained
at www.ICGtesting.com
Printed in the USA
FFHW010858080119
50035176-54816FF

9 781589 097353